CW01635881

GILT EDGE

A KENZIE GILMORE CRIME THRILLER
BOOK 9

BIBA PEARCE

LIQUID MIND
Publishing

Liquid Mind Publishing

KENZIE GILMORE CRIME THRILLER SERIES

The Kenzie Gilmore Crime Thriller Series

Afterburn

Dead Heat

Heatwave

Burnout

Deep Heat

Fever Pitch

Storm Surge

Night Watch

Gilt Edge

Scan the QR code or use the link below to find the Kenzie Gilmore series on Audible:

https://www.audible.com/series/Kenzie-Gilmore-Audiobooks/B0BT4ZMK48

JOIN WITHOUT WARRANT'S MAILING LIST

Follow the link to stay up to date with Without Warrant!

https://BookHip.com/WKDXPAV

You'll receive a **free** copy of

Hard Line: A Kenzie Gilmore Prequel.

GLOSSARY OF MODERN MESSAGING SHORT CODE

ngl – not gonna lie
fr – for real
tbh – to be honest
imo/imho – in my opinion / in my humble opinion
lmk – let me know
wdyt – what do you think
brb – be right back
ttyl – talk to you later
omw – on my way
wyd – what are you doing?
eta – estimated time of arrival
dm me – direct message me
slide into dms – privately message someone
ping me – contact me / send me a notification
bump – bringing a conversation back up
thread – conversation chain or topic
lurking – reading without participating
dead chat – inactive conversation
lowkey/highkey – subtly/obviously

bet – agreement, like "sounds good"
say less – I understand, no need to explain further
fs – for sure
nw – no worries
mb – my bad
irl – in real life
icymi – in case you missed it
fwiw – for what it's worth
tl;dr – too long; didn't read (summary)
rn – right now
sus – suspicious
cap/no cap – lying/not lying
valid – legitimate, makes sense
based – authentic, respectable opinion
touch grass – go outside, disconnect from online
chronically online – spends too much time on internet
main character energy – acting like the protagonist
rent free – can't stop thinking about something

1

Lieutenant Reid Garrett arrived at the waterfront estate forty minutes after the call came in. The place was already buzzing with activity. Patrol cars choked the long private drive, red and blue lights bouncing off the palms like the inside of a nightclub.

A news helicopter hovered offshore, its rhythmic thud reverberating against the pre-dawn air, while camera crews clustered beyond the gate, shouting questions at the law enforcement vehicles that went in. Nobody answered them.

Reid gritted his teeth as he cut the engine and stepped out of his pickup. The humidity wrapped him in its sultry embrace. The screeches of the cicadas rose above the noise at the gate, shrill and relentless. Miami in early summer.

Damn, it was gearing up to be a hot one.

He looked back toward the gate at the bottom of the long drive. The victim had been someone noteworthy; you could always tell by the reception. Problem was, that meant additional pressure from the top brass. He squinted as the hazy beams from the chopper angled down on the mansion. It also explained the media frenzy and all the shit that went along with it.

Miami PD would have loved the case, but the estate technically sat on Sweetwater's side of the line. Lucky them.

He nodded to Officer Diaz, already wearing protective shoe coverings and gloves, as she lifted the tape up for him to duck under. "What's with all the attention?"

"Wait till you see the body." She flicked her head uneasily toward the mansion.

"Is it bad?" He sucked in warm air, steeling himself.

"Not bad, just... weird."

Weird was never a good sign.

"Who called it in?"

"Landscaper. A guy named Mateo Rojas."

"Little early for gardening, isn't it?"

She shrugged. "He said he wanted to get an early start. Gets too hot to work in the middle of the day."

Fair enough.

Reid glanced around. The property was sizable, stretching for half a mile in three directions, flanked by a high fence and ringed with foliage. "You question him?"

"We got his statement, yes. Said he arrived at half-past five, found the front door open, and went inside. Discovered the victim downstairs in the gallery."

"Gallery?"

"He's an art collector."

Reid arched his eyebrows but followed her up the steps and into a vast, marble hallway where a CSU officer was waiting. He pulled a pair of covers over his shoes as he stared up at the vaulted ceiling, the enormous chandelier and elaborate cornices and whistled under his breath. "Who's the victim?"

"Name's Malcolm Hargreave. He's the co-founder of Bioneer Pharmaceuticals. That's all I got so far."

"From the landscaper?"

"No, Google. Landscaper didn't know what he did, only that he was wealthy."

"That much is evident." Reid walked around, studying the impressive display of antiquities and artwork on the walls. Most of it was Asian in origin or style. He recognized Mount Fuji, its snow-capped peak rising from a haze of mist, and nearby hung a striking abstract that suggested cherry blossoms in the fall.

"This way." Diaz led him through a heavy, soundproof door and down a short flight of concrete steps. The temperature dropped noticeably as they reached the bottom.

"It's temperature controlled," Diaz pointed out as the air became cooler and drier.

The space that opened up before them wasn't a basement so much as a private museum. Double-height ceilings, polished stone floors, and discreet track lighting bathing each piece in a reverent glow.

The sturdy display cases housed jade figurines, bronze ritual vessels, and scrolls that looked so old they might crumble if touched. Each item was accompanied by a small brass plaque bearing a date, dynasty, or provenance.

"Holy smoke," he muttered.

"Yeah." She pointed to the other side of the room. "Body's over here."

Reid followed her around a central glass cabinet containing a dazzling assortment of antique swords to where Hargreave lay. The cabinet had a jagged hole in the side where it had been smashed. Shards lay scattered over the plush velvet inside, and he tried to avoid stepping on them.

He stopped short when he saw the body. "Whoa!"

"Told you it was strange," Diaz said, staring at the prone figure of the man lying on his back with—if Reid wasn't mistaken—a katana embedded in his chest. It stood erect, the blade gleaming in the overhead lighting as if it had been positioned to show it off.

He took a tentative step closer, treading on more glass. The handle was ornate and crafted with care. It looked really old. Must be an antique. The tip had cleanly pierced the fabric of Hargreave's suit without bunching or tearing, like the blade had been lowered into place instead of slammed home.

"No blood spatter," he remarked, tearing his eyes away to look at the surrounding walls and floor.

"No scuff marks around the body either," Diaz confirmed. "Doesn't look like he put up a fight."

Reid leaned over and studied the victim's fingernails, careful not to touch the body. They appeared clean and manicured. A wealthy man's hands.

"Any sign of forced entry?" he asked, straightening up.

"Nope. The front door was open, as was this one." She tossed her head toward the heavy steel door.

"Then he knew his attacker, or he voluntarily let them in."

Diaz gave a nod of agreement.

He let out a breath and stood still for a moment, taking it all in.

"Any cameras?" he asked after a beat.

"Sure. All over the place. None of them were on."

"What?" He frowned. "Why?"

"We don't know. There's a control room on the first floor, but Vargas said everything was switched off."

"Let's collect what there is and get it analyzed."

"Vargas is already on that."

He gave a grunt of approval. Vargas was his unflappable second-in-command and probably his best detective on the technical side of things, although the surveillance cameras and footage—or lack thereof—would be analyzed by an external digital forensic team.

"Good."

He turned back to the body. Hargreave's jacket was unbuttoned, the lapels smoothed flat. His shirt was mostly pristine except for the neat puncture point where the steel disappeared into his chest. His arms lay at his sides, palms up, fingers loose. No visible defensive wounds.

The most perplexing thing was the victim's face. His expression was calm, eyes half closed, mouth slack. He looked almost peaceful, if you ignored the sword pinning him to the floor.

Reid let out a slow breath. "Okay, I've seen enough. You can call in the crime scene unit."

Diaz walked to the door and beckoned to the two waiting CSU techs clad in sterile white overalls and masks. They nodded to him as they entered.

Reid gestured to the body, then stepped back to let them pass.

"This crime scene was staged. We're going to need photographs from every angle," he said to the one with the Nikon slung over his shoulder.

"Yes, sir."

He turned to Diaz. "I'm willing to bet he wasn't killed here."

"Not enough blood?"

"Yep."

Diaz nodded at the body. "That sword looks pretty definitive to me. If I'm not mistaken, it's gone right through his heart."

"That might be, but if he'd died of that stab wound, he'd have bled out here on the floor. There's no blood underneath him. No blood around the wound."

She pursed her lips. "You're right."

"Whoever did this wanted to create a spectacle," he continued, looking up. "They even positioned the goddamn lighting to spotlight their handiwork."

"Can we dust those lights for prints?" Diaz asked the other forensic tech.

The man squinted upwards and nodded. "Gotcha."

"This why there's a crowd at the gate? Landscaper took photos?" They were probably already online.

"He didn't say, but I guess he could have done."

Reid, Diaz beside him, circled the gallery as the crime scene unit got to work. They heard the soft clicking of the camera as the photographer recorded the body in situ.

They reached the steel door and came to a stop. It was solid steel with industrial hinges and a keypad mounted beside the frame. It didn't look damaged.

"We need prints and touch DNA on this keypad," he said, thinking out loud.

"I'll let them know. You thinking the killer had the code?"

He shrugged. "Maybe, or he circumvented it somehow."

"The victim could have left it open," Diaz suggested.

"Could be. Have we searched the rest of the house?"

"Martinez is doing that now," she told him. "But at first glance, nothing."

"No primary crime scene?"

"No blood or signs of a struggle." She nodded back to the body. "This is it."

Except it wasn't. He was sure of it.

"When will the ME get here?" he asked.

"Soon. He's on his way."

"We need an accurate time and cause of death," he muttered, swiping a hand through his hair.

"May have to wait for the autopsy," Diaz said.

He knew she was probably right. This one was anything but straightforward.

Vargas approached from down the corridor. He nodded at Reid. "Boss."

"You find out why the cameras were off?" Reid asked.

"Switched off from the control room," Vargas replied. "Nothing forced or broken. Could even have been done by the victim himself."

"Did he live alone?" Reid asked.

"Looks like it. Just him and his art. His wife left several years ago, and we're not sure if there are any offspring."

"No girlfriend, boyfriend, lover?"

He shook his head. "Martinez and I just searched the whole house—it's huge—but there's no sign of another person living here or even visiting. One toothbrush, one side of the bed mussed up, food for one in the refrigerator. Guy was a loner."

"Rojas said he thought he lived by himself," Diaz added.

Rob gave a nod. "We canvass the neighborhood?"

"Hamilton and Dwayne are on it now," Diaz told him. "Although the nearest property is over four hundred yards away. Doubtful they heard anything at that distance."

"You never know," Reid said, although he suspected the same. These waterfront properties were vast, and you'd have to be pretty close to hear an altercation from inside one of them.

Anyway, Dwayne Griffith was a tough beat cop who'd transferred a couple of years ago from Miami PD. If anyone could get the lowdown on the victim from the neighbors, he could.

"The press won't make things easy," Vargas pointed out with a grimace. "They're camping out by the front gate."

"Yeah, I noticed. The crime scene online yet?"

"Not yet," Vargas said grimly. "You think the landscaper took photos?"

Reid glanced back at the body. "Wouldn't you? Wealthy art collector, an exotic weapon, ritualistic staging. It's media gold."

Martinez approached, her cheeks flushed.

"What you got?" he asked, turning to her.

"Not sure what to make of this." She handed him a sheet of paper.

Reid glanced down at it. It was the masthead that jumped out at him first. It was an article from the *New York Times*. Below the headline was a familiar byline.

By Kenzie Gilmore, staff reporter.

He exhaled under his breath.

Vargas's eyes widened. "He had a copy of an article by Kenzie?"

Martinez nodded. "It was right there, sitting on his desk. Look at the headline."

The Private Vaults of Stolen Art: How Illicit Antiquities Disappear into the Homes of the Ultra-Wealthy.

Shit.

Reid raked a hand through his hair. "She must have written this when she was in New York."

"Yeah, but why did the victim have it?" Diaz asked.

He shook his head. "That's what we need to find out."

Reid scanned the opening paragraphs. It was about a limestone head, looted from a desert site in the Middle East, photographed briefly on a phone before vanishing. A bronze figure that surfaced in a Geneva showroom with a history that began, conveniently, in the 1970s. Objects that slipped quietly out of conflict zones and into climate-controlled rooms overlooking oceans and city skylines.

Kenzie had written about the invisible journey of stolen art, the way it rarely passed through museums or public auctions but moved instead along a private circuit of consultants, intermediaries, and discreet galleries whose doors were never marked and whose client lists were never shared.

She'd described provenance not as a fixed truth, but as a story, one that could be edited, softened, or rewritten entirely if the buyer had enough money and asked the right people. Collectors, she'd noted, seldom thought of themselves as criminals.

Many believed they were custodians or rescuers of history, preserving beauty the world had failed to protect.

She argued that intent didn't change the impact. Every private acquisition created a demand, and that demand sent someone into the ground with a shovel, a crowbar, or a gun. He stopped reading there, lifting his gaze.

It was a well-written article, but then he expected nothing less from Kenzie.

"I need to read the whole thing. Can you make copies?"

Martinez nodded. "Will do."

He glanced at the others. "When you're done here, head back to the station. I'll be there soon."

"What are you going to do?" Vargas asked.

Reid reached into his pocket and pulled out his phone. "Go straight to the source. I'm going to talk to Kenzie."

Diaz shot a quick smile. “Tell her I say hi.”

He nodded, and they turned to leave.

“Hey, Vargas—” he called after them.

His deputy turned around. “Yeah?”

“Get one of the officers outside to film the crowd at the gate. I want a shot of everyone out there.”

Martinez glanced at him. “You think the perp might come back?”

“They often do.” Reid tilted his head in the direction they’d come. “Particularly if they’ve gone through all that effort.”

2

KENZIE SPOTTED Reid immediately as she drove up. He was standing in front of the mansion, hands thrust in his pockets, brow furrowed. She knew that look. He was concerned about the article, about her.

He'd given her a brief explanation on the phone but hadn't gone into any detail. Curiosity was eating away at her. One thing she knew for certain was that she'd never been to a victim's house before in her life. If you could call this a house.

She gazed through the windshield at the modern Spanish-style mansion, all white stucco and sweeping arches, its terracotta roof tiles warming as the first light of dawn crept across them. Wide balconies gazed out onto a sweeping, manicured lawn around which the driveway weaved. Tall palms swayed in the light breeze around the perimeter.

It was a gorgeous property. Whoever had lived here must have been very successful.

She pulled over behind one of the police vehicles and walked over to Reid. "Hey, I came as soon as I could."

She'd been at her condo, but lately, much of her time was spent at his place in the Glades. Once a crumbling cabin, it had been destroyed by a fire a couple of years back and been completely redone. The renovation had transformed it into a sizable waterfront property with majestic views over the swamp, completely surrounded by nature.

At first she'd thought it isolated and a little too rustic for her liking, but she'd gotten used to it and now she felt very much at home there.

Reid greeted her with a quick smile and a nod. If it had been just the two of them, he'd have kissed her, but this was a work situation. Reid didn't do public displays of affection, even when he wasn't on the job.

"Security let you through?"

"Yes. Thank goodness you gave them my name. It's chaos out there."

"Take a look at this."

He handed her the article wrapped in a plastic evidence bag. She recognized it straight away.

"This is a piece I wrote for the *New York Times*. You say it was on his desk?"

Reid nodded. "Victim was a collector of eastern weapons and artifacts."

Her eyes widened. "Can I see inside?"

He shrugged. "Sure. Don't see why not. It's all over the internet already."

"Really?" She followed him up the marble steps and into a cavernous entrance hall. "How'd it get out so fast?"

"We have the landscaper who found the body to thank for that."

Kenzie glanced up, kicking herself that she hadn't thought to look. She'd been so eager to get here, she'd dashed out without considering it might already be online. "Wow. What did you say this guy did again?"

His lips quirked. "I don't think I did. He was some pharmaceutical bigwig."

"Uh-huh. He liked his eastern art. This is an impressive collection." She nodded at Mount Fuji. "That's a Hokusai over there."

He didn't ask who. Art wasn't his forte. "Wait until you see downstairs."

"The body is still here?" She arched an eyebrow in surprise.

He shook his head. "ME removed it an hour ago, but you can see where he was found."

She shot him a sideways glance. "But not where he died?"

Reid gave a soft snort. "Exactly. ME said it wasn't the katana that killed him."

"Katana? Now I'm really intrigued." She followed him through a heavy steel door and down a cold flight of steps to a basement-level room. "Temperature controlled?"

"You got it."

Reid nodded at the officer stationed just inside, then stood back so she could take a look around.

"Holy smokes." She stepped inside and gazed in awe at the museum-grade display cabinets, their curated contents and the professional spotlighting.

Masks stared back at her through glass, carved faces frozen somewhere between ritual and threat. Tapestries depicting violent scenes hung on the walls, while an assortment of shiny weapons were mounted with obvious care.

Her reporter's brain was already making assumptions about the man who lived here amongst these treasures. Who'd loved them, obsessed over them, spent his wealth on them. Created a whole goddamn gallery to display them.

Did he allow anyone else to view them? Or were they for his pleasure alone?

She walked over to the smashed cabinet in the center of the room. "Was this where the murder weapon was kept?" Glass still sprinkled the floor, glinting like scattered diamonds.

"Yeah, we think so. It's been taken into evidence, but it was embedded in the victim's chest."

She glanced up at him. "He was stabbed?"

In response, he held up his phone and showed her a photograph of the body in situ before it was taken to the morgue.

"Wow. Okay." She leaned in to study the curved katana blade, the ornate handle, and, of course, the all-important positioning of the body.

The weapon looked to be in pristine condition, obviously very old and rare. The body had been staged, that much was clear, with the victim's hands positioned at his sides, the sword penetrating his sternum and probably going right through his heart.

She straightened up. "I see what you mean. No way he was killed in here."

"ME didn't give a cause of death," Reid told her. "He thought it could be asphyxiation or even poison. There were no obvious clues on the body."

She rounded the cabinet and stared at the spot on the floor where the body had lain. There was no blood, no spatter, no markings. If it wasn't for the chalk outline and the glaring yellow forensic marker positioned in the center, she wouldn't have known anyone had died there.

"What about defensive wounds?" she asked.

He shook his head.

Kenzie crinkled her forehead, a habit she had when she was thinking. "So the killer murdered him somewhere else, carried him down here and arranged him on the floor, before stabbing him with the sword?"

"Looks like it." His gaze fixed on her. "Any idea why?"

Kenzie shook her head. "None. I don't know the victim. I have no idea why he was reading my article other than it's obviously an area of interest. I mean, look at all this stuff." She waved her arm around in an arc. "Maybe he was trying to acquire a piece on the black market. Maybe he was interested in selling something to a buyer but didn't want to use legitimate channels. I don't know."

"You mean it could be a coincidence that your article just happened to be on his desk?"

She knew Reid didn't believe in them. "What else could it be?"

He frowned. "I was hoping you'd be able to tell me that."

"Sorry. It's a mystery to me, but one I'd love to have a go at solving."

His scowl deepened. "No way. I don't want you getting involved in this any more than you already are."

"I'm not involved." She put her hands on her hips. "I don't even know the dead man's name."

He hesitated.

At her raised eyebrow, he sighed. "Hargreave. Malcolm Hargreave."

"Thank you."

"Mean anything to you?"

She shook her head.

"Damn."

"I wrote that article for the *Times*. It was after that syndicate of art smugglers were busted by an FBI agent posing as a buyer. Do you remember?"

"No, sorry. Not my area of expertise."

"Well, the case went to trial and there was quite a lot of press attention at the time. I was asked to write a feature article on corruption in the art world as a follow-up piece."

He gave a short nod. "Hargreave's name didn't come up?"

"Not that I recall. I can go back over my notes, but I don't think I'll find anything. Your victim is clearly a collector. He wouldn't be facilitating illegal activities. Making use of the pipeline, maybe, but not part of the organization behind it."

Reid ran a hand over his jaw, stubbly since he hadn't had time to shave that morning. "Yeah, you're probably right."

"I could put out feelers. Maybe do a podcast on him for my channel," she began, but he cut her off with a raised hand.

"Kenz, please. This is an active investigation. I can't have you disclosing details to the general public. You know that."

He shot her a look that implied she should know better.

"I wasn't going to give them any details," she retorted. "What I meant was, I could name him as the victim, mention his collection and see what gives. You said yourself it's already out there. Those in the art world must know who he is."

She gestured to the artifacts. "This is a serious collection. These pieces are not easy to come by. He'll have a reputation, for sure."

Reid pursed his lips.

"We might even be able to get people to come forward. I could end the show with an appeal for anyone with information to contact the Sweetwater PD." He was considering it; she could tell by the way his gaze wavered.

"I wouldn't give them any details you didn't want me to," she added. "But it may help."

It had helped before.

During the Night Watchman case, they'd appealed for help from the public and been amazed at the response. It had helped them track down an elusive loner with crucial information on the murder.

"Hold that thought," he said. "Let me see what the day brings. We'll talk tonight."

She gave a reluctant nod.

Reid was naturally cautious, although he had been known to lose it on occasion, particularly when her life was at risk. She knew there wasn't much he wouldn't do for her. He'd proven that several times over.

They both had.

"Promise me you won't go ahead and publish anything? I know you've been cleared as a police consultant, but what I've shown you this morning is still strictly confidential. It doesn't go any further than the department."

"I know that." She gave a soft snort. "Of course I wouldn't compromise an investigation. I was just trying to help."

He squeezed her hand. "I know."

Shadows were beginning to form beneath his eyes. He couldn't have had much sleep. Her heart went out to him.

"Do you want me to look into this stuff?" She waved a hand around at the displays. "I could do some research on these artifacts. Find out how much they cost, their provenance and so on. Might help, if his death was connected to the black market or something he was into."

His brow furrowed, then he said, "Yeah, actually that could be useful. I would put Monroe on it, but he wouldn't know a Picasso if it hit him in the head."

Kenzie chuckled as she thought of the old-school detective now on desk duty. "No, probably not."

Reid waited while she took snapshots of the artifacts, tapestries and antiquities on display. It was important to capture them as thoroughly as possible when comparing them online. Every little detail counted. When she was done, they left the gallery together and walked back up the stairs to the entrance.

Kenzie shook off a shiver as they emerged from the cool staircase into the light of the central hall. Being early summer, the sun was already streaming in through the open door and wide windows. She could feel the temperature starting to climb.

"I probably won't make it back to my place tonight," Reid said as he walked her to her car.

"I know. Call me when you can." She knew exactly what it was like when they caught a case like this one. The first forty-eight hours were crucial. Already, the team would be going through CCTV cameras in the area, conducting door-to-door inquiries to see if anyone had seen anything, and researching the victim, his family, friends, and associates. It would be all systems go for Reid and his team for the next few days.

She'd be lying if she said she wasn't a teeny bit jealous.

Her dreams of becoming a cop had been smashed along with her knee while at the police academy. She'd dropped out while she recovered, but despite all the physio, it had never gotten back to full strength. Even now, it would still give in if she pushed too hard, and she knew she'd never pass a physical.

Becoming a reporter on the crime beat had seemed like the next best option, but now she was consulting for the Sweetwater PD and running her own investigative podcast. Time and the advancement of technology had meant she'd forged out a new career for herself. One that gave her immense satisfaction. Plus, she got to work for herself, which wasn't something Reid could say. No, sir. Life wasn't too bad at all.

Waving at Reid, she got into her car and started the engine. All of a sudden, she was hit by that all-too-familiar surge of adrenaline. It had been a while since her last case, and she'd been looking for something to dig into.

Now she had it, she couldn't wait to get started.

3

Sweetwater Police Department, once a practically defunct station with a poor reputation and a dismal closure rate, was now a thriving hub of activity. It had gone from being the place where old cops downgraded before they retired to being one of the most requested departments by newly graduated recruits.

As Reid strode in, he couldn't help but feel a sense of pride. It hadn't been easy getting rid of the old legacy of cronyism and corruption, but he'd done it, and now they had one of the best success rates in the state.

Vargas lifted a hand as he entered the bullpen and beckoned him over.

Reid stopped at his desk. "What's up?"

"Update from the tech team. None of the surveillance cameras were tampered with. They just weren't running. The last recording was the night before the murder."

Reid frowned. "What does that tell us? That Hargreave didn't set them to record on the night he died?"

Vargas shrugged. "Seems that way. Maybe he hadn't gotten

around to it yet, or maybe he was expecting someone so kept them off."

Reid gave a thoughtful nod. "Someone he didn't want on camera."

"Like a shady dealer or buyer?" Vargas suggested.

"Black market?" Diaz called from her desk. She was nearest to Vargas so could overhear their conversation.

"Any word on the street?" Reid asked.

"Some of the nearby properties have private security setups. Dwayne and Hamilton are following up."

"Can we get a last known location on Hargreave's cell phone?" Reid asked, even though he knew it would likely say the guy was home.

Still, they had to check. It was those kinds of details the prosecution loved to unpick—provided they ever found a suspect. "And let's pull his call records. Maybe this was an arranged meeting."

"I'll get his bank statements too," added Vargas, who knew the drill.

Reid went to his desk and sat down. He preferred working in the thick of it with the others. It kept him sharp. He wasn't the type of boss to ride a desk in a swanky back office and let his officers do all the legwork.

Not that swanky was even an option at Sweetwater PD. The place had been so rundown when he'd taken over, it hadn't even had air conditioning. Luckily, their successes meant the budget had stretched a little further in subsequent years.

"Any news from the crime scene unit?" he asked Diaz.

She shot him a "really?" look. "It's only been a couple of hours, boss. Give them a chance."

He grunted. This morning felt like a long time ago.

"What about the victim? What do we have on him?"

Diaz swung her chair around to face him. "Turns out Malcolm Hargreave was actually Dr. Malcolm Hargreave. He hadn't practiced in years, however, not since he took over the company."

"Pioneer Pharmaceuticals?" he remembered.

"Bioneer, but yeah. He took the reins over a decade ago and since then it's gone from strength to strength. Seems they struck gold with a new cancer treatment."

"What about the art?" Reid asked, stretching out his legs under the desk.

"Well, it's not clear how his interest started, but he traveled extensively to Asia for manufacturing partnerships, so he could quite easily have acquired some of it when he was there."

Made sense.

"Have we looked into his connections? Known associates?"

"Nothing untoward. I'm still checking out the wife, Sandra West."

"If she's local, get an address," he said.

She nodded and turned back to her screen just as the door opened. In strode Officers Hamilton and Griffiths. They'd been querying the neighborhood on foot and looked hot and in need of a drink. By the expressions on their faces, Reid could tell they didn't have much.

He nodded a greeting. "How'd it go?"

Dwayne Griffiths, the Miami beat cop, shook his head. "Why do they have to have such big goddamn properties? We've walked miles. Give me downtown Miami any day."

Hamilton, one of the youngest officers in the department, masked a grin. "We didn't find much. A couple of people said he was a well-respected figure but kind of a loner. Kept to himself."

"One woman thought he had a son," Dwayne added. "But thinks the family is estranged."

"Wife moved out four years ago," Diaz called, reading off her screen. "She had a son, Michael West. Not Hargreave's, though."

"Previous marriage?" Reid asked.

"Looks like it, yeah. Before she was Sandra West, she was Sandra Holton, but she was born Sandra Miller. From Kirksville, Missouri.

Both parents are deceased." She glanced up. "Seems like Sandra didn't always have money."

"Get me an address. We need to talk to her."

Diaz nodded.

"Any surveillance footage we can look at?" Reid asked the two men.

Dwayne nodded. "Yeah, the folks at 15 Palm Drive have a camera out front. They said we can take a look at the footage from last night, but judging by the angle, it won't cover the road."

"Damn," Reid grumbled. It was to be expected, though. Why watch someone else's property? "Anyone else?"

"Possibly." Hamilton glanced at Dwayne, who gave a nod.

"There's a property on the north end that's covered in cameras. Huge place, but nobody's home."

"Number?" Diaz asked.

"No number. Name." Dwayne rolled his eyes. "Sunset Villa."

Great. The end of the street didn't even have numbers, the houses were so big.

"I'll look it up," Hamilton offered, going back to his desk.

Reid itched to pick up the phone and call the medical examiner, but he knew he'd just be sidelined. The worst part about police work was waiting for results. He needed to know the cause of death, because he was willing to bet it wasn't murder by katana. That was for their benefit.

Or the media. Or someone.

It would at least give them something to go on.

"Got the wife's address," Diaz said, scribbling on a sticky note.

"Great, let's go." Reid got to his feet. He needed to do something proactive.

"Before you go." Vargas swiveled around. "There's a silent partner."

Reid frowned. "As in a business partner?"

"Yeah, Silas Ackerman. He's the money. Helped finance the research into the new cancer treatments the company was developing. He's a shareholder and member of the board. Lives in Coral Gables."

"You and Martinez take him," Reid said, delegating. "Find out if he has an alibi for last night."

"Will do." Vargas opened his drawer and pulled out his weapon.

Martinez was already on her feet.

All four walked out together.

Sandra West lived in the upmarket neighborhood of Coconut Grove. The drive took a little over thirty minutes, during which time Reid bounced off Diaz the ideas that had been buzzing around his head.

"The way the body was found," he said, as he navigated West Miami traffic, "makes me think that the killer wanted to leave us a message."

"Us?" Diaz glanced over from the passenger seat. "Why us?"

"Okay, maybe not us exactly, but the media. Other collectors. The crime scene is already plastered all over the web."

"You're thinking it was a warning? Maybe someone was trying to teach Hargreave a lesson?"

Reid frowned as he slowed at an intersection. "I think it's worth looking into any Asian connections. Maybe someone took offense to a pharma billionaire collecting Japanese national treasures."

"You think it's culturally motivated?"

"I don't know. I'm just brainstorming here. Might be nothing."

"That's potentially sensitive ground," Diaz warned, her voice tight.

"I know, but we can't disregard it just because it's sensitive."

"True."

"The provenance of the items should help," he decided, maneuvering around an eighteen-wheeler.

"Isn't that what Kenzie is doing?" Diaz asked.

"Yeah, she's looking into the artifacts, see what we can glean from them."

"If there is a cultural angle to this, it might be a good idea for Kenzie to mention it on her podcast," Diaz said thoughtfully.

At Reid's sharp glance, she elaborated. "I mean, activist groups don't like to stay silent. If the killer was ideologically motivated, there might be online support for him."

He drew in a breath. She had a point.

"I hadn't thought of it like that."

"Private chat rooms, groups, Discord servers. There's a ton of avenues where we might be able to learn something."

"Okay, point taken. I'll talk to Kenzie tonight." It seemed irresponsible to disregard the online stuff, even if it did make him feel like a dinosaur. If this killer was younger, ideologically or culturally motivated, or an activist of some kind, then Diaz was right. That is exactly where he'd hang out.

"I might contact Kenzie's friend at the *Herald*—Acosta." He was the department's go-to guy when it came to complicated tech stuff.

"Raoul? Yes, good idea. He'd know where to look. He's not at the *Herald* anymore. I heard he quit."

"He did?"

"Yeah, he's freelancing now. Private sector."

It was only going to be a matter of time. He was wasted at a newspaper, in Reid's opinion.

"Okay, I'll call him. Hopefully we can still afford his rates."

Diaz grinned. "Maybe he'll give us a deal. Repeat customers and all that."

He smirked.

"This is it," he said a few moments later. They pulled up outside a sizable townhouse. Freshly painted stucco, designer outdoor lighting, and landscaping that looked professionally maintained rather than loved. There was no charm or personality, just expensive comfort.

He studied the late-model SUV in the drive. "Looks like she's home." It was spotless, like it had recently been detailed. Pricey, too.

"She did well off Hargreave," Diaz told him, as they walked up the path to the front door.

"Does she work?"

"Runs her own modeling agency. FRAME Models. Mostly online catalogue stuff. Financials show she's barely breaking even."

Reid glanced up at the townhouse. "So this is Hargreave's money?"

"Yep."

They'd just reached the door when Reid heard scuffling around the side of the house. He walked past the entrance and peered around the corner.

A young man was trying to pry open a window. He had it a third of the way up and was about to jump up and enter the house when Reid drew his service pistol.

"Hey! Stop right there. Sweetwater PD."

4

Kenzie let herself into the apartment just as the sky over Miami was turning a bright cobalt blue. There was only a whisper of cloud on the horizon, but it was still early. Later, when the humidity had built to stifling levels, the clouds would move in, and it might even rain. But right now, it was a glorious morning.

She kicked the door shut behind her and stood there for a moment, keys still in her hand, listening to the sudden quiet. The crime scene Reid had shown her on his phone was still fresh in her mind. The sword. The stillness of the body. The way the gallery lights had been angled just so. Like a stage setting, waiting for an audience.

She crossed to the kitchen and put on a pot of coffee, then went to her office and logged onto her computer. Before doing anything else, she Googled: *Malcolm Hargreave death.*

The results were astounding. Already, there were dozens of sites referencing his murder.

She clicked on the first link and saw a photograph of the victim's body, lying prone on the gallery floor, katana glinting in the spotlights. It was similar to the one Reid had taken but with better composition. The colors were brighter too, and there was more contrast. It could have been a filter. Either way, the landscaper clearly had other skills.

The coffee machine gurgled, and she went back to grab a mug. Presumably Reid and his team would vet the landscaper. Make sure he was on the level.

She took a sip, letting the caffeine fortify her. Of course he would. He was a pro. As an investigative journalist, it was hard for her to take a back seat when a case like this presented itself. She was itching to get involved, but that wasn't her job.

At least she could help by looking into the artifacts and those glorious works of art on the walls. If there was anything shady there, she'd find it.

Kenzie uploaded the photographs from her phone to the computer. It was a large-sized iMac and she wanted the highest resolution she could get. Every little detail mattered, no matter how small. If she were going to cross-reference Hargreave's pieces with museum databases, gallery listings, and public auction records, she needed detailed descriptions.

Next, she created folders for each category of item: weapons, tapestries, ceramics, art. Within them, she created subfolders for each item, filled with its description, date, the source, and the timestamp. Basically, any information she had on that item from the mansion.

Finally, she used an AI assistant to scan the photographs and enhance her amateur descriptions, careful to make sure they were accurate. She did not use AI to write her articles or transcripts, but it was handy for research, especially when she needed to move fast.

Armed with as much information as she could get, she began to search.

First, she queried all the major auction houses like Christie's and Sotheby's, but while they had items that were similar, nothing was a match to those housed in Hargreave's gallery.

She leaned back and let out a slow breath. No matter. She hadn't expected to find anything there. Not really. Those channels were expensive and upmarket.

If Hargreave had purchased items illegally, he would have done so from other collectors, museums in financial difficulty, or unscrupulous galleries who were prepared to make exceptions for American dollars.

She searched art listings by private collectors, anonymous buyers, and old estates. Hargreave's name didn't come up. Neither did anything in his collection.

That didn't mean much on its own. Plenty of high-end buyers used intermediaries or shell companies so they wouldn't leave a footprint. She knew this from her research into art smuggling for the *Times*.

Stretching her neck, she was about to take a break for lunch when a listing from a Japanese auction house popped up, and the image of an ancient scroll caught her eye. It was mounted vertically behind glass, the calligraphy elegant but restrained, the brushwork confident without being ornamental. In the lower corner was a red stamp.

Zooming in, she magnified the seal. Her pulse ticked up a notch.

Switching tabs, she went back to the folder containing Hargreave's scrolls. Gnawing at her lower lip, she scanned the entries until she found the one she was looking for.

Opening it, she held her breath.

Yes!

The seal was identical.

This was the auction house from which Hargreave had purchased that artifact. She tapped through the database until she got to the provenance. Sure enough, it had been acquired by a US buyer two years previously.

Instead of Hargreave's name, however, it had been sold to a company called Orion Holdings LLC. The address was a post office box in Wilmington, Delaware. No street number, no suite, just a registered agent and a paper trail designed to go nowhere.

Smiling, she got to her feet. While it might seem like a dead end, she suspected that Hargreave was the owner of Orion Holdings. That he'd opened this company with the express purpose of acquiring stolen or high-risk pieces. Items that were smuggled out of Asia and into America to waiting buyers who paid top dollar for them, despite the murky provenance.

Kenzie had interviewed several buyer-collectors while researching her article for the *Times*, and she knew first-hand that they didn't buy for financial gain. They didn't buy to show off how wealthy or how cultured they were. They bought for the simple reason that they were art lovers. Genuine collectors who wanted to possess those items of cultural and historical significance, to ogle their beauty and craftsmanship. And they often didn't care how they got them.

This was what Hargreave was. This was why he had a temperature-controlled gallery in his basement, and why he had a steel-enforced door and a sophisticated alarm system.

And most likely why he was dead.

After a break when she ate lunch and processed what she'd discovered, she went back to her computer. This time, she approached her search from a different angle. She now knew which corporation Hargreave was using—or at least one of them—so she searched directly for sales involving that company.

Orion Holdings popped up in several search results. Always high-value pieces, always of Asian origin. None of which were for sale on the open market.

He'd done deals with intermediaries, other collectors, even academic institutions. Buying through a company wasn't illegal, and Kenzie couldn't find any reference to the pieces having been stolen. They shouldn't have left Japan, of course, but they didn't seem to be on any UNESCO database of cultural property violations.

Given the number of items purchased by Orion Holdings, and

how many matched her list, Kenzie was one hundred percent certain that Hargreave was Orion.

Still, she needed actual proof.

One thing she knew for sure was that the shell company had been set up deliberately for anonymity. Delaware had been chosen because it didn't require ownership disclosure.

After thinking for a moment, Kenzie googled the registered agent's name and pulled a list of every company that agent represented. Then she looked for patterns.

There were several companies formed within weeks of Orion. Some even had similar naming conventions. Vega Asset Management, Andromeda Enterprises, Perseus Holdings. All star groupings or constellations.

Feeling the grit behind her eyes, Kenzie got up and made another pot of coffee. When it was done, she took it back to her office. The sky was darkening already, the sun sinking over the horizon. She'd been at it all day. Still, she finally felt like she was making headway.

She wondered how Reid was getting on. One more hour and then she'd call him with an update.

Back at her computer, she searched the other company names.

Bingo.

They were all involved in the sale or purchase of Japanese artifacts or art.

Adrenaline making her pulse race—or maybe that was the coffee—she dug deeper, focusing in particular on the murder weapon. Her reasoning was that since that was the one the killer had chosen to use, it must be important.

She had only the landscaper's photographs and the crime-scene images Reid had allowed her to see, but the smashed display cabinet told its own story. The plaque beneath the broken glass listed the sword's age, origin, and maker—enough to give her a starting point.

She ran it through an AI-assisted search, which could cover more ground and websites than she could ever hope to. In a shockingly short amount of time, it had flagged a relevant news article in *Bijutsu*

Techō, a Japanese art journal she'd encountered once before while researching restitution cases.

It identified the blade as having been stolen fifteen years earlier from a small Zen temple in Yamagata Prefecture, where it had been held as a ceremonial object rather than a display piece. The theft had occurred during renovation work. No arrests were ever made, and the sword was presumed lost. A devastating loss to the temple and the local community.

Kenzie let out a measured breath. Hargreave *had* been buying stolen artifacts. Not just stolen, but of cultural and ceremonial significance. As was so often the case, because it had been temple-held, not museum-held, it had never made it onto any Interpol or UNESCO lists.

From her previous research, she knew that in Zen temples, items like the katana were associated with ideals like protection, discipline, and authority. Often, they weren't 'owned' but held in trust. According to Japanese cultural thinking, when an item such as this sword was stolen, it's a violation of that trust. It is a disruption of the moral balance and supremely disrespectful.

Maybe the killer wanted to send a message. The sword never belonged to Hargreave. The ritual staging was an attempt at restitution—a quiet justice to right the wrongs of the past.

5

The young man froze.

Diaz sidestepped around Reid, her weapon drawn. "Sir, put your hands where we can see them."

He lifted both hands into the air, turning to face them as he did so. "Wait. Don't shoot! I—I can explain."

"I sure hope so," Reid said, taking a few steps closer. "Because from where I'm standing, it looks like you're committing a felony."

"No, sir. I mean, yes, I am trying to get in, but it's okay. I live here."

"You live here?" Diaz frowned.

"Can I see some ID?" Reid asked, holding his gun steady. He could already tell that this guy was no threat. He wasn't armed, he was wearing board shorts and a T-shirt, a pair of flops on his feet. No way would he be burglarizing a place dressed like that. His hair was tousled and streaked with blond. Reid pegged him for a surfer or a student—maybe both.

"I don't have any on me," he said.

"Why are you trying to break into your own house?" asked Diaz.

"I've been staying at my girlfriend's place down the road. When I got here, the house was locked and my mother was out."

"Where are your keys?" Diaz asked, frowning.

He shrugged. "Didn't take them with me."

It was stupid enough to be believable.

"Who is your mother?" asked Reid.

"Sandra West. I'm Michael West. I'd show you my driver's license, but it's inside."

Reid lowered his weapon. "You're Michael West?"

"Yeah." He hesitantly lowered his arms. "Why are you here?"

"I'm Lieutenant Garrett and this is Detective Diaz." He nodded in the direction of his colleague. "We need to speak with your mother."

Diaz holstered her gun but kept her gaze on the youngster.

"She must have gone for a run. She sometimes jogs around the golf course." He gestured to the back of the house, where Reid assumed the golf course was situated. "If I can get in, I'll open the door and you can wait inside?" He phrased it like a question.

Diaz nodded. "Okay, fine. But any funny moves and we're coming in after you."

"Yes, ma'am," he said, and pulled himself up onto the window ledge. With a quick grin, he swung a leg over and dropped down inside.

"Looks like he's done that before," Reid said dryly.

Diaz chuckled. "Let's hope he really does live here."

"I'll go around the front, while you wait here," Reid said, and headed back to the front of the house.

Less than a minute later, the front door swung open and Michael stood there grinning as if to say, "told you so". He had a disarming smile with dimples in each cheek.

Reid checked to make sure he hadn't armed himself, but it was clear.

"Diaz," he called over his shoulder as he held up his badge.

The kid gazed at it, before nodding and opening the door wider. "Come in."

Reid stepped inside. "Thanks."

Michael gestured to a living room with cream leather upholstery. "Take a seat. Would you like a drink?"

"Sure, some water would be good," Reid said, as Diaz came in behind him.

They sat down as Michael came back with two glasses of water.

"So, what do you want with my mom?" he asked. "Has she done something wrong?"

"Why would you ask that?" Reid said.

"Why else would two cops be here?" He shrugged.

Fair enough.

"Hasn't she paid a parking fine or something? That would be just like her."

"No, nothing like that. We want to talk to her about her husband," Diaz said, in a softer tone. "Your stepfather."

Reid let her steer the conversation, sensing she wanted to see what they could get out of the kid before his mother returned. He looked to be in his early twenties, which meant they didn't need an adult present to question him.

"Malcolm? What's he done?"

"He hasn't done anything," Diaz said.

Michael's eyes widened. "Has something happened to him?"

There was an uncomfortable pause.

"He was murdered last night at his home," Diaz said eventually, after glancing at Reid. "I'm so sorry to have to tell you like this."

Reid watched his face for a reaction. It shifted from disbelief to shock to horror as he processed what she'd said. Genuine emotions.

"He's... dead?"

Diaz nodded. "I'm sorry," she said again.

Michael collapsed into a chair, his face ashen. "Oh my God. What happened? How? I mean... what—?" he shook his head, at a loss for words.

"Were you close to your stepfather?" asked Reid. He was surprised by how upset the kid was.

"Yeah, sort of. I mean, he raised me."

"How old were you when your mother married Malcolm?" Diaz asked.

"I was four. She was a single mom and he took us in." His voice choked up. "He was good to us."

"So why'd they split up?"

He shook his head, ignoring Diaz's question. "I can't believe he's gone."

She gave him a moment to collect himself. When he'd taken a few deep breaths and swiped at his eyes, she said, "It was four years ago, wasn't it? When they split?"

He blinked and glanced up. "Yeah, about that."

Reid got the impression he wasn't happy about it.

"What happened?" he probed, gently.

"Mom met someone else. Said she didn't love him anymore." There was a definite edge to his voice now.

"You didn't want to leave?" Reid asked him.

He stared at him for a long moment, then sighed. "No, okay. I didn't want to leave. Malcolm was a good guy. He might have been 'boring', but he was a rock. He looked after us. Always had."

Reid could feel the kid's animosity.

"How'd he die?" Michael whispered.

"We don't know yet," Reid said quickly.

A sniff. "But you're sure it was him?"

"Yeah, there's no mistake."

They would need Sandra to come and ID the body, but that was just a formality. They'd seen Hargreave's driver's license back at the mansion. It was him, all right.

Michael squeezed his eyes shut.

They heard footsteps on the driveway and turned to see a woman jog up to the door. That must be Sandra West. A moment later, she stepped into the living room.

"Michael, why is there a police car outside the house?" She stepped further into the room and spotted them sitting on the sofa. "Has something happened?"

When nobody answered, she glanced at Michael. "Are you okay?"

"Yeah, it's not me," he said through gritted teeth. "It's Malcolm. He's dead. Are you happy now?" With that, he turned and stomped out of the room, leaving them alone with a stunned Sandra.

Reid got to his feet, set his water glass down on the coffee table, and reached for his ID.

"I'm sorry for the intrusion," he began. "I'm Lieutenant Garrett and this is Detective Diaz. We came to inform you of your husband's death. Your son let us in." He left out the part about nearly arresting Michael for unlawful entry.

"He's my ex," she said, squaring her shoulders. "We're separated."

Reid inclined his head by way of apology. Seemed the shock had worn off fast. "Could I ask when last you saw Malcolm?" Better to stick with first names.

She scowled. "What's that got to do with anything?"

"He was murdered, Ms. West," Diaz said, standing up.

Sandra stared at them. "Murdered?"

"Yes. Could you answer the question?" Reid wondered if she was putting it on. She seemed more shocked than upset. Not like her son, who'd clearly been devastated by the news. Then again, maybe there was just no love lost between them.

"I don't remember when I last saw him." She shook her head as if it was all too much. "A couple of months back, maybe. We didn't talk much."

"So you didn't see him last night?" Reid pressed.

"Last night? No, of course not. Is that when—?" She gazed at them, leaving the question hanging. "Oh, God. You're asking if I had something to do with his death?"

"We're talking to everyone who might have had contact with him," Reid explained.

"Well, you're wasting your time here, Lieutenant. Neither Michael nor I have seen Malcolm in months."

"Why didn't you get a divorce, Ms. West?" asked Diaz, throwing her a curveball.

She flushed, clearly flustered. "Malcolm didn't want to. He didn't believe in divorce." She took a sharp breath. "Then again, he didn't want to look bad in the eyes of the board. All he ever cared about was that company—and his stupid artifacts."

"He was collecting when you were living together?" asked Diaz.

"Yeah, he's always loved that Japanese stuff. Kind of creepy, if you ask me. All those ancient masks and swords." She shuddered, despite the perspiration drying on the sides of her face from her run. "He loved them more than he ever loved us."

"Did he build the gallery in the basement?" Reid asked.

She gave a stiff nod. "That was a recent development. I think he needed something to occupy him after we left. I couldn't wait to get out of there. The place was like a mausoleum."

"What did Michael think?" Diaz asked softly.

"Michael? What does he matter? He's twenty-three years old. Out most of the time anyway, at that girlfriend of his. He's not the one who had to endure that place day after day."

"He seems upset by his father's death."

"*Step*father," she emphasized, then sighed, her shoulders dropping. "Malcolm was the only father figure Michael had. He didn't know his biological dad."

"Do you mind if I ask what happened?" Reid asked.

She was back to scowling. "Not that it's any business of yours, but he didn't stick around. Took off as soon as he found out I was knocked... er, pregnant. What can I say? I was young and stupid back then."

"Missouri, wasn't it?" Reid asked.

She stiffened. "That's right. You've looked into me?"

"Standard procedure, Ms. West," he explained.

"Well, I haven't done anything wrong so like I said, you're wasting your time. I'm sorry he's dead, but we weren't together."

Reid wasn't done with her yet. Casting a glance at Diaz, he said, "You stand to inherit a lot of money now that he's gone. Did you know that?"

"Do I?" She didn't appear to be all that surprised.

"Yeah. It has to go through probate, but I believe he left everything to you."

Hargreave's attorney had gotten in touch with them earlier that morning. Of course, the funds would be tied up until his murder was solved, or an arrest was made, but Sandra West would get everything. That gave her motive.

6

KENZIE LEFT a message on Reid's phone and headed out to meet Raoul. The computer-genius-turned-researcher-turned-hacker-turned-she-didn't-want-to-know-what had suggested a little-known blues bar downtown. It was the kind of place you found only if someone told you where to look.

She'd been there before. It was one of Raoul's favorite haunts. Livelier on weekends when local bands squeezed onto the small stage and the room filled with music and bodies, it was virtually empty during the week.

A jukebox hummed softly in the corner, cycling through old Muddy Waters tracks, while a handful of regulars lingered at the bar, nursing beers or talking quietly over tumblers of whisky.

Kenzie, who was early, noticed the bartender knew most of them by name and poured without being asked.

She chose a table toward the back where the lighting was low and forgiving. Not that she cared, but Raoul liked the privacy. Now he'd gone freelance, he'd turned more secretive than ever. She knew that had to do with his high-value clients who demanded absolute discretion.

A ray of artificial streetlight shot across the scuffed floorboards as the door opened and Raoul walked in. He looked around, then broke into a wide smile when he saw her, pushing his glasses up his nose.

"Hey, good to see you, Kenz." He opened his arms to give her a hug. He was dressed in jeans and a dark hoodie, with a backpack slung over one shoulder. Standard attire for him. She knew the backpack contained an electronic device of some sort, perhaps a laptop or tablet, upon which he could probably inflict more damage in a minute than any run-of-the-mill hacker could in a year.

"Good to see you too." She hugged him back, then gestured for him to sit down. "Want a drink?"

"No need." He turned and nodded at the barman, who came over with an Old Fashioned, ready-made.

"I thought you liked to keep a low profile," Kenzie teased.

"He doesn't know my name, just what I drink," Raoul said once the barman had gone.

Kenzie chuckled. "Okay, now tell me what's going on in your life." It had been a while since they'd last caught up.

He shrugged. "Oh, you know. This and that."

"Vague as ever."

"Occupational hazard," he said with a lopsided grin.

She laughed.

"More importantly, what brings *you* here?" He studied her over his glass. "As much as I love to see you, Kenz, I know this isn't a social call."

"Why can't it be both?"

He patted her hand. "Of course it can. Ignore me. It's been a long day."

"Everything okay?"

"Peachy," he said. "Let's get back to you. How's the podcast going? I haven't managed to listen in since the Night Watchman case."

The public manhunt that she'd instigated via her channel, and the subsequent outcome of the case had seen her user base grow from a few hundred to a few hundred thousand subscribers. She'd been interviewed on several local radio stations, even a couple of local news channels and other podcasts.

"It's doing well. Bigger than I ever expected, honestly. Which is kind of the problem."

Raoul's mouth twitched. "Good problems to have."

"I feel like I've set an impossibly high bar. Each episode needs to be as good, if not better than the last."

He grimaced. "The life of a YouTuber."

"At least this new case has serious potential."

That got his focus. He leaned forward. "What case?"

She hesitated, wondering where to start. Reid had already messaged to ask for Raoul's details. He needed his help in an official capacity.

"There was a murder last night. The victim was a wealthy art collector. Lives in one of those enormous waterfront properties. You might have seen the headlines already."

His brow furrowed. "The sword guy?"

"That's the one."

Raoul let out a low whistle. "Didn't know you were on that?"

"Reid asked me to do some research into the artifacts found in the victim's house," she said. "By the way, he's going to call you to ask for some help. Hope that's okay."

Raoul pursed his lips. "Sure. Always happy to help the local popo. So this guy, the victim, was a collector?"

Kenzie scrolled to the photos on her phone. "Yeah. He had an entire gallery in the basement filled with priceless antiquities. Check this out."

She showed him the pictures, and his eyebrows shot up above his glasses. "That is an impressive collection."

"I've been checking the provenance of the pieces—or trying to. I managed to make some connections."

He leaned back, folding his arms across his chest. "Do tell?"

"Hargreave was acquiring items through various shell companies. Stolen artifacts."

Raoul whistled.

"Yeah." Kenzie lowered her voice. "There was a sword stolen fifteen years ago from a temple in northern Japan, amongst others."

"Shady bastard," Raoul muttered. "And do we think the stolen treasures has something to do with his untimely demise?"

Kenzie broke into a wry smile. "We're considering the possibility."

"I see." He unfolded his arms and tilted his head. "That's why you need my help? To see if it has legs?"

"Exactly. The crime scene was deliberately staged. Whoever did it wanted it seen, wanted it talked about. I think they were sending a message."

"What do the cops think?" Raoul asked.

"Reid is following up on other leads." She wrapped her hands around her glass. "That's why he thought of you. You're better placed to look into this than they are."

Raoul grunted, as if this was a given. "It's going to cost them."

She grinned. "I know. You've already been vetted as a consultant, so just send them an invoice when you're done. Don't go overboard, though, Sweetwater PD doesn't have endless resources."

"I'll do what I can," he promised with a wink.

"I thought an ideological or cultural motive was a good place to start."

Raoul leaned back, considering. "Agreed. People like that love to talk."

"Online," Kenzie added.

"Always online," he agreed. "They find each other. Validate each other. Build little echo chambers where they feel justified. Forums, Discord servers, private groups. Spaces where cultural restitution, anti-collector sentiment, that sort of thing is being discussed."

Kenzie reached across and squeezed his hand. "I knew you were the right person for the job. Thanks, Raoul. I mean it."

He grinned. "Of course. Won't be too hard. It's not like that stuff's illegal, just buried."

"Good. And if you find nothing, that tells us something too."

Raoul lifted his glass. "To nothing, then. Or to something useful."

She clinked her beer bottle against his. "I'll take useful."

7

Reid drove in silence for a few minutes, letting the hum of traffic and the thump of tires over uneven asphalt fill the space between him and Diaz. Coconut Grove fell away behind them, replaced by wider roads and less manicured streets.

Diaz was already texting on her phone. "You think she's lying?"

"Could be hiding something," Reid admitted. "I think she knew about the will. How do we know it was Hargreave who didn't want a divorce. Maybe it was her?"

"That would make more sense," Diaz decided. "Divorced, she'd only get what the settlement afforded her. Widowed, she gets it all."

"Plus, the divorce settlement would be minimal since she was the one who strayed," he pointed out.

Diaz glanced across at him. "That gives her even more of a motive."

Reid gave a grim nod. "Let's see where her phone puts her and take it from there."

They pulled into the Sweetwater PD lot and parked the cruiser. Inside, the bullpen was quieter than earlier, but the case board was already starting to fill up with photos, timelines, and names.

Diaz headed straight for her desk and sat down at her computer. Reid stood in front of the board, studying the images. There were the crime scene photos taken by the CSU photographer. Better than his, they showed the katana in all its lethal, sharp-edged detail.

A close-up of Hargreave's face, eyes closed, skin unblemished. The familiar purple bloat of death hadn't yet begun, so he seemed oddly at peace. A picture of his hands, fingernails clean and neatly trimmed. The ME would take samples, but it didn't look like there was any DNA to be found there.

There was a full body shot to give them context. The hands resting by his sides, the suit jacket uncreased, the shirt hardly wrinkled despite the blade puncturing it.

"Any prints found on the weapon or on the other fixtures in the room?" he asked no one in particular.

Hamilton looked up. "Nothing on the sword, boss. We haven't got the rest back yet."

He tightened his jaw. It all took time. Early days, yet.

Dwayne pushed his chair back with a scrape. "I found out who owns that house at the end of the street. Sunset Villa."

Reid turned, raising an eyebrow. "Yeah?"

"Mateo and Valeria Solís."

Diaz spun around. "Solís? As in Café Pacifica Solís?"

"Who is Café Pacifica?" Reid asked.

"They're a Latin American music band, really big right now." Diaz was flushed with excitement. She was clearly a fan.

Vargas chose that moment to walk in. "Think Miami Sound Machine, only modern and with more rap."

Reid got the picture.

"So, are they going to give us their camera footage?"

"Small problemo," Dwayne said. "They're currently at their pad in Barbados, but they said they'll contact their private security company and have them pull any footage covering the street outside Hargreave's place from last night."

"When can we get it?" Reid asked.

"Your guess is as good as mine." At Reid's sharp look, he added. "I'll chase up."

Vargas walked up to him. "So I went to see the silent partner, Ackerman. He was stunned to hear of his partner's death. Even more shocked to hear he'd been murdered."

"He didn't know?" Given the amount of coverage, Reid found that hard to believe.

"Apparently not. He's old school. Doesn't use social media."

"Doesn't watch the news either?"

"To be fair, it's been less than a day, boss."

True. "Does he have an alibi for last night?"

Vargas shook his head. "Claims he was at home all evening by himself."

Reid frowned. "Can anyone vouch for him?"

"There's his wife, but she was at some event. Got back in the early hours. She did say he was there when she left and when she got back though."

"She's in publishing," Martinez added, coming up behind Vargas, coffee in hand. Reid looked at it longingly. He couldn't remember when he'd last eaten or drunk anything.

"Doesn't mean anything." He rubbed a jaw growing more stubbly by the minute. "He could have gone out, murdered Hargreave, and been back before she came home."

Vargas frowned. "No way to tell."

"Did you speak to the neighbors?" he asked.

A nod. "Neither of them noticed him leave, but then the properties are fairly private. They each have their own driveways and fences. Hard to notice anything in a neighborhood like that."

Reid gave a grunt. The lives of the rich and famous. It made policing so much harder.

"He did mention something interesting, though," Vargas added. "Apparently Hargreave wanted out."

"What? Like out of the company?"

"Yeah. Out of the day-to-day running of it. He was looking to sell off his shares, step back. Focus on other pursuits."

"Like his art collection?" Reid narrowed his gaze.

Vargas gave a little shrug. "Maybe. He didn't specify."

Reid exhaled, long and slow. "Okay, so what would happen to Ackerman if Hargreave sold his share of the company?"

"If Hargreave dumped his shares on the open market, it could spook investors," Vargas supplied. "The founder stepping away always does. The stock dips. Confidence wobbles."

"So Ackerman could potentially lose a lot of money."

"That's an understatement," Martinez said, warming to the topic. "He could see millions wiped off the board."

Reid tapped a finger against his cheek. "That sounds like a motive to me. Let's dig a little deeper into his movements and his relationship with Hargreave."

"Will do." Vargas went back to his desk.

Martinez handed him her coffee. "Take it. I'll make another one."

He shot her a grateful grin. "Thanks. It's been a long day."

And it was only going to get longer.

Somewhere along the line, the sun set and darkness fell. Someone switched on the light. The team was busy chasing up leads, trawling through CCTV footage, and waiting for the cell phone providers to send through mobile data on their various suspects.

The only reprieve came when Dwayne's wife, Beatrice, stopped by with a tray of empanadas, still warm and smelling of cumin and fried dough.

The team dove on it with gusto, and it did a lot to revive them.

The unusual murder had found its way onto national television and was being broadcast over every news channel in the state.

Reid cursed under his breath. Rojas should be fined for releasing photographs of the crime scene—but he didn't want to get into the legalities of that. They had enough on their plate.

He turned away from his screen to take a call from Perez, a captain at Miami PD. Perez previously served as Reid's boss at the Miami PD before being promoted to his current rank. Their relationship was professional yet informal, and Reid considered Perez a friend.

"You've got your hands full, Garrett," Perez said, once they'd hello-ed and how-are-you-ed.

"Tell me about it," he grumbled, rubbing his eyes.

"I know this is your jurisdiction, but if you want our help, you just have to ask."

'Our' being Miami PD, where he used to work.

"Thanks, but for now my team has it under control. You know how it is."

"Gotcha. Still, the offer stands."

"Thanks, boss," he said.

Perez snorted at the title. "Like you ever listened to me."

"I always take what you say into consideration, Captain. You know that."

"Get back to work, Lieutenant. I'll check in with you in a couple of days."

"Copy that." Allowing himself a weary grin, he ended the call.

It was after ten o'clock when Diaz turned tiredly toward him. "Lieutenant, I just got the call data from the phone company."

Reid turned to face her. "Anything?"

"Sandra West did not leave her house last night. She was home from just before six to seven fifteen this morning."

Reid felt his shoulders droop. Tiredness clawed at the edges of his concentration. They all needed to take a break soon.

Monroe was on the night shift, along with two other officers who were already taking calls and dealing with the normal evening business that came in, but the rest of them were pooped.

"At least her phone was," he amended.

Diaz gave a tight nod. "That's right. She could have left it behind to give her an alibi."

"Check CCTV in the area," he said, stifling a yawn. "We need to confirm that."

"On it." She swung back to her screen.

He was about to call it a day, when Hamilton rushed over. He seemed excited, like he'd found a lead.

"What is it?" Reid asked, praying it was something good.

The young officer grinned. "I did a background check on Mateo Rojas, the landscaper, like you asked. And guess what, he's got priors."

Reid stiffened. "He has?"

"Yeah. Nothing violent. Just theft and trespassing, but a couple of arrests. No convictions in the last eight years though, but still."

Reid frowned, his weary brain kicking into gear. "Could be a coincidence." But his tone lacked conviction.

"Could be he was planning on robbing the place and Hargreave caught him in the act," Vargas called over his shoulder.

"Then why didn't he?" Reid frowned. "This was not an impulsive attack. Besides, there was nothing missing."

"That we know of," Diaz added. "He could have stolen cash or jewelry."

"We didn't see any evidence of that that in the house search," Martinez pointed out.

Reid raked a hand through his hair. "Still, we can't ignore it." He glanced back at Hamilton. "Have him picked up. I'll interview him tomorrow morning. Formally, this time."

"Yes, Lieutenant." Hamilton pulled out his phone.

"And send me everything you've got on him," he added.

Hamilton nodded.

Reid leaned back in his chair. The uniformed cops would pick up the suspect, and he could spend the rest of the night in the holding cell. So much for going home.

He glanced up at the case board where Vargas was updating everything with a black marker. The staged body. Mateo Rojas.

Sandra West. The silent partner. Too many moving parts, and not enough facts—yet.

But they were moving forward, and that's all that mattered.

"Okay," he said, straightening up. "We follow up on all those leads. Double-check alibis with phone data and card transactions. Let's map all of their movements last night."

Diaz stretched, arching her back. "I'm going to need more coffee."

Reid nodded at her. "Fuel up, team. We're just getting started."

8

PODCAST TRANSCRIPT: EPISODE 24- GILT EDGE

(*Soft intro music fades in.*)

Kenzie Gilmore:

If you live in Miami—or anywhere nearby—you've probably already seen the news.

Last night, Dr. Malcolm Hargreave was found dead in his waterfront home. Hargreave was a wealthy pharmaceutical magnate and a private collector of Japanese art and artifacts.

Today, we're going to look at what we know about his death.

And just as importantly—what we don't.

(*Brief pause.*)

(*Traditional Japanese strings fade in briefly, then out.*)

Welcome to *Off the Record*. I'm Kenzie Gilmore, and this is Episode Twenty-Four: *The Gilt Edge*.

Here's what can be confirmed at this stage.

Malcolm Hargreave was discovered inside his home, in a private gallery designed to display his collection of antiques and artifacts. He'd been stabbed with a Japanese sword—a katana, to be precise. The blade was old, rare, and extremely valuable.

I'm not going to describe the crime scene in detail. Many of you have already seen the images circulating online, and if you haven't, they're readily available across news sites and social media. Repeating them here serves no real purpose.

What matters are the facts.

There were no obvious signs of forced entry. There was no blood on or around the body, which suggests Hargreave did not die in that room. He was likely killed elsewhere by some other means.

At this time, we do not know the exact cause of death.

We do not know what happened in the hours leading up to it.

And we do not know who, if anyone, was with him.

What we *can* say is this: the scene was staged.

There are a few reasons a killer might do that. One is performance. A desire for attention. For recognition. For an audience.

But there's another possibility—one that feels more relevant here.

The staging may have been a message.

Hargreave was known for collecting rare Japanese artifacts, some of them centuries old. Objects that originated in temples, shrines, or private collections overseas. The question that naturally follows is whether the killer believed those pieces never should have left Japan in the first place.

If that's true, then this wasn't about theft. It was about punishment.

Which opens up a number of uncomfortable questions.

Were the artifacts acquired ethically?

Did Hargreave know their full provenance?

Or was he targeted by someone who believed they were acting in the name of cultural justice?

At this stage, those questions remain unanswered.

There are details about this case that I am not able to share. This is an active police investigation, and I'm not going to compromise it. I work with law enforcement, and I take that responsibility seriously.

What I *will* say is this. A man is dead. And a family is grieving. We ask that you respect their privacy.

That said, I do have a request.

If you live near the area of Hargreave's estate and noticed anything unusual last night—anything at all—I want to hear from you.

If you work in the art or antiquities world and had direct dealings with Malcolm Hargreave, I want to hear from you. Not rumors. Not speculation. Firsthand contact only.

And if you spend time in online spaces where people discuss cultural restitution, stolen artifacts, or private collectors—pay attention right now. Look for individuals or groups who are grandstanding, posturing, or claiming moral responsibility for this death.

If you have credible information, you can contact the Sweetwater Police Department directly. Or you can reach out to me through the usual channels, and I will make sure that information is passed on to the appropriate authorities.

Over the coming episodes, I'll continue to bring you updates as this investigation develops—sharing what I'm allowed to share and discussing the theories that can be responsibly examined.

(Outro music fades in.)

Kenzie Gilmore: This has been *Off the Record.* Stay safe, and if you have real information, please get in touch.

(Outro fades out.)

9

By the time the sun came up, Reid and his team had unearthed several new leads. Silas Ackerman had met with Hargreave a total of three times in the two weeks prior to the latter's death.

According to Hargreave's executive assistant, a young man by the name of David Rankin, they'd met once in the first week and twice in the second. He didn't know what about, but in their last meeting, which took place the day before Hargreave was murdered, he'd heard raised voices coming from his boss's office. Apparently, Ackerman had marched out without a word afterwards, a stormy expression on his face.

"He's definitely a person of interest," Reid muttered after Vargas had relayed the conversation to him. "Can we get the precise times of those meetings?"

"The assistant is going to send them through when he gets into the office tomorrow," Vargas told him. Rankin had most likely been fast asleep when Vargas had called, like all normal people not working homicide cases.

The second lead to emerge that night was to do with Sandra West, Hargreave's estranged wife.

"Take a look at this, boss." Diaz gestured to her screen where a black and white still of Sandra West's street was being held on pause. Reid swiveled so he could see her monitor. Vargas got up and came over, standing behind him.

"I pulled all the city traffic cams I could find in the vicinity, as well as a couple of private feeds on her street. Most of them are garbage. Poor angles. Trees. Shadows."

"But?" Reid prompted.

"But one house down the block has a camera pointed directly at their driveway. It catches part of the sidewalk."

She hit play.

The footage was grainy and dark, but clear enough to make out a figure moving across the frame. Timestamp read 2:30 a.m. The person wore jogging gear, a dark top, light sneakers, and a black cap pulled low, obscuring their face. They moved at an easy pace, not running, not rushing.

"It could be anyone," Vargas reasoned.

"Or it could be her," Reid countered. "Height's about right. Build too."

"We can't see her face, unfortunately," Diaz said. "If we can't see her face, we can't prove it's her."

"Let's bring her in for questioning," Reid decided. "Print out a copy of this and we'll ask if it's her. I want to see her reaction when she's in front of me in the interview room."

Diaz nodded. "I'll arrange it."

That was one more person they had to speak to today.

The first of their suspects to arrive was the landscaper, Mateo Rojas. He'd been brought in neatly dressed in dark blue jeans with a white T-shirt and sunglasses perched on his head. He had thick dark hair and an astute gaze but didn't appear to be too impressed by the early wake-up call.

"Lieutenant, what am I doing here?" Rojas inquired, as Reid

walked into the interview room. The suspect had been processed, read his rights, and seated at the table. "I gave a statement at Hargreave's mansion."

"I read your statement." He placed a manila folder on the table between them. Rojas's eyes darted to it, then back up at Reid's face. "I have some follow up questions."

"Should I be worried?" Rojas asked.

Reid sat down, the wooden chair squeaking on the concrete floor. "You have reason to be?"

"No, sir."

Reid sat back and studied him. "You didn't tell us you'd taken photographs of the body."

"Is that what this is about?" Rojas shook his head. "Photography is not a crime, is it?"

Reid inhaled through his nose. "No, it's not a crime, but those pictures are hampering our investigation. The additional publicity makes it hard for us to do our jobs." He didn't expect the guy to understand.

Rojas leaned forward. "I thought the world should see what someone did to Hargreave. The sword sticking into him like that. That was some weird, ritualistic shit, man."

"We don't know what it was yet," Reid pointed out, feeling the annoyance build. "That's the whole point. By jumping the gun, you're putting ideas into people's heads. Creating a false narrative."

"How do you know it's false? You don't know who did this. It could be someone punishing him for collecting all that stuff."

Reid frowned. "Did Hargreave mention anything to you about being harassed? Was someone giving him a hard time about it?"

Rojas shuffled, uncomfortable now.

"Mateo?" Reid prompted.

Rojas sighed and spread his hands out on the table. "He didn't say anything to me, but I heard him talking on the phone a couple of times. He liked to walk in the garden when he got calls at home. Especially when he was stressed, which was pretty often."

Reid studied him. Rojas sported a neutral expression, his demeanor was calm, he wasn't perspiring. He appeared to be telling the truth.

"So you overheard?" he asked.

"Yeah, man. I overheard Hargreave saying how he was being targeted. Said he'd had hate mail delivered to the house, that they knew where he lived. He was freaking out about it."

Reid was listening hard now. "When was this?"

"A couple of days before he died. I don't remember exactly when."

"Try." Reid fixed his gaze on him.

Rojas jutted out his lower lip and screwed up his face. "Okay, man. Give me a minute." He clicked his fingers and sat upright. "Yeah, that's it. It was last Friday. So four days before he died. I'm at his place Tuesdays and Fridays, so it had to be one of those."

Reid nodded. "See? That wasn't so hard, was it?"

Rojas grunted. "Don't say I didn't cooperate with the cops."

Reid made a note in the file.

"Tell me about your criminal record," he said, without looking up.

Rojas started. "Hey, man. What's that got to do with anything?"

"Maybe nothing. Maybe something."

He sulked, his mouth turning into a pout. "That was a long time ago."

"I still need to hear it."

"Okay, fine." Mateo looked down at his hands. They were calloused. Working hands. Not soft and manicured like Hargreave's. "I grew up in Little Havana. My mom was single, my dad wasn't around much. You get the picture."

Reid nodded but let him talk.

"When I was a teenager, I was angry a lot. I got involved with the wrong crowd. We got picked up once or twice for trespassing. Once I boosted a car with some guys, but we ditched it a couple of blocks down the street. Still got booked though."

"Looks bad on the job resume." Reid flipped open the file and glanced at the printed rap sheet. The charges matched.

"I know, man. That's why I went into gardening. Nobody asks any questions when you're the gardener."

"How did you end up working for Hargreave?" Reid asked.

Rojas's shoulders lifted in a half-shrug. "One thing led to another. You do a good job at one place, the neighbor asks for your number. These rich people talk. They want their hedges perfect and their lawns like carpets. And they pay stupid money for it."

"How much was he paying you?" Reid asked.

Rojas let out a short laugh. "More than I ever thought I would make."

Reid nodded. They could check his bank statement. "So why take the photographs?"

Rojas's face tightened. "Because it was messed up."

"That is not an answer," Reid said.

"It is an answer," he snapped, then caught himself. He leaned forward, lowering his voice. "Look, Lieutenant. I walked into that basement and it looked like a movie set. Like somebody had done it on purpose so it would be found. The lights. The way he was lying there. The sword sticking out of him like... like I don't know what."

Reid held his gaze. "And your first instinct was to take out your phone."

Rojas hesitated. "My first instinct was to get the hell out of there. Then I thought, nobody is going to believe me when I tell them what I found. So I called 9-1-1 and then took a few shots. I didn't mean to sell them. It was just to show my buddies, you know? But then a reporter offered me two thousand dollars for them, so—" He shrugged, as if that was a done deal.

Reid guessed he couldn't blame him. Two grand was a lot to most people.

Rojas was right about one thing, though. That crime scene had been like the set of a movie. The killer had arranged it down to the last detail.

And Rojas had played right into their hands.

Sandra West was not as cooperative as Rojas had been. Dressed in what she said was her Pilates outfit, she sat with a towel around her shoulders, glaring at him and Diaz across the table.

"Lieutenant, I do not appreciate being picked up as I'm about to leave for my class. I have a cell phone. You could have called and asked me to come in."

He preferred the element of surprise. The inconvenience often caught people off guard. Ruffled their feathers. Just like it had done with Sandra.

"I could have," Reid agreed. "But then you might have said no."

Her nostrils flared. "I am not a criminal."

"No," he said calmly. "You are the estranged wife of a man who was murdered. That makes you relevant."

She scoffed. "Relevant. Is that a polite way of saying suspect?"

He didn't answer.

Diaz slid the printed still across the table. It showed the mysterious figure on the sidewalk at two thirty a.m. Jogging gear, light shoes, black cap pulled low.

Sandra glanced down at it. "What's that?"

"Is that you?" Reid asked.

She stared at it for a beat, then shook her head. "No. Why would you think that's me?"

"It was pulled from a CCTV camera off your street the night of your husband's murder," Reid replied.

She scoffed. "That could literally be anyone from my neighborhood."

"At two thirty in the morning?"

She shrugged. "Do you know how many people jog around there?"

He didn't, but he got the point.

"Maybe they couldn't sleep."

He threw her an agitated look.

She spread her arms and glanced across at Diaz. "What? It's possible, right?"

He sighed. "Okay, let's move on. You told us you were home all night."

"I was," she replied, like it was ridiculous he was still talking about it. "I got in early. I watched TV. I went to bed. End of story."

Reid leaned forward. "You also told us you hadn't seen your husband in months."

Her gaze sharpened. "That's right."

"Except it's not right, is it? You visited his house last week. You were seen by the gardener."

She gritted her teeth. "Dammit."

He glanced at Diaz, who shrugged.

Reid turned back to Sandra. "Care to explain what that was about? And why you lied about it?"

She heaved a sigh. "Because he called me. He wanted to talk."

"About what," Reid asked.

She hesitated, then lifted her chin. "About the divorce."

Reid held her gaze. "You told us he didn't want a divorce—or did you lie about that too?"

Her shoulders drooped. "I was ashamed, okay. Malcolm wanted to divorce me because I'd had an affair. I was embarrassed. It didn't last long. Just a fling—but I was so goddamn bored." As if that excused it.

"Anyway, I said no. I knew how it looked. The errant wife being cut off. He'd leave me with nothing."

"So it was in your best interests to stay married?" Reid surmised.

She nodded. Diaz gave a sympathetic smile, playing good cop to his bad one.

It worked. Sandra turned to her. "I was thinking about my son as well as myself. If he cut me off, we'd have nothing."

Diaz nodded and took over the line of questioning. Reid was happy for her to do it. He sat back and watched.

"Happens to women all the time," Diaz said. "They give up their jobs to support their husbands, and then when they split up, they have to start over."

"Exactly!" Sandra gave an animated nod. "I didn't work when I was married, Malcolm didn't want it. I had to start my own business when I left."

"The modeling agency?" Diaz asked.

"Yeah, but it's a competitive market out there. Hard to break in."

He didn't know anything about modeling, but he could understand that.

"So what changed?" Diaz asked. "Why did Malcolm suddenly want to speak to you?"

"I don't know. Maybe he'd met someone? That's all I can think of. I told him I couldn't survive on a measly divorce settlement, but he said that was for the courts to decide. We had an argument about it. I'm ashamed to say I pleaded with him to reconsider. He wouldn't."

"And that's how you left it?" Diaz asked, tilting her head and gazing at Sandra.

Hargreave's wife uttered a sob. "I know how it looks, but I swear, I had nothing to do with his death."

"Even though you stand to inherit, now that he's gone. You get his entire fortune, and his shares in the pharmaceutical company. That's a lot more than a measly divorce settlement," Reid said.

She stared at him, the color draining from her face.

"You wanted to know why I lied," she whispered. "This is why. Because I knew how it would look."

Diaz pursed her lips and glanced at him. He kept his gaze on Sandra. "Be that as it may, it does put you at the top of our suspect list."

She gave a strangled gasp. "Am I under arrest?"

"Not at present."

He saw her exhale in relief.

"Just don't leave town, okay? We may want to speak to you again."

10

Kenzie logged onto her computer and discovered her podcast episode had been viewed over a hundred thousand times since last night.

Wow.

She leaned back in her chair for a moment, letting it sink in. The spike wasn't just good, it was explosive. The Night Watchman case had brought eyes to her channel, but this one had hit a nerve.

She scrolled down the page. The comments were coming in faster than she could read them. Hundreds already. The 'likes' were stacking up. Threads branching into arguments, theories, counter-theories.

Her audience was wide awake, and they were thinking.

Blowing an errant strand of hair out of her face, she leaned in and started reading properly.

Could this be connected to stolen artifacts from Japanese temples? Maybe someone's taking revenge for cultural theft?

. . .

She stopped, then clicked the username. It was a new account with no other remarks or uploads. Still, the comment had nearly four hundred likes.

She scrolled on until she came to another that made her pause.

The positioning of the body seems ritualistic. Has anyone looked into whether the victim was involved in black market antiquities?

Her stomach tightened. Even though she knew it to be true, she hadn't shared what she'd found with anyone other than Reid and his team. Seeing strangers arrive at the same conclusion was an endorsement of sorts. There might be something to that theory.

What if this is about honor? Like someone enforcing bushido against people who disrespect Japanese culture?

Bushido.

Kenzie frowned, opened a new tab, and searched the term. The way of the warrior. A samurai moral code encompassing values such as courage, honor, loyalty, and respect. The commenter was asking if the killer was upholding the strict, traditional code of the Japanese samurai by murdering Hargreave.

She frowned. Were they? Was this more about honor killing than revenge or some other motive?

She kept going.

I did some digging. That collector had a reputation for buying questionable pieces. This feels personal.

. . .

Who did some digging?

How had they found out about the 'questionable pieces'? Had they gone through a similar process to what she had, starting with the sword—the katana—and gone from there?

Had they discovered the shell companies too? Traced the items to the stolen temple artifacts?

Or did they know something she didn't?

The user's handle was @InTheField. She clicked on it, but like the other one, it led nowhere. Recently created, it had obviously been set up for the sole purpose of commenting on this particular video.

On a whim, she tabbed to one of her most popular videos on the Night Watchman case and did a quick search through the comments section for the same user. Nothing. She found a @FieldMouse and a @FieldingQs but no @InTheField.

Could either of them be the same person?

Reading the comments, she bit her lip. Hard to say. Some of them were well reasoned, clearly thought out, but none of them mirrored the style of the 'this feels personal' remark. Then again, one comment wasn't really enough to base an analysis on.

Kenzie gave up and went back to reading her current comments feed.

The murderer could be sending a message about justice and consequence.

Yes, that was true. They could definitely be sending a message of some sort. The staging of the crime scene, the positioning of the sword, the body—it all pointed to that.

Has anyone considered a Japanese nationalist group? The symbolism is too specific to be accidental.

. . .

She rubbed her temples.

What struck her wasn't that any single comment was correct. It was that together, they were circling something. The same idea, approached from different angles. Theft. Dishonor. Restoration. A wrong that needed correcting.

She opened her notebook beside her keyboard and started jotting things down.

Stolen artifacts.
Bushido code?
Justice?
Message?
Nationalist groups.

They already knew the victim was buying stolen artifacts. Japanese artifacts. With that in mind, the bushido code made sense—in a warped kind of way. Could the killer be trying to get justice by murdering Hargreave? Was that the intended message?

She took a deep breath and stretched her neck. Could the user who'd mentioned nationalist groups be on to something? Kenzie got up to grab another cup of coffee, then she resolved to get back to searching and try to find out.

11

"I don't think Rojas did it," Reid announced in a team briefing later that day. Diaz and Martinez had gone home for a few hours' sleep, along with Monroe and Dwayne, but Vargas, Hamilton, and himself were still going, buoyed up by adrenaline and caffeine.

Reid was so wired, he didn't think he could sleep now even if he tried.

"He had the means and the opportunity," Vargas pointed out. He looked as strung out as Reid felt.

"Yeah, but no real motive. He saw an opportunity, nothing more." Hamilton had checked with the reporter who'd confirmed Rojas's story. Reid believed the gardener when he said he'd turned over a new leaf. Bad pun intended.

"Nothing was stolen, as far as we know," Reid added.

Vargas frowned. "Okay, so he's in the clear. What about her? She's a tricky one. I watched the live feed of the interview. Not sure I believe her whole 'woe is me' act." A couple of years back, Vargas would have fallen for her sob story hook, line, and sinker, but since then he'd hardened up.

He'd been used, in the worst possible way, by a woman he'd been ready to spend the rest of his life with. She'd hacked into his work laptop, stolen confidential case files, and used the information to commit murder. He'd never recovered.

Now he didn't trust anybody.

"You think she could be the one Malcolm was meeting the evening he died?" Hamilton asked.

"Why would he switch off the security cameras if it was his wife?" Vargas countered. "That makes me think it was someone he didn't want a record of. A black-market dealer or a buyer, rather."

Reid nodded. "I agree, that's more likely. Kenzie is coming in soon to tell us what she's found. She did some research into the artifacts."

"Oh? She find anything?" Vargas asked.

"She says she did. I haven't had time to talk to her about it, but we'll find out soon enough."

An hour later, Kenzie breezed in wearing a floral sundress, a splash of color in a room that had long since lost it. Reid was surprised by how glad he was to see her. When she sat on the edge of his desk, the light, summery scent she carried cut through the recycled air and made the space feel less oppressive.

"You're a sight for sore eyes." He managed a faint grin.

She shot him a concerned glance. "When did you sleep last?"

"Don't remember. Did you find anything?"

She nodded. "Yeah. Where do you want to talk?"

Diaz was back in the office, as was Martinez, but Monroe wasn't due until the evening shift.

He spread his arms. "How about right here? The team needs to hear this too." It would save him repeating it.

She nodded and turned to face the others who spun their desk chairs around and huddled in.

She waited until she had their attention. "Okay, well it's pretty interesting. I found proof that Malcolm Hargreave was buying and selling black-market antiquities."

There was a collective murmur of surprise.

"What kind of proof?" Reid asked.

"He was acquiring pieces through shell companies, most of which I traced to agencies in Delaware." She glanced at her phone. "Orion Holdings, Vega Asset Management, Andromeda Enterprises, Perseus Holdings. They were all set up for illicit purchases of artifacts with murky provenance. I've traced purchases all over Asia. There have been some sales too, but mostly acquisitions."

They stared at her.

Reid cleared his throat. "That puts a different spin on things. Did you manage to link them to any of the pieces in his gallery?"

Her eyes sparkled. "Sure. There was a sword stolen from a remote Japanese temple, a scroll with questionable origins, and some others that had either been bought through an intermediary, or via dealers with shady reputations." She hesitated. "There is some suggestion that his death was a revenge killing."

"For the stolen art?" Diaz whispered.

She nodded. "I released an episode last night and it's gone viral. I've had thousands of comments already. Some—I think—are worth exploring more fully."

Reid ran a hand through his hair. "Like?"

She handed him a sheet of paper. "These are the most interesting. I've looked up the users, but most are unregistered accounts, set up purely for commenting on social media. I asked Raoul to dig deeper into the users, but I'm not sure if he'll have much luck. New account users are almost impossible to identify."

Reid took it and scanned the page. "A lot of ideological or cultural theories."

"Yeah, it's a sensitive topic. Really hit a nerve."

His jaw tightened. "While I'm not dismissing this angle, it's not our priority right now. If you could ask Raoul to look into it, we'd be grateful. It would save us a lot of time."

Vargas held out his hand, and Reid passed him the page. He took a look and blew out a breath. "Wow. Everybody has an opinion."

"Yeah." Kenzie nodded to the piece of paper in his hand. "The general consensus is that this was a retaliation for the stolen artifacts. Maybe a nationalist group or a fanatic who believes Hargreave violated a sacred trust. Bushido. A loss of honor and therefore must die."

"Bushido?" asked Hamilton, shaking his head.

"The Way of the Warrior," Kenzie explained. "It's an ethical code or philosophy followed by Japan's samurai warriors. Like honor, loyalty, and respect. But get this..." She glanced at Reid. "They believe in ritualistic suicide to restore lost honor."

Reid stared at her. He'd heard of bushido but had never had any exposure to it. Until now.

Vargas handed the paper to Diaz. There was a deep groove in his forehead, a sign he was worried. "We can't go through all these users. We don't have the manpower. Even with Raoul's help, we'll need to investigate any possible leads."

Reid drew in a breath. His colleague wasn't wrong, but he didn't want to jump the gun. "Let's see what he uncovers first and take it from there. We need hard evidence, not guesses from people who think a Wikipedia article makes them experts on Japanese honor codes."

"Problem is, we can't separate the armchair enthusiasts from the people who really believe this stuff," Diaz pointed out.

That was the problem.

"You can't, but maybe Raoul can," Kenzie cut in.

Heads turned in her direction.

"He's going to look online for groups, chats, Discord servers... any place these enthusiasts might hang out."

"Sounds good," Reid said.

"So we're taking this seriously?" Vargas asked.

"It's one of many avenues of investigation," Reid replied. "Right now, we focus on Sandra West, the silent partner, and the missing camera footage. We find out who he was meeting that night. I still think that is our strongest lead."

"Agreed," said Vargas, turning back to his desk.

The others nodded and drifted back to their seats.

Kenzie pushed herself into a standing position. "I'll check in with Raoul later and let you know if he's found anything."

Reid gave a nod. "Keep me posted."

"Will do."

He hesitated, looking to see if the others were still paying attention. No one was.

"Thanks, Kenzie." He kept his tone quiet. "Appreciate your effort. I know how time consuming this is."

She broke into a smile. "No problem. It's what I'm good at."

"See you later?"

"Of course, if you can make it."

"I'll try." He was so exhausted, he couldn't go another night without sleep.

She gave a knowing nod. "See you later, then."

He watched her leave, blond ponytail swishing behind her, and felt the heaviness in his chest lighten, just a little.

12

KENZIE'S PHONE BUZZED, and she looked up from her screen, bleary-eyed.

Raoul.

Just the person she needed to talk to. She was making no headway here at all. If Japanese nationalist groups existed, she couldn't find them online.

"Hey."

"Hey yourself," he said. His voice was low, measured. That told her more than the words did. "You got a minute."

"Always." She grabbed her mug and leaned against the counter. "What did you find?"

"Quite a bit, actually," he said. "You were right about the cultural angle. There's chatter. Not mainstream stuff but not buried as deep as you'd think either."

Kenzie straightened. She'd be damned if she could find it. "Where?"

"Discord, mostly. Private servers. Some invite only, some you can stumble into if you know what to search for." She clearly didn't.

He paused. "There's one group in particular that stood out."

"Yeah?"

"It's framed around bushido," he continued. "Honor. Cultural restitution. The idea that sacred objects don't belong in private collections, especially not Western ones. They talk a lot about the looting of temples and shrines, that sort of thing."

"I know what it is," she said. "Came across it in the comments of my latest video."

"Oh, really? I'll take a look. Anyway, there is a lot of mention of moral balance, restoring honor, that kind of thing."

Her grip tightened on the mug. "How extreme are they?"

"Mostly ideological," he said. "Lots of posturing and quoting from historical sources. But there's anger under it. Real anger."

"Anyone specific," she asked. "Or is it just the group having a rant?"

"There's a user who posts a lot. I think he's the lead moderator. Goes by the username ShatteredTorii."

Kenzie wrinkled her forehead. "As in the shrine gate?"

"A broken gate," Raoul specified. "Can't tell his real name without doing a deeper dive. He uses that username consistently across platforms."

That was interesting.

"What's his deal?"

"He's a Japanese national, from what I can make out," Raoul told her. "He appears educated and fluent in English, but there are still telltale signs it's not his first language. Not a kid. If I had to guess, I'd say late thirties, early forties. He writes like someone with a deep knowledge of the ideology. Possibly a student or academic. He's been vocal for years about artifacts taken from sacred sites. Calls collectors 'grave robbers with inflated bank accounts.'"

Kenzie let out a slow breath. "Has he mentioned Hargreave?"

"Not by name," Raoul said. "But there have been several posts in the last few days about a prominent Miami collector who got what he deserved. There was a mention of that gallery you told me about. 'Blades displayed like trophies.'"

That sent a chill through her.

"He could be who Hargreave met with the night he died," she whispered. "He could have posed as a dealer or intermediary."

"Easy," Raoul warned. "There is nothing to suggest that anyone in that group knew Hargreave. I didn't find anything remotely like a confession. It's mostly ideological babble."

Kenzie closed her eyes for a second. "It's a start."

"That's not all." Raoul paused for a beat. "I found something else that may—or may not—be relevant."

She opened her eyes. "Go on."

"There's a group of true crime investigators who've latched onto the case hard," he said. "They're studying the crime scene photographs that landscaper guy took, they're mapping timelines, comparing symbolism. Some of it's a stretch, but some of it makes real sense."

"What's it called?" she asked.

He snorted. "The Evidence Room."

"Catchy."

"Yeah, it's a private forum, but easy to access. They're very active, by the looks of things, particularly in the evenings. Several hundred posts a day."

"Wow. True crime fanatics, you say?"

"Yeah, big time. I don't think this is their first rodeo, either. They've got a long history of online case solving. Some of it is actually pretty useful. Looks like they've assisted police and sheriff departments all over the state."

Kenzie gave a knowing nod, not that Raoul could see her. These groups were popping up all over the internet now. People who wanted justice for friends, relatives, or even strangers in their hometowns when cases went cold. Sometimes it was budget issues. Sometimes lack of manpower. Investigations were shelved, cases dropped or abandoned for lack of evidence.

Web chats and group environments meant civilians could now have a shot at finding the culprits. A second set of eyes. Sometimes a thousand of them. Obviously, it came with controversy and plenty of bad takes along the way. But Kenzie had seen it work. Hell, her own podcast was proof of that.

"Who's the moderator," she asked.

"User goes by RedCairn," he said. "Again, no real name attached to his profile."

"How many members?" she asked. "And can anyone join?"

"They've got about forty registered members, but only a handful are consistently active. Some dip in and out during cases, but the core group do most of the heavy lifting."

That was often the case in these online groups. It was run by a stalwart few, with others participating when they had time or the mood took them.

"They've already put together a theory about revenge, bushido-style," Raoul continued. "The group is of the opinion that the killer wanted the crime to be found, photographed, and discussed. That it was some kind of warning not to steal Japanese treasures."

Kenzie's stomach twisted. "They might have a point."

He grunted. "Which is why I thought you might be interested."

"Okay, thanks Raoul. This is a lot to digest. Can you send me some links? Is there any way I can see what's happening in these groups?"

"Not unless you join them," he said. "I snuck through layers of security to do it, but you won't be able to go in that way."

She bit her lip. "I'll just have to join then."

"The ideological one is encrypted and almost impossible to find without an invitation or direct link. They'll know something's up if you ask to join. The armchair detectives... well, that's up to you. You could ask to become a member. They don't take just anyone though. Their membership is made up of retired cops, researchers, tech-savvy individuals." He drew a breath. "But...with your pedigree, you've got a shot at being accepted into the group."

She hesitated. "Good idea. Send me the details, Raoul."

"Will do, but Kenz—"

"Yeah."

"Watch your back. Most of these groups don't trust outsiders. Don't go in asking a ton of questions. Lurk first, get the lay of the land. If anyone gives you any shit, you back out."

"Understood," she said. Even though she wasn't a novice when it came to online groups, she appreciated his concern. Raoul was a veteran, and she wasn't about to contradict him. "Thanks for the heads up."

They hung up, and Kenzie stood there for a long moment, phone still in her hand and the faint buzz of adrenaline in her stomach. This case was about to get a lot more personal.

Kenzie logged onto the Discord server using the link Raoul had given her.

The landing page was deliberately muted. Dark background with minimal branding. No splash graphics, no slogans. Just a short description at the top of the server rules panel.

The Evidence Room.

Beneath it, a tagline read: Private Investigative Discussion. The group rules were listed as evidence-based analysis only, no speculation, no doxxing. No vigilantism. No defamatory comments or swearing. Anyone not abiding by these rules would be removed and blocked from the group.

She exhaled slowly. That alone told her this wasn't a casual fan space. Most informal true crime groups led with disclaimers and emojis. This one led with boundaries.

She skimmed the visible channels. Most were locked.

#rules-and-onboarding

#case-submissions

#methodology

#active-discussions
#media-analysis
#symbolism-and-staging

That last one made her pause.

A small badge beside several channels read restricted. She hovered her cursor over it, and a tooltip popped up.

Read access granted after verification.

"So that's how you roll," she murmured.

She clicked into the public lobby channel. The chat feed scrolled steadily, but not fast. This wasn't banter and suppositions. It was deliberate conversation. Timestamps spaced minutes apart. Paragraphs of commenting, not one-liners or impulsive blurts.

She scanned the usernames. Most were understated. No skulls or edgy handles. Mostly muted names that had some bearing in reality.

RedCairn. AlexR. GrayAtlas. FieldNotes. CrossCheck. ThirdWitness.

She scrolled back to the top of the feed. They were dissecting the crime scene photos with a calm rationale. They discussed the framing, the angles, and the positioning. Asking questions like why the sword was upright. They'd also picked up on the lighting, and how the macabre tableau had been spotlit for maximum effect.

Not amateurs, then.

One thread talked about how there was no sign of struggle. Someone commented on the unrumpled clothes, the lack of bruising or grazes on the body of the victim. The hands unscuffed. One user had uploaded a diagram of the gallery layout and annotated it with dimensions.

Kenzie felt that familiar tightening in her chest. A mix of admiration and unease. These people weren't rubbernecking. They were working the case like real investigators. Using evidence available to them through news channels and online resources to construct a theory. She was impressed.

She clicked on the server info panel. Membership required approval, but as Raoul had said, they were particular about who they let join. Relevant experience was required.

She opened the join request form and perused the questions. They were pretty blunt, getting straight to it.

Why do you want to join The Evidence Room?

What experience do you bring to the group?

Do you have a public profile or body of work we can verify?

Kenzie inhaled, leaning back in her chair. This was the moment she had to decide whether she was going to open herself up to this or not. To get involved would be to commit, and she knew it would require time and effort to monitor and engage.

Did she really want to do this?

No, but what was the alternative? She couldn't see all the feeds without joining. Only the top few, the ones they allowed as an enticement to new members.

She'd viewed enough to know they were serious and were making headway on the investigation. They'd gotten off to a good start, pretty similar to what she and Reid had discussed.

But were they involved in Hargreave's death? Probably not.

Would they unearth leads the police wouldn't? Unlikely, but possibly. Maybe she should join just to keep an eye on them?

She gnawed on her lower lip, thinking. If she joined, it would be with an alias. She could keep her profile private. Nobody needed to know who she really was.

Sucking in a breath, she started typing.

Username: ReporterGirl
Occupation: Investigative journalist and podcast host
Affiliation: None

She paused, knowing she needed more to pass inspection. After a beat, she continued:

I have covered multiple active and cold cases, often in collaboration with law enforcement. My work focuses on evidence, sourcing, and responsible public engagement.

She hesitated, then added one more line.

I am frustrated with watching from the sidelines. I want to take an active role in crime solving and contribute meaningfully rather than speculate from the outside.

She reread it. It was honest—maybe too honest. But if she was going to do this, she was all in. No half-measures.

At the bottom of the form was a final checkbox.

I agree not to disclose internal discussions without moderator approval.

She checked it.

Her cursor hovered over the final button: SUBMIT.

She thought of Reid, buried under case files. Of the comments flooding her channel. Of the careful staging in that basement gallery.

Then she clicked.

The screen refreshed. A simple message appeared.

Your request is pending moderator review.

Kenzie leaned back and let out a breath she hadn't realized she was holding. If they let her in, this case was about to open up in ways she couldn't control. And if they didn't, she'd just have to find another way to keep tabs on them.

13

Reid got to Kenzie's, having driven into the blindingly setting sun, already low in the sky, all the way to her place on Bay Harbour Island. He could barely keep his eyes open.

She greeted him with a hug, a beer, and the smell of a pot roast that made his stomach rumble. He hadn't eaten properly in days.

"Hey," she said into his shoulder, holding him a beat longer than usual. He let himself lean into her, just for a second. His body felt heavy, like he was carrying the weight of the world on his shoulders.

"Hey," he managed, then cleared his throat. "That smells so good."

Kenzie laughed softly and pulled back to look at him. The smile faded into concern. "Reid. You look awful."

"That's the nicest thing anyone's said to me all day." He tried for humor but couldn't quite pull it off.

"Take a load off," she said, steering him inside with a hand at his back. "Sit down. You're eating, then you're sleeping."

He wanted to argue, to insist he was fine, but he didn't have the energy. He toed off his shoes and sank onto one of her kitchen stools while she moved around the kitchen dishing up.

He liked the rhythm they had going. They weren't living together, not officially. She often spent weekends at his place, but sometimes, so she didn't have to do all the driving, he stayed here. Usually during the week or when she was working on an article or episode for her podcast and needed her equipment. It wasn't closer, but it wasn't too far away either. Only a forty-five-minute drive door to door.

She set two plates down on the counter. Pot roast, carrots, mashed potatoes, gravy. His mouth watered.

"Let's eat, before you pass out on me."

He smirked, then picked up his fork and took a bite. "Damn, I needed this."

She chuckled. "I know."

They ate in silence for a minute, the clink of cutlery and the low hum of the fridge filling the space. Reid didn't realize how hungry he was until his plate was half empty.

Kenzie watched him with that look she got sometimes, half affection, half calculation. The reporter in her never really switched off.

"How's it going?" she asked finally.

He swallowed, took a sip of beer, and exhaled. "Well, it's going. In circles, mostly, but then it always does at this stage."

"I know what you mean."

She did, too. That's what was so great about Kenzie. Her investigative skills were top-notch, and together they made a formidable team. That's why he'd brought her on as a consultant to the Sweetwater PD. Perez had finally agreed after she'd assisted on so many cases in an unofficial capacity that there was no point in not making it official.

Thankfully, that meant he could give her case details without breaking protocol. Still, he had to be careful. She was a reporter, after all, with a highly public YouTube channel. Sure, it came in useful at times, but could also be a problem for them, particularly when he and Kenzie disagreed.

She was nothing if not independent.

"Did you get any further on Hargreave's wife?" She glanced across at him.

"Yeah." He told her about the pending divorce.

Kenzie's brows shot up. "That's one hell of a motive."

"I know. We pulled her phone data but according to that, she was home all night."

"Or she wanted you to think she was."

"Exactly," he agreed. "Her son can't vouch for her since he wasn't there. He stays at his girlfriend's place."

She pursed her lips. "What about CCTV?"

"Yeah, that..." He hesitated.

"What?" she prompted, her eyes eager. "Did you find something?"

He stroked his jaw, now so badly in need of shaving it was almost beard-level stubble. "Not sure. One camera caught a figure on the sidewalk at around two thirty in the morning. They were wearing jogging gear, but their face was hidden by a black cap."

Kenzie gave a small gasp. "Could it be her?"

"The height and build match," he said with a nod. "But it could be anyone. That's what a lawyer would say, anyway."

"Does it line up with time of death?"

He grimaced, unable to hold back his frustration. "We don't have a time of death yet. Not officially."

Kenzie set her knife and fork down. "When will you know?"

"The autopsy was scheduled for this afternoon." He stifled a yawn. "We should have the preliminary report tomorrow. If the ME can narrow it down, we can see whether that jogger matters."

"Will you keep me posted?"

Reid nodded, even though he'd probably forget.

Kenzie nudged him. "If it was the wife, then I've just joined a true crime detective group for nothing."

He frowned. "You what?"

She told him about The Evidence Room. "They're a bunch of

amateur detectives who help the police with active ones and look into cold ones."

"They also obstruct investigations, compromise evidence and leak confidential information," he countered, unable to hold back his annoyance. "Amateurs who don't know when to quit."

Kenzie bit her lip. "These guys have a decent track record," she tried to explain. "According to their Discord group, they—"

"Anything on there is unverified. You can't believe a word they say."

"I read their group discussions," she insisted stubbornly. "They've made the same headway we have on the case."

"The Hargreave case?" He rubbed his forehead.

"Yes. They've assessed the crime scene, noticed the staging, the lighting, everything."

He scowled.

Great. Now they had a bunch of fanatics to contend with.

"They could be useful," she argued, hands on her hips.

He sighed. Once Kenzie had an idea, she didn't stop until she'd either disproved or discarded it. Her stubbornness was what made her such a good investigator.

It also got her into trouble.

He was too tired to argue. "Okay, I can see I'm not going to persuade you otherwise, but just so you know, I don't approve of those groups."

"Really? I hadn't noticed."

He snorted and got up from the counter. He was just making his way to the sofa when she said, "Raoul called today. He found some nationalist group online spouting bushido ideology. He's going to keep an eye on them."

"Did they mention the Hargreave case?" He sank down and stretched his legs out in front of him.

"Sort of." Kenzie curled up beside him. "They mentioned a dead collector, just not by name. The general sentiment was he'd gotten what he deserved."

"Hmm?" Reid leaned his head back. He was close to losing his battle with consciousness. "That does sound interesting."

"Why don't you go and lie down," she offered. "It might be more comfortable than the couch."

"I'm fine," he lied.

She smirked.

"Remind me to tell you about the hate mail when I wake up," he slurred, trying to make a mental note, but failing. His brain was shutting down. It wouldn't be long now.

"Hate mail? Who's getting hate mail?"

He felt himself falling into blissful oblivion.

"Reid... Reid... What hate mail?"

Her voice floated around somewhere in the distance, just out of reach. He tried to reply, but instead a gentle snore came out. He was warm, comfy, and well-fed. Everything else could wait.

14

Once Reid was asleep, Kenzie went back to her study. She moved quietly, not wanting to wake him, though he was out cold on the sofa. His breathing was slow and even, and he sat with one arm flung awkwardly over a cushion.

Logging back onto her computer, she went straight to Discord.

The Evidence Room server icon sat there, unchanged, but when she clicked into it, something was different. The lock icons were gone from a few channels and new ones had appeared.

Her pulse kicked up. A notification banner stretched across the top of the screen.

Welcome, ReporterGirl. Your access has been approved.

She clicked into the general channel. Almost immediately, a message popped up.

RedCairn: Welcome aboard, ReporterGirl. Appreciate you taking the time to go through the screening process.

Kenzie exhaled slowly, stretched her fingers, and typed back.

ReporterGirl: Thanks for having me. I know you don't take new members lightly.

Three dots appeared, vanished, then appeared again.

RedCairn: We don't, but you sound more than qualified. You work with law enforcement, you said?

>

>

ReporterGirl: On occasion, yes. I'm a vetted consultant.

No harm in telling them that. They wouldn't know which department. She'd suspected that was one of the reasons they'd accepted her. Seemed she was right.

A few other usernames chimed in, one after the other.

ThirdWitness: Welcome.

FieldNotes: Glad to have you.

>

>

CrossCheck: What kind of podcast do you host?

>

ReporterGirl: True crime, of course.

There were a few smiling and laughing emojis at that. She scanned the usernames. These were the ones she had already seen posting thoughtful, careful analyses. Their tone was calm and professional. Nothing gave her any cause for alarm at present.

RedCairn posted again.

RedCairn: For everyone's benefit, I'll go over the rules. Confidentiality clauses apply. No cross-posting, no attribution without group consent. No last names, and you don't have to give your first name unless you want to.

>

>

>

>

ReporterGirl: Understood. I'm here to contribute, not broadcast. Your goals align with my own and my podcast.

That seemed to land well. A couple of reaction icons popped up. Check marks. Thumbs up.

She scrolled through the active discussion channel. They were mid-conversation about the crime scene staging. Someone had uploaded a still from a news clip showing the gallery from yet another angle. Another user was questioning the placement of the display lights.

She didn't jump in right away, preferring to lurk for a while and see what she could learn about the group. They were informative and logical, but that didn't tell her anything out of the ordinary.

After a few minutes, she thought she'd better participate. She wanted to give them something, something that would help but not derail the case.

ReporterGirl: I heard the front door to the property was open and the security cameras were switched off. Not tampered with, just off.

There was a pause.

Then.

ThirdWitness: How do you know this?

>

>

>

ReporterGirl: I saw the incident report.

>

AlexR: In an official capacity?

>

>

ReporterGirl: Let's just say that detail wasn't withheld from the press.

She knew the landscaper would have told his friends about how he'd found the body. It wasn't one of those crucial details Reid would have wanted held back. They had no control over who the landscaper told.

CrossCheck: That suggests the victim knew his killer.

>

>

>

GrayAtlas: Puts a different spin on it.

>

>

RedCairn reacted with a simple check mark.

Kenzie felt the tension in her shoulders ease a fraction. They discussed that point for a while, and she stayed engaged but careful, and didn't offer up anything else. An hour passed without her noticing.

At some point, a direct message notification popped up.

AlexR: Hey. Intrigued how you knew about the door and alarms. Were you at the crime scene?

Kenzie pursed her lips, considering how to reply. This was the member Raoul had flagged as critical to the group. The one with the most impact, other than the lead moderator, of course.

She replied.

ReporterGirl: Professionally adjacent. Former investigative journalist, now freelancer and podcaster. I work with law enforcement as a researcher.

>

>

AlexR: That's not a no.

Kenzie cringed. Had she gone too far? Let him know too much? These people were strangers, and she had to be careful how much she divulged about herself and the investigation.

She reined it in.

ReporterGirl: How about you?

>

>

>

>

AlexR: I'm more on the data side. FOIA requests, timelines, public records. What's the real reason you joined?

She chose her words carefully.

ReporterGirl: I'm frustrated with watching. I want to be useful. I think I could contribute a lot and do some good here. Not just on this case.

There was a beat.

AlexR: That's why most of us are here.

They talked quietly in DMs while the main channel kept moving. Alex told her about a cold case he'd worked on with the group the year before. A missing person's case that had stalled until someone in the group caught a discrepancy in phone tower data.

Kenzie shared a little more of her background, enough to prove her skill set, but without giving him enough to identify her.

She framed herself as someone who had seen how investigations could stall, how public pressure could both help and hurt.

Eventually, she asked:

ReporterGirl: I see some channels are still locked.

>

>

>

>

AlexR: Yeah, that's for the core group. We're more committed than the rest, we dig deeper.

>

>

ReporterGirl: I see.

>

>

>

AlexR: If you want access, you'll have to ask RedCairn. He controls the access.

>

>

>

ReporterGirl: Understood. Think I need to earn it before asking.

>

>

AlexR: You may already have.

She hesitated, then went for it.

ReporterGirl: If a referral helps down the line, I'd appreciate it. No rush.

A pause. Longer this time.
Then.

AlexR: Let's see how tonight goes. But yeah. I think you'd be a good fit.

Kenzie let out a breath.

Back in the main channel, they were talking about motives for the murder. He was wealthy, he was separated, estranged from his family according to witness accounts, and he was an art dealer with shady connections. He'd been killed by a katana and the crime scene staged in such a way to garner maximum exposure.

They were correct on most fronts, except one. The cause of death.

RedCairn tagged her.

RedCairn: ReporterGirl, curious on your take.

All eyes were on her now.

She sat back, thought for a moment, then typed.

ReporterGirl: Not sure if you're aware, but the victim wasn't killed by the katana. If you look at the photos, there's not enough blood. He was killed elsewhere and moved to the gallery, where he was found.

The channel went quiet. Then the responses came.

FieldNotes: You're right. We did wonder about this, but it's hard to see clearly using the photographs alone.
>

>

GrayAtlas: Thanks for the confirmation.

>

>

AlexR: Good call. That brings us back to the crime scene staging and the motive for murder.

>

>

>

ReporterGirl: Given the elaborate effort, I'd say the motive is most likely to do with some form of symbolic justice—or the killer wanted the world to think it was.

>

RedCairn: Agreed.

Kenzie felt something shift then. A subtle thing, but real. She was no longer being evaluated. She was being engaged.

Another hour slipped by. Midnight came and went. She heard Reid give a loud snore from the couch, then settled again.

At one forty-five, RedCairn posted a final message.

RedCairn: Logging off soon. Good work tonight. ReporterGirl, you're cleared for the tiered channels. Alex vouched for you.

Her chest warmed.

ReporterGirl: Appreciate it. Thanks for the trust.

She logged off a few minutes later, the clock on her laptop reading 1:53 a.m. The apartment was quiet. Reid was fast asleep, dead to the world.

Kenzie closed the laptop and sat there for a moment, letting the events of the night catch up to her. She hadn't learned anything worthwhile, that was true. But she was inside now.

Maybe with her fellow true crime enthusiasts, she'd get closer to the truth.

She knew Reid didn't like it, and understandably so. From his point of view, they were pests, poking their noses into investigations he didn't think they had any right being involved in.

But if they uncovered a lead or two, surely that couldn't be a bad thing.

15

Reid woke up in Kenzie's bed, the sunlight streaming in through a crack in the blinds, hitting him square in the eyes.

"Ugh." He squeezed them shut again, but it was too late. Blue lasers danced behind his lids. He needed to shift position or get up. He chose up.

Kenzie was still fast asleep beside him, curled into the fetal position, her blond hair splayed out like a halo on the pillow. She looked angelic. An air of innocence that belied her street smarts and savvy, and that she often used to her advantage.

Moving the cover back gently, so as not to wake her, he slipped out of bed. He didn't remember falling asleep, didn't remember coming to bed. At some stage during the night he must have walked here, because Kenz sure as hell couldn't carry him.

Geez, he must have been so out of it.

He stretched, then wandered into the kitchen to put on a pot of coffee. The morning sun leaked into the living room, pooling on the floorboards.

He liked Kenzie's place. It was near the water, it was bright and breezy, and much more luxurious than his rustic cabin. She'd bought it with the inheritance she got after her father passed and was—in his humble opinion—a worthy investment.

Armed with a cup of joe, he opened the front door and stood facing the ocean, marveling at how blue it was, and how endless. He stared out at the horizon until he had to blink and look away. In the other direction stretched the Miami skyline. Heavy and permanent, shimmering in the early morning haze.

A fresh, briny smell wafted past, and he turned his face up to the sun enjoying the warmth as it seeped into his skin. That was how Kenzie found him moments later when she joined him.

"It's a beautiful day," she announced, slipping an arm around his waist and giving him a squeeze. He reciprocated.

"It is. Pity I have to ruin it by going into the office, but duty calls."

She shot him a sympathetic smile. "You were dead to the world last night."

"Yeah." He quirked an eyebrow. "How'd I get to bed?"

"You walked, or rather sleepwalked." She chuckled. "I haven't seen you that out of it for a long time."

He gave a low grunt.

"How are you feeling now?" she asked.

"Good. Better."

She nodded.

He scratched his head. "Hey, you were telling me something when I passed out last night. What was it?"

"About the true crime group." He saw the apprehension on her face. She didn't want to get into that again—neither did he.

"No, the thing about Raoul."

"Oh, that. Yes, he did a deep dive on the web for us and found an active ideological group that might be worth looking into."

"Oh, yeah? Who are they?"

"Not sure what they're called, but they're active on Discord."

He shook his head. "Is everybody on Discord nowadays?"

"Pretty much." She grinned. "It's actually a platform for gamers. They have voice comms as well as private meeting rooms. But it's spilled over into real life. Now organizations are using it to chat and host online meetings, and so on."

"Is it secure?" he asked.

"To a degree. I don't know how to get in without an invitation, but Raoul hacked his way in and did some covert lurking. He found them."

"I'm not sure you should be telling me that," Reid muttered.

Kenzie smirked. "Anyway, he mentioned one user that was pretty prolific. He goes by the username ShatteredTorii."

"Shattered Whati?" Reid asked, frowning.

"Torii. It's a gate to a shrine or holy place."

He pursed his lips. "Learn something every day."

"Raoul thinks he's a Japanese national, probably mid-forties, well educated. Possibly a professional academic."

Reid glanced at her. "That's quite a profile sketch for a techie."

She grinned. "He is a man of many talents. It's based on the user's accent, grasp of English, and the content in his comments and posts."

"I see. And can Raoul forward this information to me?"

"He will, but I'm not sure what you're going to do with it. You can't get into the group without a password, and they're not easy to find. Raoul told me that they're purposely hidden. You'd have to have a direct link or invite to locate them."

Reid's jaw tightened. "Okay, let's put that on ice for now, then. Tell Raoul to keep an eye on them. Anything shady or incriminating, he's to let me know ASAP. I mean that, Kenz."

She gave a nod. "Understood."

At his cynical look, she added, "That's what I told him."

Reid knew he'd have to be satisfied with that. For now.

"Want something to eat before you head to the station?" Kenzie smiled alluringly. "I can make bacon and eggs."

His stomach rumbled. Last night's pot roast had been good, but he hadn't eaten in so long, he needed the calories. Glancing at the time on his phone, he figured he could spare half an hour to fuel up. God knows when he'd get a chance to eat next.

"Sure, sounds great. Mind if I take a shower?"

"Go ahead."

She strutted to the kitchen, and he left his phone on the counter and disappeared into the bathroom.

A hot shower later, and Reid felt like a new man. He was even whistling a little tune as he made his way back into the kitchen. His mood was improving by the second, helped by the thought of a good breakfast. Then he'd kiss his woman goodbye and head to the department. Not a bad start to the day.

Kenzie turned as he walked in, her forehead furrowed.

"Something wrong?" He headed for the counter.

"Your phone's been buzzing non-stop," she said. "I think it's important."

"Everything's important," he said with a roll of his eyes, but picked it up and checked the screen, anyway.

"Shit. Six missed calls from Diaz."

All in the last ten minutes.

Kenzie turned away from the pan and leaned on her side of the counter, facing him. "Has something happened?"

Reid felt his good mood evaporate like the smoke from the frying pan. "You could say that."

A bad feeling crept down his spine and tightened his gut.

"There's been another murder."

16

"What happened?" Reid asked, gripping the phone to his ear.

"Another body," Diaz told him. "In Tamiami Park. Technically county land, but we were closest. And given the linkage, they let us keep it. Literally, boss, it couldn't be any more public. It's already a circus."

Reid's stomach sank. "Shit. I'm on my way."

He hung up and looked at Kenzie.

"Another one?" she whispered.

He gave a grim nod before handing her his mug and reached for his keys. "I've got to go."

"Is it... the same?"

He knew she was asking about the sword, the ritual, the bizarre staging of the crime scene. "I don't know. Diaz didn't say. I assume so."

He looked around, unable to find his keys. They weren't where he usually left them. Then again, he'd been so exhausted when he'd arrived last night, it wasn't surprising he'd lost them.

She picked them up off the coffee table and handed them to him.

"Thanks. Sorry I can't stay for breakfast."

A shrug. "No problem. I understand."

He knew she did.

"See you later," he said, giving her a quick kiss on the cheek and turning for the door.

"I'll be here."

The drive into Miami was a frantic, high-speed sprint. There was so much traffic, he spent most of the time veering into the opposite lane, hoping like hell other motorists would see him coming. With the lights flashing and sirens blaring, he was hard to miss.

He turned off Biscayne Boulevard and saw it before he reached the park. A chaos of police vehicles and pulsing lights held back a cluster of onlookers, camera phones held high like lighters at a concert.

Teeth gritted, he parked badly, slapped his badge onto his belt, and jogged over to where Diaz was standing by the cordon.

"What a shit show. Can't we get these people out of here?"

"I've got them as far back as I can." She lifted the cordon so he could duck under. "The crime scene is two hundred yards that way." She nodded toward the west of the park with her head.

"How bad is it?" he asked, as she nodded to a uniformed officer to take over and led Reid toward the crime scene.

"About the same as the last one."

The body was positioned near a stand of palms, on a patch of trimmed grass perfect for picnics and dog walking. Instead, it was covered in white suits.

CSU were setting up a tent to conceal the body, which was something, at least. It would be hours before they were done here. The ME hadn't even arrived yet.

They got close and his gut tightened like it always did at a crime scene. You'd think after all these years it would get easier, but it never did.

He took that as a good thing.

Male. Late forties. A hundred and eighty pounds, give or take. Well dressed, but not expensively so. A good quality button-down shirt, sleeves rolled neatly to the forearms. Slacks. Loafers still on his feet. He sat upright against the trunk of a palm, shoulders resting back as if he'd chosen the spot deliberately. His head lolled just enough to look like he might be asleep, catching a moment of shade.

Except he hadn't chosen this.

A sword had been driven straight through his torso, angled slightly upward, a heavy length of steel protruding from his back. It pinned him there, body locked against the rough bark. This wasn't the curved katana used on Hargreave. The blade was longer, straighter, but still unmistakably Japanese.

The hilt was jammed hard against his chest, wrapped in dark cord. He cringed. It must have taken some force to position it like that.

"It's a samurai sword," Diaz muttered.

Reid glanced around, his mouth dry. The scene had been staged again. The victim's hands had been placed on his thighs, palms down, fingers relaxed. His head tilted slightly to one side, as if he'd dozed off after a stroll.

A folded cloth sat beside him, square and neat, like a ceremonial offering.

"What the hell?" Reid muttered, crouching down to get a closer look.

The fabric was heavy, not something you'd pick up at a souvenir shop or tourist market. Silk, maybe, or something like it. Deep indigo, almost black, with intricate motifs embroidered in gold thread catching the light.

"Yeah, not sure what that's about," she admitted. "We'll have to get an expert to take a look at it."

He shook his head and walked towards a CSU tech who knelt beside the body, his forensic case open at his side. He was taking a swab of something he'd found nearby and inserting it into a test tube.

"You got something?" Reid asked.

"Maybe. Can't be sure. We just take whatever we find in the immediate radius," he replied noncommittally.

Reid felt the tension grip his shoulders. "Okay, what can you tell me? Was he murdered here?"

"Doesn't look like it, but the ME will confirm."

Same as before.

"What about defensive wounds?"

"Nothing evident. Again, the autopsy will confirm."

He sighed. "Is the ME on his way?"

"Said he was."

"Is that a drag mark?" He studied the grass in front of the body. It looked like it had been flattened slightly, by something heavy. Or maybe he was imagining things. Seeing what he wanted to see.

The CSU tech glanced up, then nodded. "Could be. We'll take samples to analyze in the lab. We'll send through the photos in a couple of hours." The photos were always the first pieces of the puzzle to get delivered. Quick and easy, now there was no development of film involved.

"Doesn't look like he was killed here," Reid told Diaz, who was standing a short distance away, surveying the crowd.

"Which means he would have been transported, somehow. The killer must have a truck or van or something. I'll get the CSUs to comb the parking lot closest to this point."

"What about witnesses?" Reid asked, scanning the perimeter.

"A dog walker found him at six twenty this morning," Diaz said. "He called 9-1-1. By the time uniforms arrived, half the park had already seen it."

"And filmed it," Reid added grimly.

Diaz shrugged.

"Hate to break it to you, but your crime scene's already all over the internet," Vargas told them, marching up.

"Typical." Reid scowled at the onlookers behind the cordon.

"They're saying it's the same killer," Vargas said. "The *Samurai Killer*."

"Jesus," muttered Reid.

"Actually, it was a katana the first time," Diaz corrected.

"Doesn't matter." Vargas nodded to the victim. "This is a samurai sword."

Reid clenched his jaw. Damn monikers. He hated them. Gave the killer illusions of grandeur. He could picture the bastard now, scouring the socials, getting off on the attention. Reid's hands balled into fists.

Diaz nodded at something behind him, and he turned to see the medical examiner approaching. Dr. Pruitt—he remembered his name from the last time. That made him feel marginally better. At least there would be some kind of continuity.

"Lieutenant," Pruitt said. "We've got to stop meeting like this."

"Doc." He tilted his head. "Glad you're here. Take a look and tell me what you see."

Pruitt got to his knees, uttering a low groan as he did so. The ME was in his fifties and sported a full gray beard to make up for the lack of hair on his head. His face was grim as he pulled on a fresh pair of gloves.

"Looks like this is a secondary crime scene," he said straight off the bat. "Same MO as before."

Reid nodded. He'd already deduced that much. "Sword was inserted postmortem?"

He bent his head to look behind the body. "At a glance, yeah."

"Any idea about TOD?" The fact that the victim had been moved, placed outside, exposed to the elements, the temperature and humidity, all complicated matters.

"Unfortunately, all I can do is give you a wide window, then narrow it down once I get him back to the lab," Pruitt said.

Rob nodded. "If that's the best you can do."

Pruitt inspected the body. Felt the victim's neck where a pulse might be but there was obviously nothing. It was standard procedure. A checkbox.

Next, he inspected the arms and legs, checking for lividity and the onset of rigor mortis. Reid had been at enough crime scenes to know the drill.

Eventually, Pruitt said, "This man died during the night. I'd put it after midnight, but before four o'clock this morning."

"Same timeframe as before," Diaz murmured.

Pruitt glanced up. "Same MO. I'd say you're looking at the same killer."

"How can you tell?" Reid demanded.

Pruitt turned back to the body. "The precision of the wound, the undisturbed clothing, the state of the body. Also, the cause of death looks to be the same."

They all stared at him.

"What cause of death?" Reid and Vargas blurted out at the same time.

"We don't have Hargreave's autopsy report yet," Diaz explained.

Pruitt's mouth tightened. "You would have, if I hadn't been called out here. I finished my preliminary late last night. I was going to send it this morning."

Reid's throat went dry. "Don't leave us hanging, Doc. What is it?"

Pruitt hesitated for half a second, then said, "Neurotoxin. A potent one. Symptoms would have been fast onset. Paralysis, followed by respiratory failure. It's consistent with tetrodotoxin exposure."

"What's that?" Vargas asked.

Diaz frowned. "Puffer fish?"

Pruitt shot her a pleased look. "Most people know it from fugu. Ingestion, typically. But it can be delivered in other ways if someone has access and knows what they're doing."

Reid's mind snapped back to Hargreave's calm face. The peaceful expression. No struggle. No blood.

Paralyzed. Quiet. Unable to fight.

He let out a low hiss.

"It's uncommon," Pruitt continued. "But not impossible to find.

And now you have two victims with the same toxic profile and the same postmortem staging."

Reid looked back at the body, at the sword protruding out of the victim's back. At the folded cloth. The careful hands. The pose.

"I don't think this is Sandra West," he murmured to the others.

"No," Vargas agreed. "Unless there's a lot she's not telling us."

"She has no background in martial arts, or anything to do with Japanese culture," Diaz added with a degree of confidence. "I checked her out. She's a small-town girl who married well."

"Plus, she'd have to have carried the body." Reid ran a hand through his hair.

"And this takes time," Diaz noted, gesturing to the body propped up against the tree, sword still in place.

Pruitt hummed in agreement. "Getting him here, positioning his body, embedding the sword... Yep, I'd say you're looking at a minimum of an hour, if not more."

"It's pretty obvious now that this has a cultural or ideological angle to it," Vargas pointed out. "We need to expand our lines of inquiry."

Reid grunted. "Two victims. Two swords. Same message."

"This time outside in the open," Diaz nodded to the crowd, who hadn't dispersed. "Way more attention."

"He's escalating." The heaviness settled back into Reid's chest. This morning's good mood was a distant memory now.

"You think there are going to be more murders?" Vargas frowned.

He inhaled slowly. "I think it's likely, yeah."

"If the killer is on some kind of vengeance quest..." Diaz waved at the victim. "Why stop at two? There must be more collectors out there who acquired stolen artifacts from Japan."

"We've got to find out who they are," Reid decided. "We need to warn them to take precautions. Because next time, the audience is going to be even bigger."

17

Kenzie hated feeling so powerless. She wasn't directly involved in the investigation, not like she had been during the Night Watchman case. Her only recourse was to work the online groups and try to uncover something that way—or through Raoul—but even that didn't feel like enough.

She barely tasted the eggs and didn't bother with the bacon, reaching for yet another cup of coffee instead. She contemplated producing another video for her podcast, but concluded it was too soon.

The second murder had just happened, and her followers would be distracted by that, not interested in a follow-up of Hargreave's case. The news cycle had moved on, and frighteningly quickly.

Taking her mug to her study, she logged into The Evidence Room. It wasn't yet nine a.m. but, as she'd suspected, the server was already buzzing.

Glancing at the left-hand menu, she noticed a list of channels now active in the server. They were marked with the hashtag symbol and labeled active-discussions, media-dump, and scene-analysis-public.

Without anything better to do, she clicked into active-discussions, where RedCairn had already posted an update.

RedCairn: A second body has been confirmed. The location is Tamiami Park. Cops aren't letting anyone near, but witness reports are of another sword death. Police have confirmed suspicious circumstances. Gross understatement.

Kenzie frowned. That didn't sound like Reid. He didn't talk to the press. Must have been Vargas or Diaz, or one of the uniformed cops handling crowd control.

ThirdWitness: Defs sus. The scene was staged again, just like with Hargreave. Take a look.

There were several photographs beneath his post. Kenzie clicked the first one and felt her chest tighten. The body was positioned with care. Propped upright against the trunk of a palm, legs extended, shoulders squared. The kind of posture a living person might choose if they wanted to rest in the shade for a moment. Except no one rested like that, with a sword through their chest.

Another photograph zoomed in on the weapon. The blade was centered, driven straight through, the hilt pressed flush against his torso.

Kenzie shuddered and glanced at the timestamps on the images. Early morning. Just after sunrise. No police tape yet. No evidence markers in frame, like in the other more recent online shots. ThirdWitness must have been at the crime scene.

ReporterGirl: You were there?

A pause, then the response came.

ThirdWitness: Yeah, I live close to the park. Heard it on the police scanner and sped down there. Just in time too. Police hadn't closed off the scene yet.

She blew out a breath. That *was* interesting.

What did she really know about any of them? Were they just well-meaning true crime enthusiasts—or was the person responsible for the murders sitting right here, watching them dissect his work, feeding off every theory and reaction?

FieldNotes: There is so much online already. We're spoiled for crime scene pics. Every conceivable angle. Videos too.

Someone had already dropped a folder link in media-dump. Kenzie scrolled through the still frames taken from news footage, wide shots from pro photographers, close-ups taken on mobile devices, and felt sick to her stomach.

AlexR: Could be useful. Interesting the killer chose a public park this time. Thoughts?

>

>

>

ThirdWitness: imo, he wants the attention. Last time wasn't enough.

>

>

ReporterGirl: Similar staging, but the sword positioning is more dramatic. He's going for even greater shock effect.

>

>

GrayAtlas: He's escalating.

That had been Kenzie's thought as she surveyed the images too.

The killer was becoming more extreme, either to garner more attention, or worse, he was developing a taste for it.

FieldNotes: Notice the folded cloth?
>
>
CrossCheck: A cultural meaning?

Kenzie leaned closer to the screen. One of the photos showed a folded cloth positioned beside the body. She'd missed it before as it had been just out of the frame of the images she'd looked at, or behind the body in the shadow of the palm tree. It appeared to be silk, the way it shimmered in the sunlight, with a gold pattern embroidered on it.

ReporterGirl: Could be symbolic.
>
>
FieldNotes: Must mean something, else why leave it?
>
>
AlexR: Let's try to find out.
>
>
>
ThirdWitness: Anybody got a better photograph?

A long beat passed where members were obviously trawling online footage. Eventually, RedCairn replied.

RedCairn: Looks like police already took it into evidence.

Kenzie thought she could probably get a close look at the

unfolded piece, but she kept that information to herself. They didn't need to know how close her ties were to law enforcement.

ReporterGirl: No noticeable defensive wounds, at least from what's visible in the photos.

>

>

>

AlexR: Looks like the same modus operandi as before. Official C.O.D.?

>

FieldNotes: Nothing in the media yet.

Kenzie was slowly beginning to understand their different roles. RedCairn was the lead moderator, and probably one of the founders. AlexR was second-in-command and likely the sharpest analytical mind in the group. FieldNotes tracked the media obsessively, while ThirdWitness was more hands-on, the type who showed up at scenes and gathered whatever he could.

She made a mental note to look into him in more detail. His presence at the crime scene that morning bothered her. It may not have been coincidental. She smirked. Now she was sounding like Reid. Quite frankly, though, she was surprised none of the others had questioned it.

CrossCheck was a data geek, probably a researcher or some form of analyst. GrayAtlas she couldn't quite place yet, but he was clearly part of the inner circle. That made six of them in the core group. Seven now, including her.

AlexR: Police will keep that close to their chest.

ThirdWitness uploaded another image. This time a high-resolution, close-up shot of the victim's face. He must have a telephoto.

ThirdWitness: We can rule out strangulation, stab wounds, gunshot wounds, or anything marking the body.

It was a good photo. Clear and unpixellated. She studied the image, trying to look at it like a detective, and not thinking about the living, breathing human being the man had been not so long ago. It didn't work. She swallowed past the lump in her throat.

ThirdWitness was right, however. There were no visible markings on the man's face or neck. Or anywhere else on his body, judging by the other photographs and the lack of blood present at the scene.

AlexR: Blunt force trauma?

>

>

RedCairn: We'd probably see signs of that in the pictures.

>

>

FieldNotes: Poison, then. Or something internal.

>

>

>

AlexR: ReporterGirl, do you think you can find out for us?

She sucked in a breath. That's what came of telling him she worked with the police.

Now they wanted to use her for information.

Her fingers hovered, then she typed.

ReporterGirl: Not sure. It's an ongoing investigation.

>

>

>

>

AlexR: Can you try?

Damn, he was persistent.

ReporterGirl: Will see what I can do. No promises.

Several thumbs-up emojis appeared beneath her comment.

18

Back at Sweetwater PD, Reid mobilized the team.

"Listen up, guys. We've got an ID on our second victim, thanks to AFIS. Name's Reginald Burton-Holmes from Long Island."

"Reginald, really?" Diaz muttered to muted chuckles.

"What's he doing here in Miami?" Martinez asked.

"He's got a vacation house near Miami Beach," Monroe, who hadn't gone home yet from the night shift, said. "I've just run a background check on him."

"Anything flag?" Reid asked.

Monroe shook his head. "Not really. Guy's loaded, but it's old money. Inherited from his grandaddy."

Great.

Wealthy victims had well-paid lawyers and families who demanded answers. And right now, they had none.

"Anyone from his family call?" he asked.

"No, but I've got his wife's details. Do you want me to get hold of her?"

He arched an eyebrow. "She's here?"

"Don't think so. Her phone puts her in New York."

"Okay. Get the cops in Long Island to pay the family a visit but send a uniform to check on the beach house, just in case." He rubbed his jaw. "It's unlikely they haven't heard already."

Those damn images on the web. Hell of a way to find out about your loved one's passing.

"We need to know why he was here in Miami. Was it work, pleasure, or something to do with his art collection?"

"You're thinking he was here meeting a dealer?" Vargas asked.

"Yeah, or someone pretending to be one," Reid amended. "Could be the same person Hargreave met the night he was murdered."

"It would be a smart way of getting access to them," Diaz said. "Posing as a dealer, or a buyer."

Reid forged ahead, thinking fast. "We also need to know if he was receiving hate mail like Hargreave was." He nodded at Monroe. "Tell Long Island PD to ask the family. They might know. He could have been acting strangely or been anxious about it."

Monroe gave a quick nod and turned back to the phone.

While waiting at the crime scene, Reid had looked up tetrodotoxin. Google had confirmed it was an extremely potent neurotoxin found in puffer fish, blue-ringed octopuses, and certain other marine/terrestrial species. There was no known antidote. Nasty stuff.

He shared this with the rest of the team now and saw several eyes widen in surprise.

"Not many places you can get hold of that," Dwayne called from his desk at the back of the room. "The killer has left himself wide open."

"Let's hope so. Can you jump on that?" Reid asked him. "Try to trace the source."

Dwayne gave a little nod. "I'll do my best."

"The time of death has been confirmed as between two and four in the morning," he told them. "That puts our mysterious jogger right in the window of opportunity."

"I've extended the CCTV trail past Sandra West's house in both directions," Vargas said, "but there's nothing. No sign of them. It's like they vanished into thin air."

"Or knew where the cameras were located," added Diaz.

Reid's gaze drifted to the case board. The street map was pinned up, a little red dot marking Sandra West's house.

Then he saw it.

The green swath running along the back of the houses.

Frowning, he walked over to the board for a closer look.

"Have you got something?" asked Vargas, coming to join him. Everybody was watching them now. Diaz and Martinez came closer, peering over their shoulders.

"The golf course." Reid jabbed it with his finger. "Sandra's son said she liked to jog around the golf course. There must be a way to get to it from their street."

Vargas followed his line of sight, his eyebrows lifting. "It runs behind the houses, but there's a perimeter. Still, there might be a gate or something."

"That could be how the figure disappeared," Diaz said in a hushed tone. "They cut through one of the properties, breached the fence and accessed the golf course."

"Where there is minimal lighting and lots of tree cover. Easy to disappear," Reid added.

"That depends..." Vargas pulled out his phone. "I'll call the golf club. They'll have security cameras."

Reid patted him on the shoulder. "Tell them it's urgent. We need to see the footage right away."

Vargas nodded and went outside to make the call.

Reid turned around. "Martinez, you dig into the second victim, Reginald Burton-Holmes. I'm guessing he's an art nut too. We need pictures of his collection. Rare works, high-value items, the entire goddamn inventory. Send the art fraud division in New York around if you have to. We've got to check the provenance on his stuff, find out if he was buying stolen items too, like Hargreave." Reid was betting he was.

She nodded.

"Cross-check them with the list of dealers and intermediaries Kenzie sent us," he added.

"What do you want me to do, boss?" Hamilton asked.

"Get a warrant for his bank statements, call data, the usual. We need to map our second victim's last moments leading up to when he was killed. Get ahold of anyone he spoke to, everywhere he went, track all his movements. Let's try to pinpoint when he was taken."

"On it," Hamilton said, and scurried away.

Reid stared at the case board for a while longer, then went back to his computer.

Logging into his email, he discovered CSU had sent through the photographs of the crime scene, as promised. He enlarged them on his screen and studied them closely, looking for anything he might have missed when he was at the park.

The forensic photographer had captured everything in high definition, which made it easier to notice things that might not be visible to the naked eye.

He studied the grass around the body, the slight depression that looked like drag marks, the dirt on the heels of the man's loafers. Definitely dragged there from a vehicle of some sort.

Turning to Diaz, he said, "Any CCTV in the parking lot?"

"I'm looking at it now." She swiveled her screen so he could see. "This is just after two a.m."

The footage moved in real time, excruciatingly slowly. Apart from a homeless man who crossed the carpark with a tattered rucksack over his shoulder, there was no other movement.

"Can you speed it up?" he asked.

She set it to double time, and they watched as the timestamp ticked up. At two fifty-four a.m., headlights turned into the lot.

"Whoa! What's that?"

"A car's turning in," she said breathlessly.

The headlights were bright, aimed right at the camera. The halo effect meant they couldn't see jack-shit.

"Is he doing that on purpose?" Reid asked, squinting at the screen.

Diaz frowned, then snorted. "Looks like it. He knows the camera is there."

They clocked movement behind the lights—maybe a car door opening, maybe a trunk—but nothing definitive. It was hazy, the glare blinding. They couldn't even see what make of vehicle it was.

"Looks like a truck," Diaz muttered, peering at her screen.

"Hard to say," Reid grumbled, tilting his head for a better look. "Could be a van or an SUV."

Diaz's shoulders slumped. "Now what? This is useless."

"Not entirely. It tells us he has wheels," Reid said. "And he's smart. He knows how to avoid the cameras. Possibly local to the area. That's not nothing."

"Great." Diaz turned her screen back to its original position and reached for the cup of cold coffee on her desk.

Her dejection was palpable. After the hype of finding what could be the killer's vehicle, they were foiled again.

"See what else you can uncover," he told her, not letting her give up. "There's got to be more CCTV in that area. Maybe another camera on the approach road caught him. Maybe he cased the lot during the day, or at some other time."

Her shoulders perked up. "I'll get right on it."

Reid suddenly realized how hungry he was. He was about to go in search of something to eat—maybe there were some leftover empanadas in the department refrigerator—when Vargas's voice cut through the room.

"Uh, boss."

He swung around. Vargas was frozen in front of his screen, one hand still on the mouse.

"What?"

"I just got the footage from the golf course," he said.

Reid walked over to his desk. "And?"

Vargas leaned back so he could see, then hit play.

Grainy night-vision footage filled the screen. A stretch of manicured green, pale under powerful floodlights. The timestamp read 01:47 a.m.

A figure entered the frame from the left. Dark running gear, black cap pulled low.

Reid sucked in a breath. "That's it. That's them."

The figure walked with purpose across the green, sure to keep their head lowered. In this light, they looked wider, more bulky than outside Sandra West's house, but it was clearly the same person.

Out of nowhere, an animal raced across the frame, startling the figure. A cat on the prowl, maybe. Something feral.

The figure jumped and glanced up. The light hit their face and Vargas hit pause.

Reid felt his stomach drop. "Is that—"

"Yeah," Vargas whispered. "It is."

"Can you enlarge that still?"

The image pixelated, but not enough to lose the shape of the man's shoulders, his gait, the way he held his arms. Reid stared at the man's features. There was no mistake.

It was Hargreave's business partner, Silas Ackerman.

19

KENZIE MET Raoul at a café just off the beach, the kind of place with weathered wooden tables, rattan chairs, and a chalkboard menu bleached by the sun. Her friend looked out of place in the coastal ease of Bal Harbour, with his dark hoodie zipped up despite the humidity and his backpack slouched over one shoulder.

Still, she loved it here. Especially at this hour, when the beach was quiet and the sand pale and smooth, stretching out toward a calm, glassy ocean that reflected the sky in washed-out blues.

"The core group is tight," she told him after walking him through her interactions with the members of The Evidence Room. A light breeze carried the smell of salt and sunscreen, fluttering the paper napkins on the table. "I'd put money on the fact that some of them know each other in real life. RedCairn and AlexR especially."

"RedCairn is the leader?" Raoul asked.

"I think so. Lead moderator, for sure," she replied. "He sets the tone, controls the flow of the discussion. But he also respects AlexR. Defers to him sometimes, the way you would a colleague, or someone whose judgment you trust."

"That doesn't automatically mean they know each other offline."

Raoul lifted his green smoothie and took a sip. The blender at the pop-up counter behind them whirred briefly, then fell quiet again. They had both ordered from the long list of cold-pressed juices and smoothies.

"Well, they definitely have history," she said, watching a gull hop closer, eyeing their table with interest. "You can hear it in the way they talk, how they just get each other."

"Could be time spent in the group," he cautioned. "Chat rooms are like that."

"Could be." She hesitated, clutching her glass. "Raoul, is there any way we can find out who these people really are?"

He leaned back, eyes narrowing as he thought it through.

"It's possible," he said at last, with more than a touch of reluctance. "But it won't be easy—or quick. There's a lot of noise to sift through before you find anything useful."

"Can I help?" she asked.

"You can go through the account history. Read everything they've posted and see if there are any hints. Anything they've let slip."

"I know ThirdWitness lives close to the second crime scene," she said suddenly. "He admitted it when I asked if he'd been there."

Raoul's eyebrows lifted. "He was at the crime scene?"

She grimaced. "Yeah, I know. I think it's time we took a closer look at these guys."

He exhaled noisily. "Okay, that's a start, but it's not a lot to go on."

She shrugged. "I know. Isn't there anything more direct we can do?" By we, she meant him. "Like trace their IP addresses or something?"

"It's not like in the movies," he said with a wry grin. "Anyone this cautious knows how to cover their tracks. The metadata will be skewed. What I can do is look for patterns. Usernames that pop up elsewhere. Writing styles. Posting habits. But again, it's going to take days, if not weeks."

She exhaled. "We don't have that kind of time. I'll just have to do it the old-fashioned way and earn their trust."

"Be careful, Kenz," he warned. "Don't be obvious about it. They'll smell a rat."

"I won't." She took a sip of her smoothie and gazed past him to the beach where a couple strolled arm in arm. She wondered how Reid was getting on.

"Don't be disheartened, I've got a surprise for you." Raoul shot her a cheeky grin and reached for his phone.

"You have?"

It was the look he used to get at the *Herald* when they worked together and he'd made a breakthrough.

"Yeah. I dove a little deeper into your nationalist organization. They're called the Heritage Preservation Coalition—and they've even got a website."

She spun back to him. "You're kidding?"

"Nope. There's not much on it and it's all in Japanese, but if you translate it, you'll get the gist of it."

"I will! Thank you. I mean it. Wow, this is huge."

"There's more," he said, eyes sparkling behind his glasses.

"Now you're spoiling me."

He laughed.

"I was scanning the feed in the group and I found something." He paused dramatically.

"What?" she prompted, leaning forward, elbows on the table.

"There's a meeting scheduled tomorrow night."

Her eyes widened. "Like a real-life meeting?"

"Yes, IRL."

She gasped. "Do you know where?"

He hesitated, but the corners of his lips had turned up.

"You do, don't you?"

He turned his phone around so she could see the address. "Want me to send it to you?"

"Hell yeah."

He snorted. "You're going to go, aren't you?"

"Do you know what time?"

"I believe it's at nine o'clock."

She gave a slow smile. "Perfect."

His look turned cautious. "Kenz, I know you're going to go no matter what I say, so I won't try to dissuade you. But please, be careful. While these guys don't seem to be violent, if they're responsible for these horrific murders, you don't want to get caught spying on them."

She swallowed as his words hit home. Visions of the two victims, the swords piercing their torsos, flickered through her mind.

"I will be careful. I promise," she whispered.

He exhaled. "Okay, but for God's sake, let Reid know where you're going in case you need backup."

She shot him a "Yeah right" look. "Reid would crack if he knew what I was doing."

"Take someone with you," he pleaded. "Just don't go alone."

"Fine," she said, her thoughts turning to her new sleuthing buddies. This might be exactly what she needed to build trust in the group—and meet one of two of them in person.

Two birds, one stone. And what a stone it was.

The minute she got home, Kenzie logged onto The Evidence Room. The screen lit up as soon as it loaded. New messages were already stacking in the main channel, the second murder understandably still dominating the conversation.

She read the comments for a while, catching up on the discussion. They'd done a lot of analysis on the crime scene, on the suspected drag marks, deducing the body had been carried from the parking lot in the early hours.

They'd researched the sword, tracing it back to a specific area in Japan, a certain decade, a particular brand. They'd valued it, although it was mostly guesswork, and put together a rough pipeline of how it got to be in the United States.

Once again, she was impressed by how thorough they were. These guys were even more inquisitive than she was, and that was saying something.

She came across a discussion thread on the symbol on the silk cloth. One of the motifs was partially visible in a social media shot someone had taken and posted online. It was a character that meant honor, apparently. Or so ThirdWitness thought.

FieldNotes: Ties in with the whole nationalist ideology. Another revenge killing.

>

>

>

AlexR: Agreed. Are the police looking into nationalist groups, I wonder?

>

>

RedCairn: Haven't heard anything in the press to that effect.

>

>

>

ReporterGirl: A source gave me a name. Has anyone heard of the Heritage Preservation Coalition?

There was a pause. Not long, but noticeable.

Then responses started coming in.

GrayAtlas: Not me. Googling now.

>

>

>

FieldNotes: Name rings a bell. Think they popped up in a cultural repatriation forum last year.

>

AlexR: Yeah. Okay. This is not fringe.

Kenzie leaned closer to the screen.

AlexR: Translating...

>

>

CrossCheck: Found it. Reading now. Looks heavy on moral absolutism.

>

>

RedCairn: How did you get the name, ReporterGirl?

That made her stomach tighten. Then again, she'd be surprised if they didn't question it. These guys were smart. They wouldn't take anything at face value.

ReporterGirl: I've got a researcher contact I use sometimes. He passed it on to me this afternoon.

It was all true.

A reaction icon popped up beside her message. Then another.

RedCairn: Was there a reason why he flagged them?

Another good question. RedCairn was the probing kind. Cautious. Naturally suspicious. He didn't fully trust her yet, but that was fine. This was the opening she needed.

ReporterGirl: They were discussing the first victim in one of their threads. Lots of moral indignation. People saying he got what he deserved, that it was inevitable, that this was what happens when collectors cross certain lines. He thought it was suspicious.

>

>

RedCairn: Okay. Worth a deeper dive?

>

>

>

AlexR: Agreed. We need to find out more about this organization.

>

>

>

FieldNotes: Do we know who's actually behind it? Any names tied to the group?

>

>

>

>

>

ReporterGirl: There are a few usernames that keep coming up. ShatteredTorii is the most vocal. Then there's IronPine and EightfoldPath. Same tone, same ideology. But that's as far as it goes. No real names, no obvious links outside the platform.

Another pause as they digested this.

AlexR: The usernames lean heavily on Japanese symbolism.

>

>

RedCairn: That doesn't mean they're Japanese.

>

AlexR: Correct. No assumptions.

Kenzie approved of their cool-headed, evidence-based approach.

Now she just had to find a way of letting the core group know about the meeting. She didn't want to post it here in the main thread, that would be reckless. Too many eyes. Instead, she clicked on AlexR's name and sent him a DM.

ReporterGirl: This isn't for the main thread. My source flagged an offline meeting tied to HPC. Tomorrow night in Miami. I felt it was too important to ignore.

AlexR didn't reply right away. The typing indicator blinked on, disappeared, then came back again.

AlexR: How solid is the source?

>

>

ReporterGirl: Source is solid. This was in their private chat.

Another pause.

AlexR: Okay. I'm looping RedCairn in.

A few seconds later, Kenzie's screen refreshed. A new notification appeared. She had been added to a private channel called offline-leads. The participant list was short. RedCairn. AlexR. FieldNotes. And her. She made a note of the hierarchy.

RedCairn: All right. Let's keep this contained for now. ReporterGirl, tell us what you know.

Kenzie straightened in her chair, fingers hovering over the keys. This was it. She had to make sure they believed her.

ReporterGirl: My source flagged an executive committee meeting of the HPC. It's happening tomorrow night in the warehouse district, west of downtown. I don't have confirmation of who's attending, but the timing feels deliberate, given the second murder.

>

>

>

FieldNotes: You're sure it's not a discussion group or lecture?

>

>

>

ReporterGirl: I'm sure. This was in their private thread. The meeting was called shortly after the second body was found.

>

>

AlexR: It's worth considering. RedCairn?

RedCairn was quiet for a moment longer than the others. When he finally replied, his words were measured.

RedCairn: Agreed—if this is legit. We only have ReporterGirl's source to go by.

Kenzie could sense his hesitation, and she wasn't surprised. But she was prepared for this.

ReporterGirl: I'm planning on going to see who turns up. I'll take photos, find out who's involved irl. Thought I'd let you know.

>

>

FieldNotes: Alone? That's a bad idea, ReporterGirl.

>

>

AlexR: She won't be alone. I'll go.

Kenzie sucked in a breath.

Yes!

Now she'd get to meet AlexR in real life.

ReporterGirl: Thanks, AlexR. Appreciate it.

>

>

FieldNotes: If you're doing this, you're not doing it as a pair.

Kenzie held her breath.

FieldNotes: I'll tag along. I've got a camera with a telephoto. You'll need backup.

Kenzie felt a mix of relief and unease settle in her chest.

ReporterGirl: Thanks, FieldNotes.

>

>

>

RedCairn: I can't make it in person, but I want updates the moment you're clear.

The typing paused, then resumed.

RedCairn: Also, remember we're not law enforcement. We do not intervene directly. We don't trespass or break any laws. If anything feels off, walk away. Don't put yourselves at risk.

>

ReporterGirl: Understood.

>

AlexR: Agreed.

FieldNotes: Copy that.

>

>

RedCairn: Good. Then we proceed carefully. This stays in this channel only. When you're back, we'll reassess and share it with the others.

The channel went quiet after that, but Kenzie was left with a sense of anticipation. She leaned back in her chair and stared at the screen. She'd wanted to be useful. To do more than comment and analyze from a distance, and now she was getting her chance. With a bunch of people she'd never met before.

Part of her wanted to tell Reid, but she knew he'd stop her going. And he'd be right to do so. It was reckless and potentially dangerous. She had no idea if the Heritage Preservation Coalition was even involved in the murders.

It might all amount to nothing. In which case, where was the harm in going? All she was going to do was observe and snap a few photos.

She blew out a breath. Anyway, she was committed now. The wheels were in motion, and she wasn't going to stop it. Tomorrow, she'd meet AlexR and FieldNotes in the flesh. And, she'd hopefully find out what, if anything, the HPC had to do with the two dead collectors.

20

"WHAT THE HELL is he doing there?" Reid stared at Ackerman's surprised face in the black and white still. "That's nowhere near Hargreave's place."

"But it is near Sandra West's," Vargas said quietly.

"He told us he was at home all night," Reid said flatly.

"Who did?" Diaz came over to join them. "Holy shit, is that the silent partner?"

"The one and only," Vargas said dryly. "He was the figure in the street outside Sandra's house the night of the murder."

She rubbed her forehead. "Wait. That doesn't make any sense."

"I know." Reid scowled. "Let's bring him in. The alibi he gave us was bullshit. I want answers."

Vargas was already grabbing his jacket.

"And loop in the DA," Reid added. "If this turns into an arrest, I don't want any surprises."

Silas Ackerman arrived forty-seven minutes later, escorted in by a stern-faced Vargas.

Reid watched through the two-way glass as his deputy escorted him into Interview Room B.

Ackerman must have been at his club because he was dressed in a tennis outfit, his hair windswept and out of place. He was nervous, however, evident by the faint sheen of sweat glistening on his forehead and the way his eyes darted erratically side to side.

Reid had killed the AC ten minutes earlier. A small thing, but he'd found the slow increase in temperature added to suspects' uneasiness.

After he'd kept Ackerman waiting at least twenty minutes, he entered the room with Diaz, a manila folder under his arm, and closed the door behind them. Inside, the air was thick with tension.

Ackerman glanced up, forcing a smile. "Lieutenant, what am I doing here? Your deputy wouldn't tell me anything."

Reid didn't return the smile. He dropped the folder on the table, sat down, and waited for Diaz to do the same.

Once they were all seated, he leaned forward and took out a photograph. After studying it for a beat, he slid it across the table to Ackerman. It was the golf course still.

Ackerman looked at it, then paled.

"Is that you?" asked Reid.

The suspect exhaled, long and slow. "Yes."

No hesitation. Not that there was any point in lying. Still, it was easier than Reid had thought.

"You told us you were home all night," he said.

"I told *you* I was alone," Ackerman corrected. He wiped his forehead with the back of his hand. "It wasn't an official statement, and I didn't think my personal movements were relevant."

"You lied to a police officer," he snapped. "It doesn't need to be an official statement."

Ackerman hesitated. "Okay, okay. Yes, I did."

"Why?" asked Diaz, studying him.

"I had a good reason." He shifted in his seat.

"I'm dying to hear it," Reid barked, losing patience.

Ackerman gave a dramatic sigh. "If you must know, I was leaving Sandra West's house. We've been having an affair."

Both Reid and Diaz digested this for a beat.

"At two forty-one in the morning?" Reid ground his teeth together, frustrated. He should have seen this earlier. The wife and the business partner.

"Why not just stay the night?"

Ackerman shook his head. "It's complicated. Malcolm was divorcing Sandra. We kept our affair secret so that he couldn't use that against her in the court case."

Reid got it. Any whiff of an affair, even if the couple were estranged, would sway the verdict in Hargreave's favor. Sandra would get far less of a settlement if she came off looking like a cheating wife.

"You should have told us."

"Look, I was trying to help Sandra. I don't suppose it matters now, though." He gave a grimace. "You know? In light of what happened."

Reid leaned back in his chair, feeling deflated. Still, he had to go through the motions. "Walk me through your movements that night."

"Fine. I went round to Sandra's at eight o'clock and left about two thirty."

"Where did you park?" Diaz asked, pre-empting him. Ackerman's car hadn't been on the street; they would have spotted it. They'd checked all vehicles coming and going that night.

"At the golf course. I'm a member, so it's easy enough."

"You go through the club to get to Sandra's place?" Reid asked, although it was more of a statement.

"Yeah. I walk across the ninth green to the street behind Sandra's. Then I cut through her neighbor's yard to her house."

"The neighbor doesn't mind?" Diaz raised an eyebrow.

"The neighbor doesn't know," Ackerman replied with the barest hint of a grin.

Dammit.

Ackerman lived close enough for that to make sense. This was going nowhere. The only thing Ackerman was guilty of was cuckolding his business partner with his wife. As distasteful as that was, it wasn't a crime. He nodded to Diaz to finish up.

Without saying another word to Ackerman, he got up and left the room.

Reid had just gotten back to his desk when Martinez came up to him. "Lieutenant, the art squad sent through a list of all the artifacts in Burton-Holmes's Long Island residence. Looking at it, there are fewer items than Hargreave had. Apart from the swords, he had several statues, chests, and masks."

It made sense they'd have different interests.

"Does anything match with Hargreave?"

She gave a quick nod. "Actually, yeah. That's what I came to tell you."

He raised an eyebrow. "Oh?"

"I traced one of the items to a local antiquities dealer. A Ming dynasty theatrical mask, according to the description. It's just one object, but it's the same dealer Hargreave used to acquire several of his pieces. He's based right here in Miami.

Reid felt a surge of excitement. "Seriously? That's great news."

She grinned. "It's called Watanabe Fine Antiquities and specializes in Japanese artifacts. It's a legitimate enterprise, from what I can tell. No warrants or official complaints lodged against it."

Reid grabbed his jacket. "Let's go."

Martinez hesitated, unsure if he meant her. She pointed to herself.

"Yeah, come on. You're driving."

She scrambled for her weapon and badge, then—smiling broadly at Vargas, who gave her an encouraging thumbs up—followed him out.

21

The shop sat just off Calle Ocho, tucked between a botanica and a closed-down travel agency. From the outside, it was understated, easy to miss. A simple wooden sign with black brushstroke lettering. No neon or flashy window displays.

The front glass was thick and tinted, protected by steel shutters that looked like they'd gotten stuck halfway down. One of them was crooked, as if it hadn't been fully reset. A small dome camera was secured above the door, but its indicator light was dead.

"Security, but not in use," Reid noted.

Martinez glanced up and nodded before ducking her head to step inside. Reid followed.

It was like entering another world.

"Wow," Martinez whispered, gazing around.

Inside, the store was much larger than it looked from the outside. Tatami mats lined the floor. Scrolls hung along the walls. Glass cases held carvings, lacquered boxes, and delicate ceramics. The air smelled faintly of incense and old wood.

A Japanese American man in his late fifties emerged from behind the counter, bowing slightly before straightening. He wore a linen shirt and wire-rimmed glasses. His expression was open but wary.

"Can I help you?" he asked.

"Lieutenant Reid Garrett, Sweetwater PD," Reid said, flashing his badge. "This is Detective Martinez. We need to ask you a few questions."

The man frowned but didn't resist.

"Of course. Please." He gestured toward a narrow doorway behind the counter. "We can talk in the back."

In stark contrast to the showroom, the office was barely big enough for the three of them. Shelves stacked with ledgers, files and reference books lined three of the four walls. A desk cluttered with invoices and a laptop sat in the middle. A framed photograph on one of the shelves showed an older Japanese man standing proudly in front of the same shop decades earlier.

"My father," the dealer said, noticing Reid's glance. "He opened this place in 1978. I'm Kenji Watanabe."

Reid nodded. "We're sorry to bother you, Mr. Watanabe, but we need to speak to you about two of your customers. Malcolm Hargreave and Reginald Burton-Holmes."

The antique dealer looked wary.

"I don't know if you've seen the news recently," he began, and knew by the glimmer of recognition in Watanabe's eyes that he had. "Well, they're both dead. Murdered."

A pause as his words sank in.

Then, Watanabe said, "I heard, yeah. But what's that got to do with me?"

"They were both customers of yours. They bought goods from your store." He glanced at Martinez, who took a notepad out of her jacket pocket.

"If you want the names of the items, I can give them to you."

He waved a hand in the air. "No need. No need. I remember. They were both very good customers."

"When did you last see either of them?" Reid asked.

"Not for a long time. It must be months." He shrugged.

"So you've had no contact with either of them in the last few weeks?" he asked again.

"No. I've only met Mr. Burton-Holmes once, but I've dealt with Malcom several times."

"Was there anything special about the items you sold them?" Reid decided to change tack. He'd be able to tell from Watanabe's phone records if he was telling the truth.

"The pieces were very rare," Watanabe said without hesitation. "I acquired them through my Japanese contact. It's all above board. I can show you the shipping manifests."

"Sure, that would be good." Martinez had said it all looked legit. On the surface anyway.

The dealer reached for a binder on one of the shelves. It was at the top of a pile of notebooks. He set it on the desk, turned to the relevant page and prodded it with his finger.

"Here's the shipping manifest for the mask that Mr. Burton-Holmes ordered. You want a copy?"

"Please."

"What kind of mask was it?" Martinez asked.

He glanced up at her. "Mid-century Japanese. Noh theatre piece. Not sacred, but still culturally significant and pretty rare. There aren't many in existence anymore."

Diaz made a note, while Watanabe shifted a pile of books from on top of the printer to the desk and made a photocopy.

"What about Hargreave?" Reid asked.

Watanabe nodded once. "Malcolm asked me to keep an eye out for a samurai sword, late nineteenth century. Edo period. Very valuable. When it came up for auction in Kyoto, I arranged for a broker to bid on his behalf. Luckily, we secured it for a very reasonable price."

"Which was?" Reid asked.

"Seven hundred thousand dollars," Watanabe said evenly.

Martinez let out a quiet gasp.

"It was a clean transaction," he added, "and I have the document of the sale here, if you're interested."

Again, Reid nodded.

Another binder, another whir of the copy machine, and the dealer handed it to him. Reid passed them both to Martinez. "When was this?"

He frowned, then gestured to the paper. "It's all on there."

Diaz glanced down. "August last year."

That was seven months ago. "You haven't spoken to him since then?"

"No, I told you. Not for months."

Seemed the dealer was telling the truth.

Reid glanced around, wondering how the hell the guy could operate a business in such a mess.

"Sorry the place is so chaotic," Watanabe said, following his gaze. "We had a break-in a couple of weeks back, and I haven't sorted everything out yet. They totaled the place."

Reid frowned. "You were burgled?"

Watanabe shook his head once, more disappointed than angry. "They pried the security door. Titanium steel, custom fitted. Or so I was told." A faint, humorless smile crossed his face. "It appears the marketing was better than the workmanship."

Reid gave a nod. "We noticed."

Watanabe gestured toward the corner of the room. "They cut the wiring. The system went down immediately." His lips pressed together. "I've filed the claim and I'm waiting for the insurer to approve the replacement."

"Did you report it?" Reid asked.

"Yes," Watanabe replied without hesitation. "Same day, but there was no follow-up."

Reid frowned. It wasn't his department, or he'd have heard about it. Still, he'd have a talk with Monroe just in case.

"Anything of value taken?" he asked. There was a lot of pricey stuff in the store.

"That was the strange thing," Watanabe replied. "With all the artifacts in my store, they went straight for the office. Pulled everything out. Took the files containing my customer records. What they needed those for, I have no idea?" He shook his head.

Reid felt an icy chill sweep over him. He glanced at Martinez who'd gone pale.

"Would that include names and addresses?" he asked, quietly.

"Yes, everything."

"You don't keep them on your computer, or the cloud?" Martinez asked incredulously.

"I've got all the recent records digitized, but my father was old school. Didn't trust computers. I'm still working through the older records."

"We're going to need a list of the records that were stolen," he said.

Watanabe scratched his head. "I can't tell you exactly which were taken. Some weren't even on the system yet."

"Jesus," Reid muttered.

"Give us what you can," Martinez said, her tone gentler than his. The man was clearly frazzled by the state of his office and the resulting mayhem.

Martinez handed him her card. "You can email them to me directly or call me on that number."

"It's confidential information," he said.

"And this is a double homicide investigation," Reid countered.

Watanabe gave a reluctant nod and took the card.

"You think that's how they were targeted?" Martinez asked when they stepped outside. The sunshine felt good after the dim interior.

"The timing fits," he said as they walked toward the police cruiser.

Martinez paused, her hand on the door. "That means those murders were planned. The killer broke in here to get the names, tracked those men down, and—" she broke off as she pulled it open.

"They're organized. But what's worse, is that whoever killed

Hargreave and Burton-Holmes has a long list of other potential targets."

Martinez started the engine and pulled out into the sparse traffic, her face scrunched into a worried frown. "There are going to be more murders, aren't there?"

Reid nodded. He couldn't bring himself to say it out loud, as if that would confirm it somehow. But several more collectors were going to die if they didn't get to them first.

They weren't just chasing a killer anymore. They were racing one.

22

KENZIE STEPPED out of the car and eased the door shut so the sound didn't echo down the street. She'd dressed in black leggings, a tight-fitting long-sleeved top, and black running shoes to blend into the darkness.

Half a block ahead, a man in navy jeans and a black hoodie pulled over his head leaned against a dark sedan on the west side of the road, where Alex had said he'd be.

As she approached, he straightened up.

"ReporterGirl," he said quietly.

She nodded. "Kenzie. You must be AlexR?"

A nod. "Call me Alex."

In person, he was older than she'd expected. Late thirties, maybe early forties. Tall, lean, with a watchful stillness that made him seem less like an amateur sleuth and more like someone who'd done this before. Military, maybe?

A third set of headlights swept past them and slowed. The truck parked behind Kenzie's car, and a broad-shouldered man climbed out, camera strap already slung across his chest.

"FieldNotes," he said, walking up to them, but keeping his voice low. "Good to finally put faces to handles."

Kenzie gave a friendly nod as they all shook hands. That meant FieldNotes and Alex had never met before.

Leaving the vehicles where they were, they set off in the direction of the warehouse. It wasn't far—maybe half a mile. They stuck to the shadows of the buildings, keeping out of sight of the road.

The warehouse squatted at the edge of a dirty canal. The corrugated metal walls were streaked with rust, the windows were boarded up, and there was no signage of any kind. If you didn't know it was here, you'd drive straight past it without a sideways glance.

The streetlights had thinned out and there wasn't much traffic. The only sound was the occasional screech of a cicada and the low hiss of water moving somewhere nearby.

They were early. There was still half an hour until the meeting was due to start. It was all part of the plan. Be in position by the time the committee members arrived. That way they'd see them go into the building. It would give them the best vantage point from which to take photos.

A single car was parked in the small lot behind the building.

Kenzie frowned. "At least one person is already here," she whispered as they snuck past.

Alex pointed to a light flickering high on the south side of the warehouse. Kenzie deduced it came from an office or storeroom where the meeting was likely to take place.

They crept a little closer, then split up without speaking. Kenzie slipped between a stack of wooden pallets and a chain-link fence. The gaps between the boards gave her a narrow view of the lot without exposing her.

Alex peeled off to the opposite side, positioning himself behind a rusted utility shed and disappearing into the thick shadow. FieldNotes, who had a bulkier frame, crouched behind a large dumpster streaked with old grease and peeling hazard stickers. Its width shielded him while affording a clear line of sight to the warehouse entrance. The flickering light above it would hopefully illuminate their faces enough so they'd be visible on camera.

The second car arrived at eight fifty-two. It was a black sedan with tinted windows. Two men got out, both wearing dark jackets over crisp white shirts. In her peripheral vision, she saw FieldNotes raise the camera to his face.

One of them paused, scanned the lot, then knocked on the door. It opened just long enough for them to slip inside—by the person they hadn't seen yet.

More cars followed. They drove in and parked, their tires crunching on the gravel. Two men and one woman, all in business attire. Even the woman wore a pencil skirt and a smart navy jacket over a cream blouse. They bowed respectfully to each other before they stepped inside.

Loyalty. Honor. Respect. The bushido code.

The way of the warrior.

The last member arrived on a motorcycle but didn't remove his helmet until he'd been admitted so FieldNotes wouldn't have been able to get a decent shot of him.

He was very careful. Or paranoid. Probably both.

She wondered which one was ShatteredTorii. Maybe the one who'd been inside?

Not trusting FieldNotes completely, Kenzie had also snapped some photos of her own. She wasn't in the best position, but if FieldNotes didn't post his photos in the group or they didn't come out for some reason, then at least she had backup.

An hour later, everybody had gone inside. No more vehicles turned into the lot.

Kenzie and Alex crouched-ran to where FieldNotes was still hovering behind the dumpster. He was checking the images on the tiny screen attached to his camera.

"Get them?" Alex asked.

He adjusted the screen so they could see. "Yeah. I couldn't get all their faces, though."

"You did what you could," Kenzie said, studying the photos. Three clear shots, two semi-side views and one of the biker with the helmet.

"Not bad," Alex murmured. "Okay, we should get out of here."

"Sure," FieldNotes put the lens cap on his camera.

Kenzie glanced back at the warehouse, biting her lip.

"What are you thinking?" he asked, his gaze on her.

He'd read her pretty well, which was vaguely disturbing.

"I thought I might hang around a while, see if I can overhear anything."

FieldNotes shifted uncomfortably. "How? There's only one window and it's closed. You won't be able to see anything, it's too high up."

"There are a couple of boarded up windows round the back," she said. "I thought I might try to get in that way."

"Break in?" hissed FieldNotes.

She shrugged. "Why not? We're here. Might as well see what else we can find out." Out of the corner of her eye, she saw Alex regarding her curiously.

FieldNotes shook his head. "RedCairn made it clear not to break any rules."

"What rules?" she asked. "It's an abandoned property. I checked out the management company. They dissolved in twenty-four. Nobody owns this place." She nodded at the door. "They're just using it as a secret meeting location."

FieldNotes slung his camera around his neck. "Count me out. I've got to get home, anyway. Wife will be wondering where I am."

Another personal detail.

Kenzie nodded. "Sure, if you've got to go."

"I'll stick around," Alex decided. "You're going to need help. Those windows won't be easy to get through. You'll have to remove what's remaining of the glass and the wooden boards."

So he'd clocked them too. Interesting.

The more time she spent with Alex, the more she suspected he had been, or was in, some form of military or investigative organization. He was too comfortable in the shadows, too observant to be a rank amateur.

She'd also noticed he was carrying a concealed weapon. It wasn't obvious, but there was a gun-shaped bulge in the small of his back, under his hoodie.

FieldNotes gave a brief salute and disappeared back toward the street.

"Let's go," Kenzie whispered. The adrenaline was starting to kick in again, making her pulse race. They circled back to where the broken window was, keeping close to the wall. Stopping beneath it, they inspected the damage. One pane had already shattered inward, and jagged teeth of glass still clung to the frame.

Alex pulled a multi-tool from his pocket and worked carefully, easing the remaining shards free one by one, letting them fall silently onto the dirt below. When the frame was clear, he lifted the loose board out. There was just enough space for them to squeeze through.

Kenzie went first, bracing her hands on the sill and hauling herself up. Heart hammering, she slipped one leg over, then the other, and dropped softly onto the concrete floor.

Alex followed a moment later, landing without a sound beside her.

She crinkled her nose. The inside smelled of damp concrete, rotting timber and something musty, probably mold. They stood still, listening. The low murmur of voices drifted toward them from somewhere deeper in the warehouse.

Alex signaled in the direction of the voices, and Kenzie nodded. Slowly, one step at a time, they crept through the derelict room and out into the dark hallway. Kenzie had a penlight in her pocket that she pulled out and switched on. The beam was subtle, just enough to cast a low glow on the floor in front of them.

Alex gave a grunt of approval.

Kenzie wondered if his heart was hammering too. Judging by the stealthy, confident way he moved, she doubted it. She, on the other hand, was acutely aware of every sound her body made. Her faster-than-normal breath. The squeak of her soles on the concrete. The brush of fabric as she walked.

They edged closer until the fragments of conversation grew loud enough to hear clearly. Her heart sank. They were talking in Japanese. Even this near, there was no way they could understand what was being said. Unless, of course, Alex spoke the lingo.

Raising an eyebrow in his direction, he shook his head. That was a no, then. She was about to suggest they leave when a thought struck her.

Taking out her phone, she opened the voice memo app and pressed record. They might be able to get this translated or use AI or something.

Hell, it was worth a shot.

Suddenly, a sharp metallic ping cracked through the space, making them both jump.

"What was that?" Kenzie mouthed.

He shrugged, but the sound had been loud enough to alert the group inside the room. Cautious footsteps were heading in their direction.

Shit.

Before she had time to react, Alex had grabbed her arm and hauled her into a nearby room. At first glance, it appeared to be a storage room of some sort. Empty crates and boxes were scattered around, a metal ladder rested against a wall, and she heard a scurry as something darted across the floor.

Alex shoved her behind the door and ducked behind two crates. The speed with which he moved startled her. The guy knew what he was doing.

The footsteps grew louder, and a flashlight beam shone into the room. Kenzie held her breath as her pulse pounded in her ears.

Please don't find us, she prayed.

23

Alex crouched, still as a statue, behind the crates. She knew he was there but he'd blended so seamlessly with the shadows that she couldn't pinpoint exactly where.

The beam swung in a lazy arc around the room. It was about to hit the crates where Alex was when it flickered and went out. The man cursed under his breath, hit it with his hand, and cursed again.

The beam flickered again but wouldn't stay on. They heard rustling as the man searched in a pocket, probably for his phone. A weaker, whiter light came on.

A few seconds later, an impatient voice called from the meeting room. The man with the light called out something in Japanese, then retraced his steps back the way he'd come.

Kenzie let out a shaky breath. That was close.

Once she was sure the coast was clear, she came out from behind the door. Alex appeared from behind a box to her left, not from where she thought he'd hidden.

"You okay?" he whispered.

It was pitch black in the storeroom, so she turned her penlight on. The pale beam picked up a random piece of paper on the floor. She was sure it hadn't been there when they'd come in. Still, they'd been moving quickly so she might have been mistaken.

"Yeah, let's get out of here."

"Good idea."

As Alex led the way, Kenzie bent to pick up the scrap paper before following after him and shoved it into the pocket in her jeggings.

They inched their way back along the hallway to the room with the broken window. At least the man with the flashlight hadn't come in here. They might have searched harder if he had.

Alex went first this time, easing himself up through the frame and out into the night. Kenzie climbed out after him, the metal rim cold under her palms.

When she dropped back onto the gravel, her bad knee almost gave out. She felt the twinge and grimaced.

"Okay?" Alex asked again.

"Yeah."

They crouched there for a moment, backs to the wall, listening.

Nothing. Just the canal water shifting and the far-off hum of traffic.

They moved away from the warehouse without a word, sticking close to the fence line until the building was a derelict outline behind them. Only when they reached the darker stretch of road did Kenzie finally breathe properly.

"That was exciting," he said as they walked the short distance to their vehicles. She didn't miss the sardonic tone.

"I'm sorry I dragged you in there. I put us both in danger, and for nothing. I should have realized they'd be speaking Japanese."

Alex gave a short huff. "We didn't know. Besides, you got a recording. Once you translate it, it might be useful."

"If it picks up their voices."

They walked the rest of the way in silence. Kenzie felt the adrenaline ebbing, and her knee started to throb.

She was acutely aware of Alex beside her, the near-silence of his footsteps, the way his gaze never stopped tracking the perimeter, alert to every movement, every shadow.

At the cars, they stopped. Alex rested a hand on his door but didn't open it right away.

"I don't think we should tell RedCairn about this," he decided, looking pointedly at her.

"What if there's something on the recording?"

"If there is, we'll decide what to do."

"FieldNotes knows we went in," she pointed out.

"We'll just say we changed our minds. He won't know we didn't."

Kenzie hesitated. She didn't want to get either of them into trouble with RedCairn, but she felt uncomfortable lying.

"Will he be very mad?" she asked.

"I don't want you pinned as reckless," he said, after a beat. "Considering you've just joined us."

Okay, that was a solid point.

"Thank you," she whispered. "I appreciate you looking out for me. Back there as well." She nodded at the warehouse.

"You're welcome."

She hesitated. "Can I ask you something, Alex?"

His gaze narrowed. "Maybe."

"I know we're not supposed to talk about who we are, but... Have you done this kind of thing before?"

He met her gaze, but his expression was unreadable. "Something like that."

It wasn't a yes, but it wasn't a denial either.

She didn't push, just nodded, flashed him a weak smile, and turned and walked back to her car.

By the time she pulled away, Alex had already left. She'd memorized his license plate, just as she'd done with FieldNote's, but she wasn't confident she'd get anything from it. He wasn't the type to use his own car. That would be too obvious.

Alex was an enigma, and one she very much wanted to solve.

What was his backstory? Why was he so cagey, so careful? And most importantly, was he one of the good guys—or one of the bad ones?

The next morning, after a restless night's sleep where she had a convoluted dream involving swords and rats and broken glass, Kenzie drove out to Reid's place in the Glades. As soon as she turned off the freeway and onto the recently paved road that led into the swampland, she felt a strange kind of calmness sweep over her.

It was Saturday, so she'd opted to spend the weekend with Reid. Or at least as long as she was able. With him in the thick of an active case, that probably wouldn't be very long, but even a few hours were better than nothing.

Besides, she was curious as to what progress they were making.

As the road wound on, it felt like the vegetation was closing in on all sides, cutting her off from the rest of the civilized world. At first, she'd found it unnerving, but now she enjoyed the peacefulness that came with it.

After the night she'd had, she needed some downtime. Unfortunately, the recording was too poor quality to translate. The technical team at police headquarters might have more luck, but she had to tell Reid about her little adventure before she could hand him the audio file.

She was not looking forward to that.

Several miles later, she turned onto a dirt road flanked by wide canals. The surface was hard and dusty and her little car bounced and shook as it drove over the washboard ridges.

Eventually, she pulled over outside Reid's two-story cabin that he'd built from scratch after the old one had burned down. It was erected on chunky stilts to elevate it above the swampy ground, and—not that you could see it from this angle—the front sported a wide, wrap-around deck with a wooden walkway that led down to his own personal launching dock where he kept his airboat.

There was nothing Kenzie enjoyed more than sitting out on the deck with Reid, watching the sun sink over the water, and listening as the swamp came to life. It had become something of a ritual when she was there.

Getting out of the car, she glanced up as an eagle screeched overhead. She'd learned to appreciate sounds of the swamp. It had music all its own. The chirp of cicadas, the cries of the birds, and the splash as something entered the water. Sitting out on Reid's wooden deck, she'd learned a lot about the wildlife. What was natural, and what she should be afraid of.

Reid came out to greet her. He wore beige pants and a khaki shirt, which looked good with his early-season tan. Circles ringed his eyes, though, and she thought he looked tired.

It was the same with every case. She knew the feeling well, not from a cop's perspective, but from a reporter's. While Reid was after justice, she was a teller of the truth.

That didn't mean the victims didn't play on her mind, or that she slept easy knowing that the killer was still out there. That could eat away at you and she knew the responsibility weighed heavily on Reid. That's what made him such a good detective.

"Hey, how's it going?" She stood on her tiptoes to kiss him. He wrapped an arm around her waist and held her to him for a moment.

Then releasing her, he said, "As well as can be expected."

She didn't ask questions, knowing there'd be time to talk about that later. He took her overnight bag and led her inside. It was cooler inside than out in the heat, even though Reid didn't have the air conditioning on.

He'd only installed it as part of the rebuild, having preferred a rickety old ceiling fan prior to that. If the useless thing hadn't burned to a cinder, Kenzie would have put her foot down. It was ridiculous trying to exist in the intense summer heat of the swamp without AC.

They had a coffee out on the deck, during which Reid asked her if she'd made any headway with the online group she was infiltrating.

"Some," she replied vaguely, staring past him at the sea of sawgrass and cattails. "I've been accepted and I'm starting to get to know the core characters."

"Anyone interesting?" he asked, although she could tell his mind was elsewhere. If he'd been focused on what she was saying, he'd have noticed her deliberate skirting of the question.

"Maybe. I'm still deciding."

He nodded, distractedly.

"What's up?" She sat back in her chair and studied him.

"Nothing, why?"

She smiled. Typical Reid. Always fine, even when he wasn't.

"Something's preying on your mind."

"It's just this case."

She arched an eyebrow. "Might help to talk about it."

He looked at her, hesitated, then said, "We found an antiquities dealer yesterday who sold artifacts to both victims."

She stared at him. "You did? That's a good thing, isn't it?"

When he didn't reply, she said, "Is he the link between them?"

"Yes, but not in the way you think."

At her confused look, he said. "The guy's store was burgled. His customer files were taken."

She gasped. "Holy crap!" That's how the killer is targeting them. He's going through the files."

Reid gave a somber nod.

"Do you know whose records were stolen?"

The killer would be moving on to the next one soon. No wonder Reid was so distracted.

"Not everyone," he said. "The ones we do know of are being contacted as we speak. I've got half the team working overtime chasing them down."

She bit her lip. "I'll understand if you want to get back to the department." Reid wasn't the type to let his team do all the legwork. It was one of the things she admired about him.

"I might go in tomorrow," he said. "Right now, they can handle it. I'm on call if anything else happens."

She gulped. "Like another murder."

He shot her a grim look. "Let's hope it doesn't come to that."

24

As IT TURNED OUT, he did drive back to the department that afternoon. Dwayne called with a lead on the toxin and he wanted to go check it out.

The rest of the team were tied up speaking to Watanabe's customers and warning them to take precautions. They were also trying to find out if any of them had purchased stolen artifacts, or acquired items from less than reputable dealers.

That information wasn't forthcoming, from what he could gather. Most collectors neither confirmed nor denied, as was their right. Reid was learning that they kept their sources very close to their chest. Perhaps to their detriment in this case.

"Who is it?" he asked Dwayne, who'd been calling and visiting drug stores, botanicas and suppliers for the last twenty-four hours. He deserved some time off.

"Her name is Solange Baptiste, and she lives in Little Haiti. According to the man I spoke to, she goes by Mambo Solange."

Stood to reason she'd be a voodoo practitioner.

"Where do I find this Mambo Solange?"

"Maison des Racines, although I'm not entirely sure where that is. You know how hard these places are to find. They don't appear on any map or street directory."

"I'll find it. Now go home to Mrs. Griffiths or she'll be forgetting what you look like."

Dwayne grinned. "Thanks, boss. I could do with a good home cooked meal and my bed. In that order."

Not so for Reid.

He took his truck and headed out to Little Haiti. Dressed purposely in casual jeans and an old shirt, he hoped he wouldn't immediately be pegged for a cop. Locals were more likely to talk to a tourist or a curious city resident than they were to law enforcement.

He stopped at a pop-up burrito spot that he frequented whenever he was in town. Vargas had introduced him to it a couple of years back, and he'd been several times since. Their breakfast burritos were legendary.

While ordering, he asked the man at the counter where he could find Maison des Racines. The man didn't answer right away.

"I heard she knows plants," he said, trying to sound nonchalant. The man knew him by sight, not what he did for a living, but he'd have to come back here, so he didn't want to be too elaborate. "My girlfriend and I are trying for a baby. We're looking for some... fertility herbs."

The man's face brightened. "Mambo Solange can definitely help you with that, my man. You'll find *Les Racine*s a few blocks off NE 2nd Avenue, between the tire shop and a bakery.

Reid noticed he'd used a shortened form of the store name. Must be a local thing. He thanked the man, took his burrito, and got back into his truck.

The drive to 2nd Avenue took no time at all, and he hadn't even gotten halfway through his snack when he spotted it. The store occupied a narrow concrete building with a faded turquoise exterior.

The front windows were cluttered rather than curated, and crowded with glass candles bearing saints' faces, bundles of dried herbs tied with twine, small bottles of dark liquid, and strings of beads hanging like curtains.

A hand-painted sign above the door read: ROOTS. REMEDIES. PROTECTION. Yep, this was the place alright.

Reid pushed open the door and stepped inside. The air was thick with incense, and he resisted the urge to sneeze. Floor to ceiling shelves stocked with jars of powders, seeds, bones, feathers, and roots labeled in a careful, looping script lined the walls.

As he progressed further into the store, he saw a low counter separating the public space from a back room. The beaded curtain told him this was likely where Mambo Solange conducted her private consultations.

He went up to the counter and rang a small brass bell. There was no cash register in sight, but lying on the surface was an open ledger with transactions written by hand.

There was a shuffle and Mambo Solange appeared from behind the curtain in a rustle of beads. She was in her early sixties with tightly coiled hair shot through with silver and wrapped in a patterned headscarf. More beads rested against her chest, clinking as she moved.

She looked him over with dark, probing eyes that seemed to see right through him. "What can I help you with?" Her voice was soft and musical, the accent unmistakably Haitian Creole.

For a moment, he contemplated lying, but he had the funny feeling she'd see straight through him and then he'd have ruined his one chance at getting the name of her buyer.

"Madam Solange," he began, sticking his hand into his jeans pocket and pulling out his ID. "I'm sure you've guessed by now that I'm law enforcement. I need to ask you some questions about a certain substance that I believe you stock in your store."

Her gaze flicked to the badge, then back to his face.

"I appreciate your honesty," she said, smiling at him. "It's very rare to find a policeman who's not trying to pretend he's someone else."

Glad he'd read that one correctly, he bowed his head. "Thank you. I'm not here to bust you, but I do need to know who you sold the tetrodotoxin to."

She blinked at him.

"The puffer fish poison," he clarified.

Her gaze sharpened. "How did you know to come here?"

"People in the neighborhood," Reid replied. He wasn't about to throw the burrito guy under the bus. Madam Solange didn't look like the kind of woman you wanted to cross.

She gave a suspicious nod. "Why are you interested in my *coupe poudre*?"

"Because it was used to kill two innocent men," he replied.

"Men, yes," she said quietly, tilting her head. "Innocent, no."

He frowned, rubbing his forehead. "How do you know they weren't innocent?"

"Because it wouldn't have worked otherwise. The spell is only for the guilty." He was willing to bet that, ingested, the toxin would floor most people. Even more so, when injected. But he didn't say as much.

"That might be true, but I still need to know who bought it."

She glanced down at the leather-bound ledger. "It will be written there."

Reid's heart sank. No way the perpetrator would have given his real name.

"Do you remember who it was? What he looked like?" he asked. Maybe she could describe him, sit with an artist.

She turned back several pages and then traced a long, lacquered nail over the entries, her bracelets jangling as she did so, and he shelved that thought. He couldn't imagine her sitting with a sketch artist.

About halfway down she paused and tapped her finger against the page. "This is the one. Here." She turned the ledger toward him.

He looked down.

John Meadows.

Reid snorted. That was only marginally better than John Smith. She must get a lot of Johns.

"Was he of Japanese descent?" he asked.

She didn't reply.

"Did you ask for identification?" he pressed, exasperated.

She shook her head. "I ask for reasons. I don't care who buys it, so long as the purpose is pure."

How could the motive for poison ever be pure?

"What was the reason?" he asked.

She gave a sly smile. "I cannot tell you that. A person's reason is their own private business."

"But you know?"

She inclined her head. "Aye. I do."

"And is it pure?" he asked.

Another nod. "I wouldn't have given it to him otherwise."

Reid left the store shortly after that. Madam Solange wasn't going to divulge any more information on her customer. He'd tried to ask for a description, but she didn't give much more than he'd been a man with dark hair and dark eyes. That described half the population of Miami.

"It would help if we knew whether he was Japanese American or not," Reid growled when he got back, pacing up and down the bullpen. He knew he shouldn't vent his frustration in front of the others, but Mambo Solange withholding information had really rubbed him the wrong way. Short of arresting her, he wasn't sure what else he could do.

"We could arrest her," Vargas suggested, voicing what he was thinking. "Force her to cooperate."

"Do you want to be the one to bring her in?" asked Reid.

Vargas shuddered. "Hell no. I don't want her turning that voodoo shit on me."

Reid looked around the room, but everyone either shook their heads or slunk back to their desks. Cowards. No matter. He got the feeling arresting her wouldn't make a stitch of difference. The woman was a vault.

"What about CCTV in the area?" Diaz asked.

Reid gave a shrug. "You can try. Anything in those areas is usually destroyed or damaged. They don't like being spied on."

"Still, it's worth a shot," she said, turning back to her screen.

"What have we got from forensics?" he asked, finally coming to a stop and perching on the edge of his desk.

Vargas consulted the notebook which lay on his meticulously tidy workspace. "Nothing at the first crime scene. The killer was careful not to leave any trace at the gallery. They found two wine glasses in the dishwasher, which suggests Hargreave had a drink with someone before he died."

Reid narrowed his gaze. "That could be how he ingested the toxin."

Vargas inclined his head. "Except forensics tested the glasses and there was no residue left. They'd been thoroughly cleaned."

"Goddammit," Reid muttered. When were they going to catch a break? "What about fingerprints on the dishwasher or in the house?"

Vargas shook his head. "Again, nothing specific. The maid's fingerprints, of course, but she wasn't working that day. She was visiting with her sister upstate. Her alibi checks out. The landscaper's prints were on the front door and the door leading down to the gallery, but then we know he discovered the body."

"Wasn't it left open?" Reid queried, frowning.

"Handprint on the door, not the handle. Suggests it was ajar, like he said."

"Okay fine. They're in the clear. Let's move on. What about Burton-Holmes's family? What did Hamilton find out?"

"He's not back yet," Martinez said, looking up from her desk.

"Call him," Reid said. "I want an update."

She reached for the phone.

Reid slumped down at his computer and pulled up the list of

customers that Watanabe thought might be missing. It was slow going as the dealer was still emailing names through to Martinez, but according to the shared spreadsheet, all of the customers they'd been given had been notified.

He scoured the list, feeling an ache begin to build behind his eyes. Twenty-seven names so far. How many of them were serious collectors? How many of them were targets for the killer? Which one of them was next?

They had to expand their suspect list now that they'd ruled out those who'd had direct contact with the victims. It was time to consider the nationalist angle, but to do that, he needed to speak to Raoul, Kenzie's newspaper buddy.

The tech whiz picked up on the first ring. "Lieutenant, I was wondering when you were going to call."

He grunted. "I meant to get in touch earlier, but I've had my hands full."

"Understandable."

"Can you come in?"

"Sure. Today?"

Reid glanced at the clock on the wall. It was already nearly five o'clock. "If possible, yeah."

"I'll be there by eight."

Reid thanked him and hung up. It was turning out to be another long day.

Next, he called Kenzie. "Hey, it's me."

Her voice was a balm to his ears. "Hi, how are things there?"

"Fine. Raoul is coming in this evening to give me an update. Anything I should know about the online groups?"

He heard the hesitation in her voice. "Not really. Raoul located a group that he thought might be of interest, but he can tell you about that. I can't infiltrate them, they're members only and I don't fit the bill."

"Okay, I'll get the info from him. You think they're involved in this?"

"I don't know. Maybe. You should look into them."

"Has Raoul said anything to you?"

"Only what he'll tell you. They're active online, they discussed the first victim, but after the fact. I don't know if there was any mention of the second."

"I'll ask him," he said, making a note. "Anything else? What about those true crime fanatics? Have they come up with anything we haven't?"

"I don't know what you've got," she said carefully. "Maybe you can fill me in later?"

"I'm going to be late here, but I could come to yours afterward. That okay?" He felt bad for abandoning her today. They usually spent weekends together.

"Sure, I'll be here. If it's late, just let yourself in, but I'll probably still be awake."

"Great. See you later."

"See you, Reid."

He put the phone down and frowned.

"What's up?" Vargas asked, coming over.

"Kenzie's acting weird."

He grinned. "Weirder than normal?"

He didn't reciprocate.

"Okay, weird like how?" Vargas asked, more serious now.

"I don't know. Can't put my finger on it. Like she knows something she's not telling me."

"Maybe because her buddy's coming in?" he suggested.

"Yeah, could be."

The more he thought about it, the more he thought Vargas was probably right. She didn't want to rain on her friend's parade. If Raoul had information to share, it was his job to do it. That's what the department was paying him for, after all.

25

Raoul arrived just after eight, looking like a grungy student in his hoodie, messy hair, glasses, and a messenger bag slung across his chest. It was hard to believe he was a technical genius. He signed in at the front desk and waited, hands in his pockets, scanning the bullpen with open curiosity.

Reid didn't waste time. He intercepted him and offered him a coffee.

Raoul shook his head. "I'm good. Thanks."

"Okay, then let's get down to business. Follow me." Reid led him through a door and down a corridor to the interview rooms. He chose the first one. This time the AC was on and the room a pleasant temperature.

"Mind if I record our conversation?" He nodded to the digital recording device bolted to the table.

"No problem." Raoul sat down, took a tablet out of his bag and placed it on the table. Then he set his bag on the floor beside his feet.

"All right," Reid said, once he'd pressed 'record'. His notebook was open on the table in front of him. "Talk to me."

Raoul tapped the tablet, and the screen lit up. "I started by trawling social media and the online chat rooms for nationalist or ideological rhetoric," he said without glancing down, "and I came up with a couple of names. After digging deeper, I found one that was particularly active. They call themselves the Heritage Preservation Coalition."

Reid frowned. "What alerted you?"

"They were talking about the repatriation of artifacts stolen from Japanese temples and shrines. About restitution and cultural retribution."

"Okay," he said slowly. "That's not really enough to raise suspicion."

"You're right. But then came the discussion about your first victim and the manner in which he'd died."

"Malcolm Hargreave?" Reid asked. "They mention him by name?"

"Not by name, but it was obvious they were talking about him. The details were exactly what was in the press."

Reid let out a breath. "Everybody saw those photographs online. Doesn't mean they had anything to do with it."

"No, but these guys weren't exactly shocked by the outcome," Raoul elaborated. "In fact, they praised it." He turned the tablet around and laid it on the table.

Reid scanned the text.

Justice was not carried out by law, but by necessity.

Followed by:

Let this be a reminder that some debts cannot be negotiated.

He let out an apprehensive breath. "I see what you mean." He thought for a moment. "Any idea who these guys are?"

"I have their online handles." Raoul reached into his hoodie pouch and pulled out a scrap of paper. He slid it across the table.

Reid liked that he'd come prepared.

He glanced down and frowned. "ShatteredTorii? IronPine? EightfoldPath?" He remembered Kenzie mentioning the Shattered-Torii one, but the others meant nothing to him.

"They couldn't just be normal names, could they?"

Raoul smirked, then pointed to the first handle. "ShatteredTorii is the Lead Moderator in the private group. He posts long comments with historical references. Really knows his stuff."

"Kenzie told me about him." He massaged his forehead. "Thought he might be an academic or something."

"Correct." Raoul nodded to the paper again. "IronPine talks a lot about consequences."

"I don't understand," Reid said.

"Says things like 'justice is inevitable' and 'balance must be restored'—that sort of thing."

"Gotcha," Reid muttered.

"Definitely worth checking out."

"What about EightfoldPath?"

"Moral absolutist," Raoul replied. "Frames everything in terms of balance and karmic debt. Less violent in tone, but just as rigid in his beliefs."

Reid narrowed his gaze, ignoring the throbbing in his head. "What about timing? How does any of this relate to the murders?"

"Most of that rhetoric was after the first murder," Raoul said with a shrug. "But there was some activity *before* the second."

"Oh?"

"Yeah, a breakaway group took the discussion offline."

"Offline? Like in real life?"

"Probably using an encrypted messaging service," he explained. "There were seven of them that fell silent for a while."

"How many in this private chat?" Reid asked.

"Over twenty. It's a large group by usual standards. Not everyone is active, however. They tend to dip in and out, but that's pretty common too."

"So the core group goes offline just before the murder happens?" Reid said thoughtfully.

"Yep. Thought that might interest you. It looks like they had a meeting afterward too."

Reid glanced up. "A meeting? Like physical contact?"

Raoul laughed. "IRL, man. Yeah."

Reid stared across at the techie. "Let me get this straight. These shady-as-hell ideological nuts met in real life and you didn't think to tell me about it?"

Raoul spread his hands. "Hey, don't shoot the messenger. I wasn't sure they were involved. I'm still not. You need to look into them yourself. That's not my job, man."

Reid tightened his jaw. "We could have intercepted them."

"They have a website," Raoul said in a more conciliatory tone. "The address is at the bottom there."

Reid glanced back at the slip of paper. "It's a legitimate organization?"

"Bona fide," Raoul stated with a nod. "You can look them up. They don't name names, but they aren't trying to hide their existence."

Reid straightened, suddenly more alert. "Can you keep monitoring them?"

"Already am," Raoul replied. "They don't know I'm there."

"Good," Reid said, conveniently forgetting about the obvious 'gray area' there. "I want alerts on any hint of involvement. Anything about potential targets or a hit list. Dates. Locations. You got that?"

Raoul nodded.

"Okay, good." He pushed himself up.

Raoul leaned back in his chair. "Sorry about not coming in sooner. Thought you were going to get in touch."

Reid knew he was partly to blame. He hadn't been giving this lead the attention it deserved. That was on him.

"Don't worry about it. Next time, call me. Okay?"

"Copy that, Lieutenant."

Reid let himself into Kenzie's condo a little before ten o'clock. He was pretty sure she'd still be awake. As expected, she was working in her study and came out to greet him.

"How'd it go with Raoul?" she asked, as they sat side-by-side on the couch.

"Fine. Good actually. We're looking into this Heritage Preservation Coalition, like you suggested. Looks like it warrants further investigation. We're trying to identify the leader, so we can question him."

"ShatteredTorii," she murmured.

"That's it. I should have paid more attention at the start, but the other suspects were lining up, and—" he shrugged.

"I know." She squeezed his hand. "They all had a motive. Understandable you'd want to clear them first."

He gave a tired nod. "Then there's Mambo Solange."

Kenzie raised an eyebrow. "Sounds fascinating. Who's she?"

"Annoying, rather than fascinating." Reid recounted his experience at *Les Racines*. "I tried to get a description out of her, but she sidestepped it. Gave me some vague description that could be anyone."

Kenzie sighed. "I'm not surprised. If they ratted on their customers, nobody would go to them."

"They aren't allowed to sell that stuff," he argued. "I could have her shut down."

"She'll know it's you," Kenzie cautioned.

He let out a huff. "Yeah, maybe I'll wait a while. That toxin has to come off the market, though."

"Agreed." Kenzie frowned. "Did she give you anything at all?"

"Only to say the motive was pure."

Kenzie shot him a confused look. "Huh?"

"The reason the person bought the poison. She doesn't sell it unless the buyer has a 'pure' motive."

"Well, that's something, I guess." She cocked her head. "Did she tell you what the reason was?"

He scoffed, feeling the tension rise. "Of course not. What the hell does pure mean, anyway?"

"Justified?" Kenzie suggested, then dropped her voice. "As in someone trying to restore a cultural balance."

Reid met her gaze. He'd had the same thought. "Or getting revenge..."

"That too," she whispered.

He arched both his eyebrows. "Your nationalist group is becoming more and more interesting by the day."

She paused. "Raoul might be able to trace them for you."

Reid studied her. There it was again, that vague look.

"Apparently there was a clandestine meeting last night between the core members of the group," he said quietly. "Did you know about that?"

She bit her lip.

That's when he knew. That's what she'd been hiding from him.

"Jesus, Kenzie. Please tell me you didn't go to it?"

She grimaced. "I mean, I could but—"

"For fuck's sake. Are you trying to get yourself killed?" He leaped up off the couch and began marching up and down in front of her. "Do you know how dangerous that was?"

"I know, but—"

"Of all the stupid, pig-headed things to do! You didn't think to tell me? I could have come with you. Could have provided backup."

"You would *not* have backed me up," she said tartly. "You know that and I know that. You wouldn't have let me go."

He stopped pacing and stared at her. "I would have sent a team."

"To do what? They just had a meeting. It was nothing dramatic."

"They could have been discussing a third murder." He put his hands on his hips. "Did you think of that?"

"Yes, Reid. I did. That's why I went. I wanted to see for myself if they were involved or if they were just another harmless group of complainers."

He tried to control his breathing. Honestly, she drove him mad sometimes. Impulsive didn't even begin to describe it. When he could trust himself to speak calmly, he said, "I'm assuming you didn't find anything, since you lived to tell the tale—or not tell it, as the case may be."

She had the sense to look embarrassed.

"I wanted to tell you," she said after a beat. "But I know how you get about these things, particularly when I'm involved." She gave him a pointed look.

He pressed his lips together to prevent himself from saying something he'd regret later.

"I know it's because you care about me," she said, more softly. "But if it's any consolation, I didn't go alone."

He scowled. "Who'd you go with?" Then the penny dropped. "It was those true crime nuts, wasn't it?"

"They aren't nuts," she said, getting to her feet. He could tell by the flush in her cheeks that he'd finally succeeded in pissing her off. "They're actually extremely good at crime solving. You should see some of the things they've come up with."

"They are not authorized to investigate this case," he fumed.

She shook her head. "There is no law that says they can't do their own research. They aren't making any arrests; they aren't obstructing your investigation."

"What do you call last night?" he countered. "What if something had happened to you, Kenzie? Or if this fanatical group had seen you and been tipped off? We might have lost the one shot we had at bringing them in."

She spread her hands. "For what? Having a meeting?"

He shook his head and forced himself to relax. There was a tense pause.

"Okay, let's dial this down a notch." He lapped the living room. The movement helped calm him.

When he'd gotten himself under control, he said, "What did you find? Were they up to something?"

She glared at him for a long moment, then sat down again, but in the armchair this time. "We observed, that's all. And took some photos of the attendees."

He did a double-take.

"You've got photographs of them? Can I see them?"

"Sure, I was going to share them with you anyway, once I'd had a chance to explain how I got them."

He shot her an exasperated look. "And when was that going to be?"

"Tonight."

"Right."

There was a short silence where they both got their breath back.

"The photos should help you identify them," Kenzie said, standing up and walking to her office. He followed, regretting the tension between them. Damn her for not filling him in. He hated it when she went off on a tangent like this. He'd played catch-up too many times.

"I also managed to get a recording of part of the meeting," she called over her shoulder.

He grabbed her arm and turned her to face him. "How did you get that?"

"Through a broken window," she said, not quite meeting his gaze.

He sucked in a breath but shelved that argument for later. "What does it say?"

"I don't know. They spoke in Japanese."

He snorted, releasing her arm. His headache returned with full force. "Jesus, Kenz. What am I going to do with you?"

Her shoulders dropped and some of the tension left her body. "Work with me in identifying these guys," she said softly, gazing up at him. Her usually clear blue eyes were indigo in the lamplight. "Then you can bring them in for questioning and see for yourself if they had anything to do with your two homicides."

Sighing, he gave a reluctant nod and followed her into the study.

26

It was time to come clean.

Kenzie sat Reid down and showed him the activity in The Evidence Room. He read without speaking for a long time, then glanced up at her.

"You have been busy," he said softly.

She swallowed. "Yeah, well it was one of the few things I could help with. You were off chasing leads, and I was left here doing nothing. So I infiltrated them." She nodded to her computer.

"These characters, RedCairn, AlexR, ThirdWitness, did you meet them the other night?"

"I met AlexR and FieldNotes." She went on to describe them. "I got the feeling Alex had done that sort of thing before."

"What sort of thing?"

"You know, covert ops, undercover work, sneaky stuff. He might be ex-law enforcement, or former military, or something along those lines."

He frowned. "Is Alex his real name?"

"Don't know. I memorized their license plates, and I was hoping you'd run them to see if you could identify them.

He was silent for a beat. "That was smart," he said, eventually.

She smiled. "I thought so."

He shook his head. It was a small consolation. She knew he was still mad as hell at her for going in the first place.

"Let's see this recording then," he said.

She leaned over him, reaching for the mouse. A few clicks and she'd pulled up the audio file. "I tried to run it through a translation site but it said it was unreadable. I think there's too much static, or background noise."

She hit play. Faint Japanese voices could be heard talking, but there was a low hum overriding everything. "I think it's the nearby street," she said.

"Send this to my work email and I'll get the tech team to have a look at it. Maybe they can isolate the voices."

She nodded. "These are the photos I took on my phone. FieldNotes took better ones, but he hasn't uploaded them to the channel yet."

She stood back while Reid clicked through the murky, grainy pictures she'd taken from behind the crates. "It's going to be hard to make a formal identification from any of these," he said.

"I know. Let me check the private chat."

Reid moved out of the way, and Kenzie sat down. She tabbed back to The Evidence Room and clicked on the private channel RedCairn had created with just her, AlexR and FieldNotes.

"It's here!" She opened the folder where FieldNotes had uploaded a dozen images, all taken outside the warehouse.

Reid leaned in closer as she clicked through them. "How many were there?"

"At least seven. We saw six arrive, and someone opened the door to let them in. There could have been more inside, but I didn't wait around to find out."

He shot her a look as if to say, "This is why you should have told me. We could have cased the joint and taken an accurate count."

"I know, okay," she said, reading his mind. His lips tilted at the sides. "But I didn't want to risk exposure. We'd been there long enough already."

"Okay, so who took these?"

"FieldNotes. He arrived in a sedan, said he had a wife at home, so he couldn't stay late, and took off early."

"Describe him to me." Reid fixed his gaze on her.

"Five eleven, broad shouldered, stocky build, but not huge like a powerlifter or anything. Slight gut, like he has a sedentary lifestyle. Brown hair, brown eyes, unremarkable features." She shrugged, not knowing what else to say. FieldNotes wasn't that memorable.

"Okay, fine. What about Alex?"

"He's slim, slightly shorter than you but not by much. He's light on his feet, moves quietly, like a panther. And has this uncanny ability to disappear into the shadows."

"Suspicious?" Reid asked.

"Definitely, but not because I think he's involved. Because he's good at this stuff. Too good for an amateur."

"Didn't you say he's the one the leader trusts the most?"

"Yeah, I think he's second-in-command. Highly respected by RedCairn."

"And we've got no idea who this RedCairn is?"

"None. He said he was busy so couldn't join us at the stake out. Raoul says they're too careful to have online footprints leading to their real identities."

Reid tapped his fingers on the side of his arm. "Okay, I'll get these photos to the team and maybe we can find out who they are. Run facial recognition or something. If they're American, they'll have driver's licenses and social security numbers. Shouldn't be too hard now we have their faces. Or most of them."

He nodded to the man in the helmet. It was a full facial helmet with a visor over the eyes. It could even have been a woman for all they knew.

Kenzie nodded but gestured to the screen. "One of the true crime members, ThirdWitness, was at the crime scene."

Reid glanced at her startled. "Which crime scene?"

"The one in the park. He loaded all these close-ups to the chat and I just knew. When I questioned him, he said he'd heard it on the police scanner and got there early, before the cordon went up."

Reid frowned. "That could be true. It took us some time to get there and shut the scene down. A couple of beat cops had tried to secure it, but there was already a crowd of onlookers when they arrived."

"I thought it might be worth a deeper look into him," she said. "He said he lived nearby."

Reid frowned. "We did see the perp pull into the parking lot in the early hours, before the body was found. We reckon he dumped the body. Dragged it from the lot to the palm tree."

"You've got the killer on CCTV?" Kenzie stared at him. "Why didn't you say?"

"Because he drove in with his high beams on. The lens flare killed the camera. Can't see a damn thing."

"Crap, really?"

"Yeah, the guy knew what he was doing."

Kenzie paused for a moment, thinking. "He knew where the camera was. He already knew where he was going to place the body. He could be a local."

"That's what I thought," Reid agreed.

Kenzie thought back to ThirdWitness. "You see anything at all from the camera footage?"

"Nope. Just a shadow moving behind the light. We can't even tell what vehicle he was driving."

She sighed and shook her head. "What a bummer."

"You're telling me."

The feed in front of them began moving. Now FieldNotes had uploaded his photographs, the others were looking at them, analyzing, assessing.

Kenzie glanced at Reid. They'd be able to see she was in the chat room, so she couldn't pretend she wasn't there. His gaze narrowed as he watched the dialogue feed.

AlexR: Great job, @FieldNotes. Pity about the helmet.

>

>

RedCairn: How'd it go?

>

>

AlexR: Good. We took the photos, waited for a while, then left.

>

FieldNotes: You didn't go inside?

>

RedCairn: Inside?

>

>

AlexR: Too risky.

Kenzie glanced at Reid. "I've got to respond. They know I'm here."

He gave her a nod. She began to type.

ReporterGirl: Didn't want to push it.

>

>

RedCairn: Good move. Glad you're back safe.

Kenzie gave that a thumbs up.

RedCairn: Any way to identify them?

>

>

FieldNotes: Not without facial rec software.

>

>

>

AlexR: What about your researcher connection, @ReporterGirl?

"You told them about Raoul?" Reid pulled up a spare chair and sat down next to her.

Kenzie bit her lip. "Not by name. Told them that's how I knew about the meeting."

He gave a stiff nod. She could tell he was still resentful she hadn't included him.

ReporterGirl: I could ask him.

>

>

RedCairn: Might be the play.

>

ReporterGirl: OK brb.

She turned to Reid. "I'll just pretend I've sent them to him. You'll have better luck running the facial rec."

"Nothing we talk about gets repeated to these guys," he warned her. "Even if we do identify ShatteredTorii, you can't tell them."

She pulled a face. "I know the rules."

"Good." He nodded at the screen. "Can we turn in now or are you going to stay up all night talking to these guys?" Was that a touch of jealousy in his tone?

"One second," she said, turning back to the computer.

ReporterGirl: He's agreed to take a look. Will update you asap gtg.

There were three thumbs up.

Kenzie signed off, and her screen went dark.

"I can see the appeal," he said, as they got ready for bed. "But these guys are loose cannons, Kenz. You don't know anything about them. Meeting them like that was impulsive and dangerous."

"Reid—"

"If something had happened to you..." She saw his jaw tense. "I wouldn't have known where you were or who you were with."

She could see how concerned he was and walked around the bed to embrace him. "I'm sorry. I know it was reckless. I won't do it again." She hesitated. "I was just eager to help. I feel so useless."

He wrapped his arms around her. "I know, but you have to be more careful. Promise me?"

She glanced up and saw the worry mixed with love in his eyes. Guilt clutched at her chest. Not once had she considered Reid in all this—or how he would feel if something terrible happened to her.

She did know, however, how devastated she'd be if she lost him.

"I promise," she whispered.

27

The first thing Reid did when he got to the station the next morning was run the license plates Kenzie had given him. He didn't pass them on to Vargas or anyone else. He didn't want to have to explain how she'd obtained them.

If they were going to pursue this organization, it had to be done properly—through official channels, on their own time, with evidence that would stand up in court. A covert stakeout conducted by a group of true-crime enthusiasts wasn't something he could condone, let alone build a case on.

FieldNotes's family car was registered to Jeff Oliver at 11247 SW 8th Street, Miami. When he ran it through the DMV, he got a driver's license with the photograph of a stocky man with brown hair and dark eyes. It matched the description Kenzie had given him.

AlexR's vehicle was a rental. Not a mainline rental agency either, but a small independent setup in Hialeah that didn't ask too many questions.

When he spoke to them, they told him the name on the form was Alexander Russel. AlexR. Could be that was the guy's real name.

He ran it through the police database, but he got too many hits to count. Turns out Alexander Russel was more common than he thought. He trawled through some of the photographs but didn't really know what he was looking for. Maybe he'd get Kenzie to take a look.

Taking out his phone, he messaged her to come into the department. Said he'd run the plates and wanted her to look through some mug shots.

She replied almost instantly.

On my way.

He allowed himself a small smile. He knew she'd only acted impulsively because she'd wanted to get involved. Kenzie was an investigator through and through and would have made a terrific detective if she'd been given the chance. Unfortunately, her injury killed that dream.

Her built-in curiosity and need to expose the truth were things that had drawn him to her when they'd first met. Now she was freelancing, she could explore the topics she wanted to, but when it came to police cases, even as a consultant, she still felt like a civilian on the outside. He could only imagine how frustrating that must be. As concerned as he was, he got it.

Putting that thought aside, Reid turned his attention to the photographs Kenzie had emailed him. Before doing anything else, he logged them into the system as coming from a civilian source. It was deliberately vague, just enough of a paper trail to justify what came next.

He uploaded the images to the department's facial recognition database and queued them for comparison against state and federal records. The system warned him that the process could take a while, depending on image quality and match confidence, so he left it running in the background and headed over to Diaz's desk.

She glanced up. "You okay, Lieutenant?"

"Was tech support able to clean up that parking lot footage at all?" he asked, thinking about the second victim and the drag marks.

Her face fell. "No, I wish. They called an hour ago saying there was nothing more they could do."

"Damn. Thanks for trying."

She nodded. "Sorry it wasn't better news."

Hamilton raised his hand to beckon him over. He had a phone to his ear, which he set down as Reid approached.

"Hey, boss. I visited the Burton-Holmes' beach house, like you asked. It was empty save for the housekeeper."

Some beach house, if it had a housekeeper.

"His wife didn't come to Miami with him?"

Hamilton shook his head. "The housekeeper confirmed it. Violet Burton-Holmes stayed in Long Island. She rarely comes down to Miami, apparently. Prefers to go to the Hamptons with her parents. They've got a place there."

"Of course they have." He pursed his lips, thinking. "When was the last time the housekeeper saw her employer?"

"That afternoon." Hamilton consulted his notes. "She left the house at five and went home. She lives in Westchester. When she arrived at work the following day, she noticed his bed hadn't been slept in."

"She didn't think to call the cops?" he asked.

"No. She did wonder where he was, but it wasn't until she saw the news that evening that she realized what had happened."

"So she saw that her boss had been skewered by a samurai sword in Tamiami Park and still didn't call us?" He shook his head in disbelief.

"Said she didn't want to get involved."

They got that a lot. People didn't want anything to do with the cops anymore. They didn't trust them, didn't engage with them, and sure as hell didn't want to be on their radar.

He sighed. "Okay, fine. But you got her statement?"

"Yeah, on record."

"Okay." He paused, thinking. "What about mail? Were there any letters at the house? Had Burton-Holmes been acting strange at all lately? Agitated or anxious?"

Hamilton shook his head. "Nothing that she'd noticed, and they don't get a lot of mail there. It's a vacation home."

"The killer could have sent the hate mail to his Long Island address," Reid muttered. "Where's Monroe?"

"Not here yet. He's working the graveyard shift tonight."

Reid grunted, then went back to his desk. So Burton-Holmes had been in Miami alone when he was killed.

Why? Were he and his wife estranged like Malcolm Hargreave and Sandra, or was he here on business? Art business, perhaps. Had he arranged to meet a dealer or a buyer?

"Did we have any luck tracing his cell phone?" Reid asked, turning to Vargas.

"Kind of. The last known lookup was in Allapattah, near the warehouse district. After that it goes dark."

"Switched off?" Reid asked.

"Or destroyed," Vargas said with a shrug.

He frowned. "What was he doing there? Meeting somebody?"

"It's a good place for it," Vargas said. "I mean it's full of warehouses, repair shops, and wholesalers but the lighting's poor, there's inconsistent CCTV coverage, and people mind their business."

"Get over there," Reid said. "Take a look around. Try to map his last movements. If he was taken, someone might have seen something. Take Diaz with you."

Vargas nodded and reached for his jacket. Even on a day like today, he was sharply dressed—unlike Reid, who was still in yesterday's clothes, save for a clean shirt he'd grabbed from Kenzie's place.

Kenzie walked in with Monroe as the other two walked out. They were laughing about something, but then Monroe's expression changed when he saw Reid. He muttered something to Kenzie and peeled off toward Reid's desk.

"Hey, boss. I got something," he said without preamble.

"Yeah?"

"You were right. Burton-Holmes was receiving hate mail, and quite a lot of it. His wife confirmed he'd been on edge recently, and drinking more than usual. When she'd asked him about it, he'd confided that he'd been spooked by the letters he was getting."

"Did she send any of them through?" Reid asked.

"Yeah. She photographed them and sent them over. I printed them out. Weird stuff—talk of honor and retribution, about violating the sanctity of temples and all that bushido stuff you mentioned."

Reid exhaled. "I knew it. Put them on my desk so I can take a look."

He turned to Martinez. "Call back all of Watanabe's customers and ask if any of them have been receiving accusatory letters. Anything that says they're going to be punished or can expect retribution. You get the picture."

She nodded and reached for the phone.

Kenzie, who'd been chatting with Dwayne while she waited, drifted over. "Looks like things are happening?"

"Slowly," Reid said. "Both victims were receiving hate mail. We're checking whether the same is true for the other clients whose records were stolen from the antique dealer."

"That tracks." She glanced around the bullpen. "Where is everyone?"

"Chasing down leads," he said. "We're trying to pin down the second victim's last known movements."

"He wasn't taken from his house?"

Reid shook his head. "Doesn't look like it. His phone last pinged in Allapattah."

"Hmm... that's a strange location to go to. Do you think he was meeting someone?"

"That's the current theory." Reid led her to Diaz's vacant desk. "Take a seat. I want you to look at some mugshots and see if any of them are Alex."

"AlexR? I thought you meant you'd run the plates from outside the warehouse."

His lips tightened. "I did. One rental, a corporate car, an embassy vehicle, and the motorcycle didn't have plates at all."

Her eyes widened. "Embassy? Like the Japanese Embassy?"

"Exactly like that," he said with a stiff nod.

"What about the corporate vehicle? That shouldn't be too hard to find."

"You'd think. Except it's an electronics company with over a thousand staff at their Miami facility. The vehicle is available to any number of people. We're still looking into who could have taken it."

"Ah," she said. "Could take some time, then."

"Yeah, so while I was waiting, I ran the plates you gave me of your two buddies."

"Okay, and—?"

"The first guy checks out. FieldNotes?"

She nodded.

"His real name is Jeff Oliver and I've got his address."

Her eyebrows shot up.

"No, Kenz," he added. "I can't let you have it. I know what you're like. Unless we have reason to suspect him of anything, we're not going to harass the guy. We've got enough on our plate right now."

She pouted.

"Don't give me that look. You know this is how it has to be."

"Fine," she said with a dramatic sigh, but he could tell her brain was already ticking over, looking for alternatives now that she had his name. Kenzie would be able to pinpoint Oliver's location without him. That's the only reason she was acquiescing so easily.

"What about Alex?" she asked, moving on.

He hid a smile. "I ran him through the database. There are a ton of Alexander Russels with criminal records, so I'm trying to narrow down whether our guy is one of them."

She scratched her head. "You really think he could be an ex-con?"

"Can't rule it out. Running criminal records is step one."

"Guess so, but I'm not feeling it. He didn't strike me as someone on that side of the law. The other, maybe. But not a criminal."

"So we rule it out, then look at other avenues."

She nodded and watched as he pulled up the Miami-Dade inmate search portal. Mugshots and booking photos began loading on the screen.

Kenzie sat down at Diaz's desk and started scrolling.

"There are so many of them," she muttered.

He shrugged. "That's Miami. Yell if you find him."

"Will do."

Reid heard the distinctive sound of a results notification popping up on his own screen. A hopeful spark tightened his gut. Facial recognition had flagged a possible match.

Returning to his desk, he was relieved that no one could see his monitor. Sitting down, he opened the file. The photo that had rendered a result was of a man in his early forties standing beneath the warehouse's exterior light, his features bright and sharp enough for the system to lock onto.

Reid studied the name at the top of the screen.

Kenji Nakamura.

With Vargas and Diaz out of the office, and Martinez tied up on the phone, Reid got Dwayne to go and pick up Nakamura. Once they'd identified him, it wasn't hard to look up his address.

Nakamura worked in the education sector and was a professor of Japanese studies at Florida International University. He lived close to campus, which happened to be in Sweetwater, in a quiet residential complex favored by faculty and long-term staff.

While Dwayne was out, Reid read a couple of the letters Burton-Holmes had received. They were very similar to the ones they'd found at Hargreave's house.

You took what was never yours. Sacred objects do not belong behind glass. They must be returned to the place that gave them meaning.

Honor is not abstract. When it is broken, it requires restoration. You have been judged, and the judgment is not in your favor.

You display stolen blades as trophies. Such disrespect does not fade with time. Warriors remember. So do those who inherit their duty.

He let out a low whistle. The letters were handwritten in a tidy, slanting cursive. Whoever penned them had a neat, steady hand.

"Are those the poison pen letters?" Kenzie asked, coming up. She'd surprised him. He'd been so engrossed in studying the threats, he hadn't heard her.

"Yeah. These are very definitely threatening. Whoever wrote them mentions sacred objects, restoration, disrespect, and honor. That's what makes me think these were written by someone whose first language isn't English."

Kenzie stood beside him and looked down at them. "The English is excellent, but you're right. I don't think it reads like a native speaker. More like someone translating their thoughts as they go."

"I got an ID on one of the people from the warehouse," he said, enjoying the surprise on her face.

"You did? How?"

"Facial recognition flagged him. Kenji Nakamura. Apparently, he is something of an activist. He was cautioned at a repatriation rally six months ago. That's how we had his photograph in the system."

"You going to speak to him?" she asked.

"I've sent Dwayne to pick him up. We're going to have a nice little chat in Interview Room One."

Her eyes grew wide. "Can I watch?"

He glanced around. There weren't many people here, and she was a cleared consultant. "I guess it's okay."

"Great. I was going to go home, but I think I'll stay and watch the show."

"You didn't find anything?"

She shook her head. "No, but then I didn't expect to. I went through all your Alexander Russel's but the AlexR I know wasn't one of them."

He gave a disappointed snort. He would have enjoyed discrediting one of those amateur sleuths.

28

Kenzie stood with Martinez and Dwayne near the bullpen monitors, her arms folded and eyes fixed on the live feed from Interview Room One. The sound was on, Reid's voice carrying clearly through the wall-mounted speaker.

Kenji Nakamura sat at the table with his hands folded neatly in front of him, back straight, posture immaculate. He didn't tap his fingers or fidget. There was no shifting in his chair. He looked more like he was waiting patiently behind a lectern for a class to quiet down than being interviewed by the police under fluorescent lights.

"Mr. Nakamura," Reid said, calm but firm. "Thank you for coming in voluntarily."

"I want to help," Nakamura replied, voice smooth and respectful. "These murders, they disgrace everything my organization stands for."

Kenzie tilted her head as she listened. He had perfect diction, a measured tone, and didn't sound defensive or offended that he was being questioned. Media-trained, she thought. Or just very used to explaining himself.

Reid leaned back in his chair and studied his subject. "Tell me about the Heritage Preservation Coalition. What do you actually do?"

Nakamura didn't rush his answer. "We advocate for the return of illegally exported Japanese cultural artifacts. We educate. We liaise with museums, private collectors, and of course, law enforcement." He gestured at Reid. "We've helped recover more than two hundred items over the past decade."

"He's convincing," Dwayne muttered under his breath.

Kenzie gave a reluctant nod.

"Have you or your organization ever taken more direct action?" Reid asked.

A faint smile touched Nakamura's lips, as if to suggest what an absurd notion.

"Detective, I'm a cultural liaison, not a vigilante. My work involves documentation and diplomacy. I fill in paperwork and arrange meetings. It's mostly academic and not at all glamorous."

Kenzie watched Nakamura's eyes as he spoke. He looked earnest, steady, and engaged. No darting glances. He believed what he was saying, or he was very good at appearing to.

Reid slid a photograph across the table. Even through the feed, Kenzie recognized the Hargreave crime scene. She made out the katana, recognized the spot lighting, and saw the glittering glass covering the floor.

Nakamura looked down at it without flinching.

"He didn't react," she whispered.

Dwayne nodded, his expression grim.

"Whoever did this," Nakamura said, glancing back up at Reid, "doesn't understand bushido."

Reid frowned. "Can you explain that?"

"The samurai code is about duty, restraint, and accountability," Nakamura said with a flourish. "Not a spectacle. These scenes"—he nodded to the photograph—"are performances. Nothing more than poorly researched theatrics. The symbolism is shallow. Incorrect. Frankly, it's offensive."

"You sound more upset about the inaccuracies than the murders," Reid observed.

Nakamura paused then. It was the first real break in his rhythm. "I am angry about both, particularly because it turns my community into villains on the evening news."

Kenzie felt a flicker of sympathy. The murders had made the headlines. There was a general skepticism growing for Japanese cultural heritage groups because of it.

Reid fixed his gaze on Nakamura. "Where were you the night of March fourteenth?"

"At a fundraising dinner," Nakamura replied without missing a beat. "With approximately two hundred other attendees."

"Where?" asked Reid, picking up his pen.

"Four Seasons."

Reid frowned. "What time did you leave the event?"

"Around one in the morning."

"The time of death was after two a.m. You could still have had time to get to the victim's house after you left the party."

"Not from Palm Beach," he said coolly.

Shit. From where she was standing, Kenzie could see Reid cringe, frustrated at being caught out.

"We'll still have to check it out," he replied stoically.

Nakamura tilted his head. "Of course."

Kenzie exhaled slowly. His polite, unflappable demeanor was unnerving. It was hard to believe this respectable academic had anything to do with those horrible murders.

Reid wasn't ready to let go. "Do you know anyone in your organization who might have taken your advocacy further than you intended?"

Nakamura considered that carefully. "We have passionate members, Lieutenant. Some have lost family heirlooms to smuggling, and there are others who felt powerless to do anything about it." He met Reid's gaze. "But passion doesn't equal violence."

"That isn't a no." Reid kept his gaze on him. Kenzie knew first-hand how disconcerting a Reid Garrett stare could be.

"No," Nakamura agreed. "It's me refusing to speculate. But if I have concerns, I'll contact you. You have my word on that."

Kenzie actually believed him.

She saw Reid's chest rise as he took a deep breath, recalibrating.

"There's something else I want to ask you about," he said, after a beat. "Your organization had a meeting last night, at a warehouse off the canal."

Nakamura inhaled slowly. "Is that a question?"

"Was there a meeting?" Reid looked annoyed that he'd slipped up.

"It appears like you know there was," Nakamura replied smoothly.

"Why all the secrecy?" Reid asked. "Why not have the meeting at your offices, or on campus. Why choose the abandoned warehouse, out of the way?"

"Because we were concerned about optics," Nakamura replied without hesitation. "And our members' safety. Emotions are running high right now. There are people who would happily misinterpret a gathering of Japanese cultural advocates as something far more sinister."

Kenzie watched his hands on the screen. Still folded. Still steady.

"What were you discussing?" Reid asked.

"The murders," Nakamura said simply. "The impact. The damage. To our work, to our community. How this looks in the media."

Reid studied him. She could almost see the wheels turning in his head. He didn't trust Nakamura, but he couldn't discredit him either. Not yet.

"It's plausible," she murmured to Dwayne. She could see how that could be a problem for them.

"And what did you conclude?" Reid asked.

"We condemn violence, Lieutenant. So we discussed how to answer questions and to protect our members."

Reid gave him a hard look. "Who else was there?"

Nakamura hesitated. "I can't give you names. It wouldn't be fair to those members. They've done nothing wrong."

"As unfortunate as it may be, your organization held a clandestine meeting tied to an ideology that is now linked to two murders. I need to know who was at that meeting."

"They are not suspects," Nakamura replied calmly. "They are academics, advocates, historians. People who believe deeply in cultural preservation."

"And who follow the bushido code," Reid said.

"Yes." Nakamura leveled his gaze at Reid. "That is not a crime."

"Which emphasizes honor and duty and accountability."

Nakamura inclined his head. "Correct."

"You're telling me none of those men would kill for it."

"I'm telling you," Nakamura said, voice firm but measured, "that anyone who truly understands bushido would not commit murder. Especially not like this."

Reid leaned forward slightly. "Even if they believed someone had violated sacred trust. Even if they believed honor had been stripped away."

For the first time, Nakamura didn't answer.

The silence stretched.

Kenzie felt Dwayne shift beside her.

Reid let it hang just long enough to matter.

"Mr. Nakamura," he said finally, "honor codes don't always stop people from doing violent things. Sometimes it gives them permission."

Nakamura's jaw tightened. Just a little.

"I won't speculate," he said. "And I won't betray people who trusted me enough to gather in a moment of fear."

Reid sat upright.

"All right," he said. "I'll respect your decision. For now."

Kenzie turned to Dwayne. "He didn't deny it."

"No, ma'am," Dwayne agreed. "He just didn't give an answer."

Kenzie gnawed on her lower lip. Sometimes, that told you everything you needed to know.

The interview wrapped up. Nakamura stood, shook Reid's hand, thanked him for the opportunity to clarify matters, and left behind a business card.

"You wouldn't think he was a suspect," Monroe murmured, coming up to them. "Looks like he just attended a goddamn business meeting."

The screen went dark as Reid turned off the camera in the interview room.

Nakamura had been calm, respectful, and articulate—but that didn't mean he was innocent.

It could just mean he was very, very good at lying.

29

Reid said goodbye to Kenzie, got a cup of coffee, and went to talk to Monroe. He nodded at the senior detective who'd been around for nearly forty years. He wanted to tap into his experience now and get his read on Nakamura.

"What did you think?" he asked, pulling up a chair.

Monroe shrugged. "He's composed, totally controlled. I couldn't get a read on him. On the outside, he looks innocent. I mean, I believed that stuff about condemning violence, murder not being part of the code, and so on."

"Yeah." Reid gave a tight nod. "It looked real, but like you, I don't know if we can trust him."

"Let's check out his alibi and see," Monroe suggested.

Reid took a thoughtful sip. "Get in touch with the Four Seasons in Palm Beach and confirm Nakamura was there that night. Check the surveillance cameras. At an event like that, I'm sure they had several."

"Sure."

"See if you can find out what time he left. If it was around one o'clock, there's no way he'd have made it to Coconut Grove by two, or anytime within the window of the crime."

"It's over an hour's drive," Monroe said with a nod.

"Exactly. Even twelve is pushing it, considering the care that went into placing the body and staging the scene."

"Also, Hargreave's not going to meet a 'dealer' after midnight, is he?"

Reid crinkled his forehead. "Good point."

"Could be the guy was telling the truth," Monroe said, arching his bushy brows.

Reid got up, taking his coffee with him. "Could be, Detective. Could be."

Vargas got back a couple of hours later, his suit marginally more rumpled than it had been when he'd left, tie loosened, sweat darkening the collar. Allapattah did that to you.

"How'd it go?" Reid asked, already on his feet and heading over. "Where's Diaz?"

"Left her there to follow up on some camera footage." Vargas peeled off his jacket and draped it over the back of his chair. "We found a bodega on Northwest Twentieth Street where the owner remembers Burton-Holmes coming in late last night. Clear as day."

"What'd he buy?"

"Pack of nicotine gum and a Diet Coke."

Reid pursed his lips. "Quitting smoking?"

Vargas shrugged. "Looks like it. Anyway, the owner watched him leave, cross the street, and head west—toward the warehouse district, along Seventeenth Avenue."

Reid nodded slowly. "Not much out there at night."

"Not unless you're meeting someone," Vargas countered. "I got one of the auto body shops halfway down the block to show me their external camera footage. Diaz is getting a copy, but we watched it on-site. Could see Burton-Holmes walking, still on foot."

"He didn't drive?"

"Not down that stretch," Vargas said. "Uniforms located his rental car parked a few blocks east, near Twenty-Seventh Avenue. Still locked. No signs of a struggle. It's been impounded."

Reid scratched his jaw. "So he never made it back to the car."

"Nope." Vargas broke into a faint grin. "And I canvassed a few more businesses. A print shop, a produce wholesaler, and a tire place. Checked whatever cameras they had. He disappeared completely in about a two-block window between Nineteenth and Twenty-First."

"A dead zone," Reid murmured.

"Exactly," Vargas agreed. "There's not much light that time of the evening, stores closing up for the night. If someone wanted to intercept him, that's where they'd do it."

"Good work," Reid breathed, grinning through the fatigue. "Now we just have to find out who took him."

"I'm going to take a look at any traffic cams I can find feeding into the area. It's thin, but you never know."

Reid clapped him on the shoulder. This was the first real progress they'd made on either of the two victims. "Keep me posted."

Vargas nodded and sat down at his desk, already reaching for his notebook.

"Hey boss," Dwayne waved him over as he was making his way back to his desk. "I've got an update on the vehicles outside the warehouse."

"Yeah?" Reid reached to take a gulp of his coffee, now going cold.

"The embassy won't give out any information, even with a warrant. Diplomatic immunity and all that."

"Shit," Reid muttered. "Let's take a look at who works there, see if we can cross check with any online groups, that kind of thing."

"Sure. There's something else."

"Oh?"

"The electronics factory. I've got a list of employees. They were very accommodating."

"So now we just have to narrow it down?"

"Yeah. From forty-seven possible employees."

"Seriously?" His smile faded.

"Seriously."

Reid sighed. "Okay, well good luck. Let Hamilton know if you need any help."

He gave a nod. "Might have to do that. Young gun is faster than me online."

Reid grinned, but it was short-lived. Martinez came rushing over, a worried expression on her face.

"What?" Both Reid and Dwayne said in unison.

"I've been calling around, asking if any of Watanabe's customers have been receiving threatening letters," she began. "Three of them have, and I asked them to send them through." She paused to take a breath.

"And?" Reid prompted.

"I spoke to the third customer's husband, and he said the letters have got them both spooked."

"Fair enough," Dwayne muttered.

"But get this, his husband didn't come home last night. He's not answering his cell phone and he doesn't know where he is. He's missing, Lieutenant."

30

"What is his name?" Reid felt the surge of adrenaline—or maybe it was dread—hit him hard in the gut.

Dwayne rubbed a hand over his head, a gesture that told Reid he was just as uneasy.

"Arthur Whitmore," Martinez said. "He and his husband, Kevin, live on Brickell Key. Arthur's an interior designer and art collector. He's not as narrowly focused on Japanese artifacts as the other two victims, but he does own several high-value pieces. Kevin Whitmore said Asian art was a particular passion of his."

One he was paying for now, Reid thought grimly.

"Okay." He sprang into action. "I want a full timeline of his last forty-eight hours. Pull phone records, credit card activity, ride-share history, the works. Get patrol to do a welfare check at the residence and start a neighborhood canvas. I want marina security, building security, and traffic cams reviewed on and off the Key."

Martinez nodded, fingers already flying over her keyboard.

"We're issuing an APB," Reid continued. "Missing endangered adult. Notify Miami PD, Coral Gables, and County. Loop in Port Authority and Marine Patrol too. We need to find this guy ASAP."

He didn't have to explain why.

"I'll handle the APB," Dwayne said, and Martinez nodded without looking up.

Reid got Kevin Whitmore to come into the station. When he arrived, Reid pulled out a chair at his desk rather than putting him in the interview room.

"Have a seat." He gestured to the chair.

It wasn't protocol, strictly speaking, but the man looked like he might crawl out of his own skin if he were boxed in under fluorescent lights with a recording device ticking away.

Kevin was in his early forties, expensively dressed but rumpled, tie loosened, jacket folded over one arm and forgotten. A certified public accountant by trade, Reid guessed he was the kind of man who liked structure and predictability. This was neither.

Kevin sat, stood again, then sat properly, clasping his hands together so tightly his knuckles went white.

"Talk me through the last time you saw Arthur," Reid said gently.

Kevin swallowed. "Y–Yesterday. Around one." His voice wavered but held. "We had lunch in the city."

"Where did you go?" Reid prompted, hoping to loosen him up.

"Oh, uh, we went to Il Gabbiano. We do that sometimes when our schedules line up."

"Anything unusual about the lunch?" Reid asked, reaching for his pen. A notebook lay open on the desk in front of him.

"No. God, no." Kevin shook his head. "We talked about work. He was excited about landing a new client. A condo redesign on Fisher Island. He teased me for ordering the same thing I always do." His mouth twitched, then fell. "Everything was normal."

"What happened after lunch?"

"We went our separate ways," Kevin said. "I went back to my office. Arthur went back to his. He texted me around three—asked if I wanted to try that new place in Wynwood this weekend."

"What happened when you got home? How did you know he was missing?"

Kevin shifted in his chair. "I didn't, at first. Arthur goes to the gym three nights a week, straight from work. I wasn't expecting him till around seven thirty."

Reid nodded. "Did you try calling him?"

Kevin scoffed. "Of course. He didn't pick up. It just rang and went to voicemail. When he wasn't back by nine, I started to panic."

"What did you do?" Reid asked, wanting to document Kevin's steps.

"I called the gym first," he explained, a woeful expression on his face. "They said he hadn't been there."

Reid frowned. "So he didn't arrive at the gym at all?"

"No. I asked them to check the logs, you know? You have to scan in with your phone. They said he hadn't used the app."

Reid felt an icy dread clutch at his chest. He glanced over as Martinez approached.

Her voice was low. "Can I speak to you privately, Lieutenant?"

He nodded and got up.

"I'll be right back," he said to Kevin, who gave a tiny nod.

"Sorry to interrupt," she said quietly, "but we just got confirmation on Arthur's vehicle."

Reid turned to her. "You found it?"

"Yeah, it's still parked at his office building—Bayfront Towers. It's in the underground garage and hasn't moved since yesterday afternoon."

"How do they know it hasn't moved?" Reid asked.

"The staff have to scan out at the exit. Didn't happen."

Shit.

"Doesn't look good, boss," she whispered, her gaze flickering nervously to Kevin.

No. It did not.

"Did you speak to anyone in his office?"

"Yeah. According to the showroom manager, Whitmore left just after five o'clock, like he always does. Told them he had to hit the gym."

"Except he never got there," Reid murmured.

"Uniform found his gym bag in the trunk of his car." She shot him a meaningful look.

Reid exhaled. "At least we know where he was taken."

"He's been taken?" Kevin's voice pitched above the noise in the bullpen. There was a hysterical edge to it that Reid didn't like. The accountant had leaped to his feet, his jacket falling to the floor. "Arthur has been *kidnapped*?"

"It's looking that way." Reid turned to face him.

Kevin's complexion drained of color. "But why—? Who would want to kidnap Arthur? He's not important. He's an interior designer for Christ's sake." Then understanding dawned, and he gasped. "It's to do with those letters, isn't it? Whoever was sending him those hateful letters took him."

"It's possible," Reid said carefully, as Martinez shot him a sympathetic look and went back to her desk. "Did you bring them with you, like I asked?"

"Yeah. Here, take the damn things. I don't ever want to see them again." He fished them out of his jacket pocket and threw them on Reid's desk.

"Only three?" Reid asked, picking them up.

"Yeah, that's all he got. If there were more, I didn't know about them."

Reid nodded as he peeled one open. It was in the same vein as the others.

The silence stretched out as he read them.

Exhaling, he set the letters down and cleared his throat. "Kevin, I need you to think carefully. Did Arthur mention anyone bothering him? Anyone he'd met who was giving him a hard time?"

Kevin hesitated, appearing close to tears. "No, I don't think so. You mean in person?"

Reid nodded.

"Not that I know of—just those letters." He glared at the pieces of paper on the desk as if they were contaminated.

Reid thought for a moment, scenarios flashing through his mind. None of them good.

"You've got to find him," Kevin begged, holding his jacket to him like a security blanket. "Please, you've got to bring him home."

Reid tightened his jaw. "We're doing all we can."

The problem was that Arthur Whitmore had vanished, they had no leads other than the letters, and he had a real bad feeling they had already run out of time.

31

It had taken Kenzie all of ten minutes to find an address for Jeff Oliver, and she'd done it on her phone in her car before she'd even left the station.

11247 SW 8th Street.

She'd driven forty minutes east and now sat outside his house as the sun dipped behind the buildings. The light had turned a dusky mauve, a hazy softness settling over the street—the kind that came when a humid day met the cooler breath of the sea.

The first thing she noticed was the sedan parked in the drive. It was the same as the one he'd driven to the warehouse. That checked out, then.

The curtains of the house were drawn, which meant she couldn't see directly inside. Damn, that was annoying. Still, they were sheer enough that she could make out figures through them, silhouetted by an inside light.

A woman's shape passed the window, holding something in her hand. A phone, possibly. She had it to her ear so was likely having a conversation. A smaller figure ran by, then disappeared. A child, maybe around five or six. That tracked with FieldNotes's age. He must have been late thirties. A couple of years younger than Alex, but chubbier and out of shape despite his stocky physique.

Her gaze drifted to the other window, also visible from the front of the house, but the room was in darkness, so she couldn't tell if it was occupied.

A fence surrounded the house, and if she wanted to peer into the side windows, she'd have to cross the property line. She didn't fancy getting caught trespassing. Reid would not be impressed if he had to bail her out of jail over a misdemeanor.

So she stayed put and watched from the relative privacy of her car.

Ten minutes later, a bigger bulk crossed in front of the curtains. She strained her eyes, trying to focus.

Yep, that was FieldNotes. She recognized the stockiness, the thick neck, the protruding gut. He stood in front of the woman, gestured with his hands, then moved out of the frame. Kenzie exhaled.

Okay, at least he'd been successfully identified. She started her engine. That was one member of The Evidence Room confirmed. There were still all the others to go.

"Jeff Oliver," she murmured, as she drove away. "It's a pleasure to meet you."

It was dark by the time Kenzie hit the causeway that led to Bay Harbour Island. She'd been driving on autopilot, thoughts elsewhere, the familiar route blurring past her windshield. It wasn't until the road narrowed and the water opened up on either side that she became aware of a set of headlights behind her.

They had a faint blue tinge to them—cooler than most—which was what made her notice. They'd been there for a while. A few miles, at least.

A chill crept up her spine, but she pushed it down.

Don't be ridiculous, she told herself.

Of course no one was following her. She was tired, keyed up, and seeing patterns where there were none. Plenty of people lived on Bay Harbour Island. It wasn't unusual for someone to be heading the same way.

Still, unease prickled at her. Enough that she decided to test it.

She deliberately missed her turnoff and continued on, circling the block instead. Past a row of waterfront condos not unlike her own. Around a small park at the end of the street. Then back onto the road that would loop her toward her building.

The headlights stayed with her.

Her stomach tensed.

Okay. So now what?

She couldn't go home with someone on her tail. This wasn't the first time she'd been followed, and last time it hadn't ended well. She'd been lucky then—her foster son had been around to scare them off. Tonight, her place was empty. She was alone.

Kenzie made a split-second decision and turned back toward the causeway. She'd drive into the city, straight to the nearest police station. No one looking for trouble would follow her there.

She didn't make it that far.

The moment she merged back onto the causeway, heading away from the island, the blue-tinged headlights dropped back.

A sharp, humorless laugh escaped her. Got you.

They knew they'd been made.

Part of her wanted to turn around, chase them, find out who the hell had been following her. But the smarter, saner side wanted to stay safe. She'd had her fair share of run-ins lately, and her promise to Reid was still fresh in her mind. She wouldn't take any more unnecessary risks.

There was a sudden screech of tires as the car behind her executed a fast U-turn and sped off in the opposite direction.

Kenzie leaned forward, peering into her rearview mirror, trying to catch anything useful. The make. The plates. Anything. But the vehicle vanished too quickly, swallowed by darkness and haze. Visibility was poor, the air thick and indistinct.

"Shit," she muttered, gripping the steering wheel.

All she'd caught was that the car was light-colored. Maybe gray. Maybe pale blue. Not nearly enough for identification.

But she'd remember those lights. Would recognize them instantly if she saw them again.

Heart pounding, she changed lanes, earning an angry blast from a horn behind her, and turned back toward her condo. This time alert, focused, and no longer on autopilot.

Back home, Kenzie double, then triple-checked the locks on the doors and windows. The tail had rattled her more than she wanted to admit, and now that the adrenaline was waning, she was only just beginning to think logically about it.

Who on earth would want to follow her?

A member of the Heritage Preservation Coalition? Had they seen her at the warehouse and realized she was the one who'd reported them to the cops?

No. That didn't make sense.

No one had spotted her that night. And even if they had, she hadn't been alone. Alex and FieldNotes had been there too. Besides, Nakamura hadn't seen her at the station. She'd left well before he had.

So who else?

The thought crept in reluctantly. One of the sleuths from The Evidence Room.

She'd been trying to work out who they were. It wasn't such a leap to imagine one of them doing the same to her. RedCairn, maybe. Or Alex. She dismissed FieldNotes almost immediately—she'd seen him at home.

The irony wasn't lost on her, though. Someone following her, following one of them.

She shook her head. Tiredness and the day spent at the station were weighing on her. What she needed was a good meal and an early night.

And yet the feeling lingered. A sense that tonight, she'd come closer to real danger than she realized.

Wanting a distraction, she thought about doing another podcast. It was time. A lot had happened since her last one, and her viewers would be getting antsy. She usually released one a week, but two murders had accelerated everything.

After eating, she set up her lights and microphone. No script this time. She knew what she could say and, more importantly, what she couldn't. Talking it through would help her impose order on the chaos and force her to stick to facts.

She took a breath, hit record, and began.

32

PODCAST TRANSCRIPT: EPISODE 25- GILT EDGE

(*Soft intro music fades in*)

Kenzie Gilmore:

If you're listening to this in Miami, you already know why I'm recording sooner than planned.

There has been a second murder.

Earlier this week, police confirmed that another man was found dead, this time in a public park within Sweetwater's jurisdiction. Like the first case, the scene was staged. And like the first case, a Japanese sword was used.

Before we go any further, let me be very clear about what I can and cannot say.

This is an active investigation. I am not here to speculate wildly or interfere with police work. I am here to lay out what is already public, what can be confirmed, and what information law enforcement may still need from the community.

Here is what we know.

The second victim was discovered in an open, public space. Unlike the first crime, this was not a private residence. It was visible. Accessible. And within minutes of being discovered, it was already being photographed and shared online.

Police believe the victim was killed elsewhere and moved to the scene. There were signs of dragging, and the lack of blood at the location supports that conclusion. The sword appears to have been placed postmortem, not the cause of death.

That mirrors the first crime.

Both scenes show intent. Deliberate positioning. Deliberate symbolism.

Authorities have not officially confirmed a cause of death yet, but they have acknowledged that they are treating the two murders as connected.

Which brings me to the obvious question people are asking.

Yes, it appears to be the same killer.

The escalation matters. The first murder was private, almost curated. The second was public. Messier. Impossible to contain. That tells investigators—and should tell all of us—that whoever did this wanted a wider audience.

There is one additional detail I want to highlight, because it's something only the public can help with.

Security footage near the second scene captured a vehicle in the vicinity hours before the body was discovered. The headlights obscured the camera's view, making identification difficult. If you were in the area that night and noticed a vehicle idling, circling, or leaving abruptly, police want to hear from you.

I also want to thank everyone who reached out after the last episode. Some of you sent thoughtful messages. Some of you shared information that has already been passed on to the Sweetwater Police Department. That matters more than you know.

If you live near either crime scene, if you saw something that felt off, or if you work in the art or antiquities world and have had contact with collectors matching this profile, please come forward.

Do not post it in comment sections. Do not try to investigate on your own. Contact Sweetwater PD directly. Or, if you're unsure, you can contact me through the usual channels, and I will ensure anything credible is passed on responsibly.

Two men are dead. A murderer is still out there. And the pattern suggests they're not finished.

(*Outro music fades in, restrained and tense.*)

Kenzie Gilmore:

This has been *Off the Record*. Stay alert, look out for one another, and if you know something, say something.

(*Outro fades out.*)

33

Things moved quickly after that. The APB went out on all channels, and within minutes patrol units across Miami were scanning streets, parking structures, and traffic cams for any sign of Arthur Whitmore.

It was late, the sun had already sunk behind the skyline, and darkness brought its own complications. Visibility dropped, witnesses thinned out, and whatever window they had was narrowing by the minute.

Arthur Whitmore had been missing for over twenty-four hours already. The probability of finding him alive was rapidly decreasing.

While Reid's team worked the phones, chasing down the parking garage management company for surveillance footage, and combing through the threatening letters for overlaps or handwriting tells, the night shift picked up the slack elsewhere.

They dealt with the usual grind—domestic disturbances flaring after dinner and drinks, noise complaints from high-rise condos, a rollover on the Palmetto that tied up two units, and a steady trickle of intoxicated arrests coming in from Brickell and Wynwood. Routine calls, but time-consuming ones. Every diverted unit was one less set of eyes looking for a missing man.

Reid watched the bullpen hum under fluorescent light and felt the pressure building.

Where was Arthur Whitmore now? Was he even still alive?

There must be something more they could do. Making a decision, he called Captain Perez on his cell. To his surprise, his former boss picked up on the first ring.

"Lieutenant Garrett."

"Hey, Captain. You said to call if I needed anything."

No hesitation. "Shoot."

"You've heard we've got another missing art collector?"

"Hell, yeah. It's all over the wire. Been keeping a lookout myself."

"Thanks, man. Listen, I have a suspect, and I wondered if you could arrange for one of your uniforms to keep an eye on him. If he's responsible, he'll be acting suspiciously."

A pause, then Perez said, "Sure, I can do that."

"Off the record, you understand?" Reid said. "I don't have any just cause to put surveillance on him."

"Understood," he replied. "Text me his name and address and I'll get on it ASAP."

"Thanks, Cap. Appreciate it."

"No problem. Glad to be of assistance. Let's find this bastard."

"Amen to that."

Reid hung up, composed a text message, and sent it to Perez. Then he sat back, feeling a small weight lift.

If Nakamura or one of his Heritage Preservation Coalition buddies had kidnapped Arthur Whitmore and were holding him somewhere, it should be pretty obvious.

The reports started coming in slowly, one after the other, and then a barrage all at once.

Monroe's phone rang, then rang again before she could finish the first call. Dwayne was already on another line, one hand pressed to his headset as he tried to keep out the confusion in the bullpen. The noise level rose fast—keyboards clacking, chairs scraping, voices overlapping.

"Okay, slow down," Monroe said for the third time in as many minutes. "Where are you right now? Sir—sir—take a breath. Start again."

Reid looked up from his desk, irritation sharpening into something colder as he took in the room. This wasn't a domestic. This wasn't a traffic pileup. He could feel it in the air, the way everyone had gone still except for the phones.

"What've you got?" he asked, already standing.

Monroe covered the receiver with her hand. Her face had gone pale beneath her freckles. "Wynwood. Multiple callers. Art festival at Wynwood Walls. People are screaming about a body."

Reid's stomach dropped.

Dwayne swiveled in his chair. "Same here. They're saying it's... Jesus." He swallowed. "They're saying the guy's been decapitated."

For a split second, the bullpen went quiet.

Reid didn't need any more details. He already knew.

"Local patrol?" he asked.

"On scene," Monroe said quickly. "They're trying to push people back, but it's chaos. Phones everywhere. Someone pulled a tarp off a planter and—" She stopped herself, eyes flicking to Reid. "They're waiting for us."

Reid grabbed his jacket off the back of his chair. "Vargas. Diaz. With me. Now."

They were moving before he finished the sentence, training kicking in. Diaz snagged her go-bag. Vargas was already on his phone, barking orders as they headed for the door.

Outside, the Miami night pressed in—warm, loud, alive. Reid slid behind the wheel, lights and siren cutting through traffic as they tore toward Wynwood. The radio crackled nonstop: patrol units calling in, EMS staging, requests for crowd control that were already too late.

"It's packed," Diaz said, reading updates off her tablet. "The festival's been running all day. Food trucks, live murals, DJs. Thousands of people."

Reid's jaw tightened. "How the hell did he place the body there with all those people?"

Vargas glanced at him. "Guess we're about to find out."

They hit gridlock three blocks out. Patrol cars were already lining the streets, blue and red lights strobing against painted walls and half-finished murals. The air smelled like spray paint, fried food, and sweat. Music still thumped somewhere nearby, incongruously cheerful.

They got out and moved toward the crowd of people, where uniforms were trying, and failing, to hold a perimeter. Yellow tape fluttered uselessly as people ducked under it, phones held high. Someone was crying. Someone else was livestreaming, narrating breathlessly to an unseen audience.

"Back up!" an officer shouted. "Everybody back!"

Reid flashed his badge and pushed through. "Lieutenant Reid, Sweetwater PD. Where is it?"

A patrol sergeant pointed, grim. "Center courtyard. Planter near the east wall."

Reid felt his chest tighten as he followed the line of sight. The planter was a massive, concrete structure, filled with waist-high flowers that had been wilting under a heavy taupe tarp all day. The tarp now lay crumpled on the ground, a faded MAINTENANCE sign still clipped to one corner.

"Oh, God." Diaz clutched his arm, her face ashen.

"Guess that's how he did it," Vargas muttered, sucking in a breath.

Inside the planter, amid crushed blooms and dark soil, lay the body.

Or what was left of it.

Reid forced himself to look. The man had been placed on his back, limbs arranged with deliberate care. His head was gone—cleanly removed—and set a short distance away, nestled among the flowers as if it belonged there. Blood had soaked into the soil, rich and black under the floodlights. A sword rested across the torso, laid straight and centered, the blade soiled, the hilt aligned with the sternum.

"Samurai," Diaz whispered, turning away.

"The murder weapon?" Vargas, usually unaffected by most things, was turning slightly green.

Reid gave a grim nod, forcing himself to breathe evenly. It didn't get much worse than this.

"It's Arthur Whitmore," he breathed, gulping over the bile forcing itself up his throat. "Fuck, we were too late."

Vargas put a hand on his shoulder. "We did everything we could."

He ground his jaw. "It wasn't enough."

Something about the sheer audacity of the crime, about the crowd, the art, the flowers, made it harder to compartmentalize.

"The bastard didn't just want witnesses." Reid couldn't stop the fury rising inside him. Cold rage surged through his body and he couldn't switch it off. "He wanted a goddamned audience."

Diaz glanced around. "The planter was covered all day. Everyone would've walked past it completely unaware the body was here."

Vargas moved closer. "Looks like he's been here a while. Can't say for sure, but the pooling in the lower limbs suggests at least five or six hours, maybe more."

"Is the ME on the way?" he asked Diaz.

She took out her phone.

"Call Pruitt," he added, wiping his forehead with the back of his hand. "I want him on this. We need continuity. I hope to God he was dead before his head was chopped off."

She pulled a face and turned away to make the call.

Reid took a deep breath and attempted to catalog the details. "The maintenance sign meant nobody would question it. He knew what he was doing."

"He must have cased the place beforehand," Vargas said. "Just like the park parking lot."

Reid pulled his lips into a thin line. They needed to nail this fucker to the wall. Three deaths in two weeks—and on his turf. No way was he going to settle for that.

Diaz returned, her face drawn. "Pruitt's on his way. Disturbed him at a family dinner."

"I don't give a shit." This took priority. He closed his eyes for a second, and when he opened them, he found both Diaz and Vargas looking at him.

"You okay, boss?" Vargas asked.

He shook his head. "This is an escalation over the other two. He's getting progressively more violent. More performative."

They both nodded.

"Just what the hell is coming next?"

34

Kenzie scheduled the podcast to go out the following morning, then let out a long, slow breath.

It was done.

Unable to stay upright, she grabbed her laptop and took it to bed with her. Before she could sleep, however, there was one more thing she had to do. She ought to check in with The Evidence Room before they began to wonder what had happened to her.

What could she give them to explain her absence? Certainly not that she'd been looking at mug shots of AlexR. Or that she'd tracked FieldNotes, aka Jeff Oliver, to his family home.

Biting her lip, she logged on. She still hadn't decided when RedCairn noticed she was online.

RedCairn: Hey ReporterGirl, good to see you. We were getting concerned.

>

>

>

ReporterGirl: Sorry, I've been busy. Had to take care of some personal stuff.

>

AlexR: Everything okay?

>

>

ReporterGirl: Yeah, all good.

She paused, thinking. On a whim, she took out her phone and messaged Reid who she knew would still be at the station.

Can I give the license plates to the true crime group? They might be able to pinpoint who they belong to. Save you the trouble?

There was a lag when nothing happened. Then she saw the three dots as Reid started typing. After a while, they stopped.

Maybe he needed a nudge. She added to her previous message.

They'll find out, anyway. Only a matter of time.

The three dots were back.

Go for it.

She frowned. It wasn't like Reid to be so accommodating. He must be distracted. Still, she didn't have time to dwell on it.

ReporterGirl: Heard back from my researcher. Gave him the plates from the warehouse. Got some details for you.

>

AlexR: Oh, yeah?

FieldNotes: Really?

>

>

ThirdWitness: Cool.

>

>

>

ReporterGirl: Black SUV with diplomatic plates belongs to the Japanese embassy.

>

GrayAtlas: wtf?

>

>

RedCairn: Makes sense. What else?

Could he sense there was more?

ReporterGirl: The Toyota was a carpool vehicle from NovaCore Electronics in Doral. Any number of employees could have used it. Work needed on that one. Any ideas?

>

>

>

CrossCheck: I can look into it, but we need an employee list.

>

>

ReporterGirl: Could probably get that.

>

RedCairn: Legally?

>

>

ReporterGirl: ngl probably not

For a moment no one said anything. Kenzie thought they were probably waiting for a reaction from RedCairn. A thumbs up or a hard no.

Eventually, AlexR stepped in.

AlexR: Maybe we could bend the rules just this once?

>

>

RedCairn: Authorities won't be able to use it.

>

>

>

ThirdWitness: If we do find the guy, we can give them a tip-off. They can act on that.

>

ReporterGirl: They don't need to know it came from us.

She knew RedCairn was worried about the group's credibility. Using unauthorized methods would cast them in a bad light. She didn't disagree, but there wasn't any way around this one. They needed a starting point.

RedCairn finally gave a thumbs up.

Kenzie felt a surge of adrenaline. Yes!

She messaged Raoul. *Need to talk. Call me first thing.*

Her phone rang immediately, just as she suspected it would.

Raoul's voice held a teasing note. "Why are you still awake?"

She laughed. "Why are you still awake?"

He chuckled. "I'm working, what's your excuse?"

"I need your help with something." She just managed to stifle a yawn.

"Is this on your Lieutenant's dime?"

She crossed her fingers, thankful he couldn't see her. "Absolutely."

"Okay, shoot."

"We traced a license plate to an electronics company based in Doral. Is there any way you can get us a list of their employees? Only those that work at the plant."

He hesitated. "We being…?"

"Not the police."

"Ah." A beat passed. "How's it going with them?"

"Good, I think. So far, they seem harmless."

"That's a relief. You figured out their real identities yet?"

"No, but not sure it matters. The only ones I'm concerned about are ThirdWitness, who was definitely at the second crime scene, and

AlexR, who's just a mystery. I'm sure he's got a law enforcement or military background, but he's not telling."

"Hmm... I can look into those two, if you like?"

"That would be good. I'm not getting anywhere myself."

"Any progress on the murders?" he asked.

She sighed. "Not much, to be honest, but maybe they'll be able to figure out who borrowed this pool car."

A hesitation. "Does Garrett know you're doing this?"

"I cleared it with him," she said. Close enough.

She heard Raoul exhale. "I'm good with it, then. What's the company name?"

"NovaCore Electronics."

She heard his keyboard clicking as he made a note. "I'll see what I can do."

"Thanks, Raoul." She hesitated. "Any movement from the HPC?"

"No red flags, if that's what you mean. Just the usual rhetoric."

"Alright, thanks. Let me know if that changes."

"Obvs, Kenz. Garrett made it clear to call him, though. Sorry. I think your little sleuthing stunt must have pissed him off."

She pulled a face. "You have no idea."

He sounded concerned. While he didn't particularly like dealing with the cops, he did care about her. "Trouble in paradise?"

"We're fine," she said. Her relationship with Reid was the one thing that kept her grounded.

"Glad to hear it. Be in touch."

"Thanks, Raoul."

A few moments later she'd switched the light off with the intention of mulling over everything that had happened during the day then formulating some kind of plan. Next thing she knew, she was waking up to the sun streaming in through the window.

35

None of the team had slept a wink. They'd been at the crime scene until the early hours, trying to learn as much as possible. Pruitt had been as forthcoming as he could, professionally speaking.

Unlike the other two, this body had been decapitated at the scene. The amount of blood left no doubt about that. But the pattern told a different story—no arterial spray, more pooling. It suggested the victim had already been dead when the blade fell.

Thank God for small mercies.

"Poison again?" Reid had asked.

Pruitt nodded, already slipping into that careful, clinical tone he used when he didn't want to over-promise. "He's presenting with the same indicators—no internal trauma consistent with the blade, no hemorrhaging that would suggest it was the primary cause of death. I'm seeing signs consistent with the same toxin. I'll confirm once I've got him back at the lab and run tox."

Unlike the previous two victims, Arthur Whitmore bore clear signs of a struggle. Dark bruising ringed his forearms, finger-shaped and uneven, as if someone had grabbed and restrained him. His fingernails were jagged and torn, one cracked deep enough to have bled.

Reid was hopeful there'd be some trace DNA there.

"Looks like this one fought back," Pruitt said after his preliminary inspection.

"Good for him," Diaz had muttered.

Now, back at the station, Reid wasn't sure it mattered. Whitmore was still dead, for all the good it had done him.

After he'd left Wynwood Walls, Reid had gone straight to the Whitmore residence. He owed Kevin that much.

Thankfully Diaz had come with him because Arthur's husband had collapsed, sobbing, when he heard the news. They stayed with him for an hour, then called in a victim support advocate to keep an eye on him until a relative could get there. Seeing the man's grief had made it much starker.

It struck Reid, and not for the first time, that it was the consequences of crimes that had the most wide-reaching effects. No matter how bad the crime scene, the repercussions were just as bad.

He put his dark thoughts aside and called Perez. This time the police captain didn't pick up on the first ring—and when he did, he sounded groggy, like he'd been sleeping.

"Garrett, tell me you caught this psycho son of a bitch?"

"I wish I could, Captain. I'm calling to find out if your boy was on my suspect last night? I know it's twenty-four hours too late, but is there anything to report?"

"I'm going to text you the officer's number, and you can ask him yourself. He's one of my best and he'll have just come off shift."

"Thanks." Even better. He could question the guy himself.

Five minutes later, he was on the phone with a surprisingly alert Officer Morales.

"I proceeded immediately to the suspect's address, as Captain Perez asked," he said, getting straight to it. "He lives in a high rise, so I left my vehicle, accessed the building and rode the elevator up to his apartment."

"You went up?" Reid asked, surprised.

"Yes, sir. My instructions were to keep eyes on him, and I couldn't do that from my vehicle."

Reid pursed his lips, impressed. Not that the officer could see.

"Was he home?"

"Yes, sir. I walked along the communal corridor, past the window and clearly saw your suspect, Kenji Nakamura, in the kitchen."

"Was he alone?"

"He was. Judging by the furnishings, I'd guess he lives alone, sir."

"What gave you that idea?" Reid asked, intrigued. This officer was good. No wonder he was one of Perez's best.

"He was sitting at the small table eating alone. There was only one plate in the washing up rack and one mug on the side. There were no feminine touches or things you'd expect to find if he had kids, sir."

"That's very observant of you, Officer Morales."

"Thank you, Lieutenant." He hesitated. "Can I just say I am a big fan of your department, sir? I applied there out of the academy but didn't get accepted."

They'd had such an influx of applications after they'd brought in Maria Lopez, notorious head of the Morales cartel, that he'd told the central human resources department no more. He was sorry to have missed Morales, though. He sounded more than competent.

"Nobody did," he said, by way of explanation. He paused for a beat. "But there might be an opening soon. Why don't you forward your resume to me, personally, and I'll take a look. If you're still interested, that is."

Perez would not be happy if he poached his best officer, but it was the kid's decision.

"Yes, sir." Morales's tone expressed his delight. Reid smiled despite the situation. At least people still wanted to come and work for them. It wasn't all bad.

"Did Nakamura leave the apartment at all last night?" he asked, circling back to the issue at hand.

"No, he did not. I watched the entrance to the block all night. I also conducted a walk-by every two hours, just to make sure he hadn't left on foot somehow."

"Good to know," Reid said, not wanting to go too heavy on the praise. "Was he acting suspicious at all?"

"In what way, sir?"

Reid didn't beat around the bush. "Like he'd just committed a homicide."

There was a shocked pause, then Morales said, "Er, I don't think so. I'm not sure how a murderer would act, but he seemed pretty normal to me. He ate supper, washed the dishes, and made tea around ten o'clock. He turned in just before midnight."

"You saw him go to bed?" Reid asked.

"No, sir. But I saw the lights inside go off, and when I checked at two a.m. there was no change. Same at four. When I left at five o'clock, the flat was still in darkness."

Reid exhaled. "Okay, thank you for that, Officer. I appreciate your diverting from your usual beat to help us out."

"Anything for Sweetwater PD," he said, then hesitated. "Lieutenant, is this to do with those sword killings?"

"It is, Officer Morales, but it looks like our suspect is in the clear."

"Sorry I couldn't help catch the perp for you, Lieutenant," he said.

"You did good." Reid thanked him again, gave him his work email address, and ended the call.

"What did he say about Nakamura?" Diaz asked from her desk. She was still pale and Reid suspected the dark shadows beneath her eyes had more to do with seeing the decapitated body than from tiredness.

Vargas had regained his normal complexion and seemed to be coping well enough. Reid glanced around at the rest of the team. Martinez was rounding up surveillance footage from every camera within range of Wynwood Walls, while Hamilton was still working through the employee list at the electronics company, trying to identify which staff member had signed out the Toyota used to attend the warehouse meeting.

Monroe had gone home to grab some sleep, but before he left, he'd delivered one crucial update: Nakamura had been confirmed at the Four Seasons in Palm Beach on the night of Hargreave's murder. Hotel security footage showed him leaving just after one a.m., clear as day.

So if Nakamura hadn't killed Hargreave, and he wasn't acting like a man who'd just beheaded Arthur Whitmore, could Reid reasonably rule him out?

His gut said no.

There were multiple people tied to the Heritage Coalition—hence the name. A coalition didn't act alone.

Nakamura could have had help. One person could have handled Hargreave. Another could have taken Burton-Holmes, driven him to the park, and staged the body for discovery the following morning.

Whitmore's death, too, could have been a coordinated effort. One person to abduct him from the parking garage. Another to carry out the beheading. Someone else could have returned later, covering the planter with a tarp and a maintenance sign, then waited until peak foot traffic to remove it, exposing the body in front of a crowd.

Reid blew out a breath. It might not be just one killer they were after.

36

Kenzie woke to find social media awash with the terrifying details of the beheading. She knew at once it was the same killer.

He wasn't just escalating. He'd gone for a full-blown spectacle. A public park, in the middle of an event, with thousands of people milling around.

A decapitated body in the middle of it.

It was gruesome, shocking, and totally audacious.

Needing to talk to someone about it and loath to call Reid, knowing he'd be busy, she logged on to The Evidence Room. As she'd hoped, most of the members were online.

AlexR: A shocking escalation. How'd he place the body there without being seen?

>

>

GrayAtlas: Must have done it earlier in the day. It only gets busy at night.

>

>

ThirdWitness: There was an event on. Some music festival.

>

RedCairn: Risky.

>

>

ThirdWitness: No CCTV in that area. I went to take a look.

Kenzie gave a grim nod. Typical ThirdWitness. He always had to get in on the action. Or was there more to it? She wondered how Raoul was getting on identifying him.

ReporterGirl: Any pictures of the crime scene?

>

>

>

ThirdWitness: Still cordoned off. CSU processing the scene. They've got a tent up.

>

>

FieldNotes: Murder weapon was another samurai sword.

>

RedCairn: Media assumes the same killer.

>

>

FieldNotes: MO is the same. Sword left with the body. Suggests ideological link again.

>

ReporterGirl: Not the same MO.

>

RedCairn: Explain?

Kenzie peered at some early photographs of the crime scene before the police had gotten there. The visuals were sickening. The body separated from the head, which sat upright in the planter like it was growing there. It was freakish and upsetting. She wished she hadn't seen it, but it was too late. She couldn't unsee it now.

ReporterGirl: Blood in the flower bed. A lot of blood. Early photographs confirm. He must have been beheaded there.

>

>

AlexR: You're right. He was killed on site. That's different.

>

>

GrayAtlas: Hard to transport a head and a body.

Kenzie cringed at the additional mental image. He was right, though. Maybe the killer had beheaded the victim there out of necessity.

FieldNotes: Same killer?

>

>

AlexR: I'd say so.

There were a series of thumbs ups.

RedCairn: We can't assume anything.

>

>

>

CrossCheck: Everything else is the same. Would be good to know how he died.

>

>

ReporterGirl: I heard it was some kind of toxin.

>

>

AlexR: Police connection?

>

ReporterGirl: Yeah.

>

>

FieldNotes: Do you know what toxin?

Kenzie hesitated. She could tell them, but the puffer fish wasn't common knowledge, and if it came out, Reid would know it was her.

ReporterGirl: No. Also no cloth or symbolic reference other than the sword.

>

>

AlexR: Only the second victim had the cloth.

>

>

ReporterGirl: That's different again.

>

>

RedCairn: What's the killer trying to say?

>

ReporterGirl: idk
FieldNotes: Different ideological meanings?

>

>

>

ReporterGirl: But why the katana, then the samurai sword and the cloth, then just the sword?

>

AlexR: Puzzling.

It was indeed a mystery. Kenzie frowned as she thought through their brainstorming session. It really helped free her mind up to think openly about the murders. The killer was sending mixed messages. Like he was unclear about exactly which message he wanted to get across. She'd never thought about it like that before.

She remembered what Nakamura had said about bushido. That it was all about honor and control. His organization condemned violence.

Could it be that the killer was trying to lay the blame at the Heritage Preservation Coalition's feet? Were Nakamura and his society just the most obvious scapegoats?

She went back to the chat.

ReporterGirl: Theory... could the killer be trying to pin the blame on the HPC?

There was a pause, then two comments appeared at once.

RedCairn: What makes you say that?

>

>

AlexR: Not following.

She explained what she'd been thinking, about how different the messages were, about how the escalation had a theatrical element to it. How it didn't sound like the warrior code.

Alex responded first.

AlexR: You could be right.

>

>

>

RedCairn: Food for thought. Let's see if anything supports that theory. Regroup in an hour?

Kenzie gave him a thumbs up and left the chat.

The thought ricocheted around her head, and she was unable to get rid of it. The more she thought about it, the more sense it made. ThirdWitness had been at two of the three crime scenes.

She knew that killers sometimes returned to the scene of the crime. A compulsion, psychologists said. A need to relive the act, to feed off the attention it generated. Was that what this was? Was he watching the aftermath, measuring the reaction?

The macabre nature of the crime indicated he was going for effect, rather than a noble justice or honor killing.

Kenzie felt the need to move, to get the blood flowing.

She'd go for a walk, she decided, pulling a dark sweatshirt out of her closet. It was the same one she wore the night of the warehouse stakeout. It rustled as she pulled it on, and she suddenly remembered the note she'd picked up off the warehouse floor and shoved in the pocket.

Taking it out, she uncrumpled it and read what it said.

It was only the address of the warehouse.

Disappointed, she was about to throw it away when the handwriting made her pause.

That sloping cursive. Neat and precise.

She'd seen that before.

Her heart began to beat a little faster. Unless she was very much mistaken, this was the same handwriting as in those threatening notes Reid had lying on his desk at the station.

A shiver ran through her.

There was only one explanation. Someone who'd been at the secret warehouse meeting had written those letters to the victims.

She'd been wrong. The HPC did have something to do with the murders. They had to. This proved it.

With shaking hands, she reached for her phone.

37

Reid saw Kenzie's name appear on his screen. He answered, preparing to keep it short. "Hey, I can't talk right now. We've just had a break in the case."

"Oh, really?"

"Yeah, can I call you back later?"

"Sure, but I think you're going to want to hear this."

She was breathless, and he could tell by the note in her voice that she'd found something important. He only hoped it wasn't via that crackpot group of armchair detectives.

"What is it?"

Vargas beckoned from across the bullpen, and Reid raised a finger.

"When I was at the warehouse that night, I picked up a scrap of paper lying on the floor. I forgot about it until now. Reid, it's in the same handwriting as those threatening letters."

Reid froze, his mind processing what she'd said.

"Are you sure?"

"Pretty much, yeah. I've sent you a photograph of it. Take a look and tell me what you think?"

His phone pinged, and he clicked on the incoming message. The image opened, and his breath caught in his throat. It was the same handwriting, no doubt about it. He'd looked at those letters long enough to know it on sight.

"It's a match," he croaked.

"Reid, there were seven people at that meeting. All members of the Heritage Preservation Coalition."

"I know," he said, his brain firing on all cylinders. "This actually ties in with our current theory, that there was more than one killer."

She fell silent, and he grimaced. Shit, he probably shouldn't have told her that. They were just exploring the option themselves.

He was so used to talking freely with Kenzie, it was hard to rein it in sometimes. "Don't repeat that," he said quickly.

"I won't," she reassured him, and he exhaled.

"Look, I've got to go, but thanks for this. Really, it's a big break."

"Do you know who they are yet?" she asked.

"Not yet. We're working on it, though."

"So are we."

He frowned. "Keep me posted if there are any results. This is important Kenz. Under no circumstances are you to take any action yourselves."

"What action could we take?" she asked, and he could hear she was offended. "I'm not going to jeopardize this investigation, Reid."

"I know, sorry. There's a lot going on."

"I realize that," she exhaled noisily. "I'll leave you to it. Just wanted to pass that on."

"Thanks, Kenz. Take care."

There was an odd pause. "Will do."

He hung up, not sure what that last hesitation was all about. Still, he didn't have time to think about it, not with all that was going on.

He stared at the image of the scrap of paper again. Then picked up one of the letters on his desk. Not that he needed side-by-side confirmation, but they were a dead-on match.

Diaz came over. "What are you looking at?"

He showed her.

"Holy crap," she hissed. "So we're on the right track. It was them."

He gave a slow nod. "Looks like it."

Martinez called him over as he was making his way to Vargas's desk. "Lieutenant, I've got one of Watanabe's clients on the phone. He's also received hate mail and is worried he's going to be next."

Vargas held the phone away from his ear. "Same here. Watanabe says he's been inundated by calls from his customers who have also received letters."

Shit.

"They can't all be victims," Dwayne said, coming over.

Reid thought about the scrap of paper Kenzie had found at the warehouse. "We need an explanation for these," he said, pulling out his phone.

"Who are you calling?" Vargas asked.

"Officer Morales," he replied, walking away so he could hear better.

Behind him, he heard Vargas ask Dwayne, "Who's Officer Morales?"

Thankfully, the young officer picked up straight away. Despite the fact that he'd been up all night, and must have been in bed, he sounded as alert as he had earlier. "This is Morales."

"Lieutenant Garrett," Reid said, by way of identification.

"Yes, sir. I recognized your number."

"Good. Listen, I need you to do me a favor."

"Anything, sir."

"Arrest Nakamura and bring him to Sweetwater PD."

"Now?" Morales asked, without hesitation.

"Yes, right now. If he's not at home, track him down at work. He lectures at the International University."

"I'm on it," Morales said, and Reid heard movement in the background. Morales was mobilizing as he talked.

"And bring a sample of his handwriting with you," Reid added. "A notebook, documents, anything written by hand."

"Understood."

"Take backup if you need it," Reid cautioned. "I don't think he's dangerous, but you never know."

"Will do," Morales said.

Satisfied, Reid cut the call.

Morales brought in Kenji Nakamura just after nine. Reid got Hamilton to take him to the interview room, while he thanked Morales.

"Good job, Officer."

Morales glowed. It turned out he knew Hamilton from the academy. Their paths had crossed once or twice, so Reid left them to catch up and prepared to talk to Nakamura.

The academic was dressed for work, his shirt perfectly ironed, his trousers creased, his suit jacket immaculate, and his shoes shining. He appeared annoyed but composed when Reid entered the interview room.

"What is this about, Lieutenant? I've already given my statement."

Reid took a seat opposite him, then fixed him with his gaze. "We need to talk about the letters."

Nakamura didn't reply straight away, but his expression didn't change. There was no surprise, no indignation or denial. Just a slow measured breath.

"Do you deny you wrote them?" Reid asked.

"No," came the quiet reply.

Reid exhaled, surprised by the admittance. He got the impression lying was above Nakamura, and he planned to use that to his advantage. Leaning over, he positioned the letters over the table in a grid pattern, then watched Nakamura's eyes as they flicked between them. Still, he didn't react.

"You sent these letters to three collectors, all of whom are now dead," Reid said.

"Yes," Nakamura replied calmly. "They're mine."

Reid digested that for a beat.

"You want to explain why?" he asked, puzzled by the lack of resistance. Could he be about to get a confession? Did the way of the warrior mean Nakamura would admit to being the killer? His gut told him nothing was that easy.

Nakamura inclined his head slightly, as if acknowledging the weight of the question. "They were not death threats, Lieutenant. They were warnings."

"Warnings that talk about judgment and retribution," Reid said. "And now the recipients are dead."

"I sent these to a lot of people," Nakamura said. "Not all of them are dead."

Not yet.

"Are you saying you didn't kill Malcolm Hargreave, Reginald Burton-Holmes, and Arthur Whitmore?"

"I didn't kill anyone," he replied, meeting Reid's glare with a frank gaze. "I'm sorry that you think I did."

Reid rubbed his jaw. Part of him wanted to believe Nakamura, but the cop in him couldn't afford to.

"Then why send them?" he asked.

"My intention was to point out what they'd done. To get their attention. It was a passive protest. Some of our later letters suggest repatriation. That's where we come in. My organization facilitates that."

"So this is a repatriation attempt?"

Nakamura leaned back in his chair. "Exactly."

Reid sucked in a breath. "You've got a funny way of showing it."

"Can I share something with you, Lieutenant?"

"Please." He folded his arms and waited. He couldn't wait to hear this.

"My grandfather was a curator at a regional museum in Kyoto. After the war, several pieces disappeared from temple collections. Items that were never meant to be sold, never meant to leave Japan. They surfaced years later in private collections overseas."

"What does that have to do with this investigation?" he asked. While he sympathized, he had no time for this. Not if it was an attempt to justify what they'd done, or to distract from it.

"It's why I founded the Heritage Preservation Coalition," Nakamura explained. "That's why I believe in the bushido code. It's not about killing. It's about restoring order. It's about working with collectors to repatriate my country's stolen artifacts. It's about my responsibility to do the right thing."

"Does that include murder?" he asked.

Nakamura gave a little sigh. "No, it does not."

Reid studied him. "You ever meet any of these recipients in person?"

"No."

"Ever follow them?"

"No."

"Ever suggest that someone else should take matters further?"

"Absolutely not."

His tone was steady and his demeanor controlled. Believable.

"You might not be responsible," Reid said, narrowing his gaze. "But what about your compatriots? The other members in your organization?"

"I can vouch for them," he said.

"I'm afraid that's not good enough. I need names. Alibis."

"They are not part of this," Nakamura said firmly.

"No offense, but I'm not going to take your word for it. If they're innocent, you can give me their names."

"It wouldn't be honorable," Nakamura said. "When we formed

the organization, we promised we wouldn't divulge anyone who was involved. I plan to keep that promise."

Reid balled his hands into fists in his lap. "Here's the problem, Mr. Nakamura. Unless you give me those names, I'm going to hold you responsible for their actions. And if I can't prove their innocence, I'm afraid I can't let you go."

Nakamura nodded once. "I expected as much."

Reid got to his feet. "If you change your mind, let one of us know."

"I won't."

That was one thing Reid felt sure of.

As he walked out, Reid felt the same unease he'd felt after the first interview. Nakamura sounded principled and sincere, but the evidence was all pointing in his direction.

So why was his gut telling him something wasn't right?

38

Kenzie walked along the beach. A fresh breeze had sprung up, cutting through the humidity and offering welcome relief. It helped clear some of the confusion in her mind, too.

At first, she'd been convinced the killer was working independently—that they had nothing to do with the Heritage Preservation Coalition. Then the note had changed everything. Suddenly, she was back to thinking the group was responsible.

But as she walked, she let her thoughts settle.

Just because the HPC had written the letters didn't necessarily mean they were involved in the murders. Her original theory could still stand. If anything, the existence of the letters only reinforced it.

It made the HPC even more of a target.

The beach was quiet—just a scattering of walkers and no one swimming. Only a handful of surfers bobbed along the break line, waiting.

Did that mean the killer knew about the letters? They must have, if they'd deliberately chosen the HPC as the group to pin the murders on. Years of reporting on the crime beat had taught her that the best way to get away with murder was to provide an alternative theory.

Lawyers did it. So did criminals.

It was a classic diversion.

Look left. Exit right.

She exhaled, the wind stealing her breath. Adrenaline was pumping now, her pulse ticking faster. Something told her she was getting close. Or closer, at least.

Then there was the person who'd followed her home.

If it wasn't a member of the HPC—and she didn't think it was—then it could only have been someone from *The Evidence Room*. One of them checking her out.

The most obvious candidate was RedCairn. It was his group. He was the lead moderator. She was the newest recruit. It made sense he'd want to assess her. He just hadn't counted on being made.

Next on her list was Alex.

He was an enigma to her—so why not the other way around? They'd spent time together. Bonded, in a way, in the dark warehouse. It was feasible he'd want to learn more about her. Except given his obvious skill, she doubted she'd ever know if he was following her. He'd be too careful. Too good.

Then there was ThirdWitness.

Like Reid, she didn't like coincidences. Being present at two crime scenes felt excessive. She understood obsession—true crime fanatics lived for moments like these. Many of her podcast subscribers were just like that.

Still, it would help if she could identify him. Rule him out.

She was so wrapped up in her thoughts—the rhythm of the waves, the wind rushing in her ears—that she nearly missed her phone vibrating in her pocket. It buzzed insistently until she gasped and grabbed it just before it cut off.

"Yeah?"

"Kenz, it's Raoul," he said. His voice was faint beneath the background noise. "Where the hell are you? In a washing machine?"

"Hang on." She turned sharply and jogged up the sand toward the walkway. Ducking into an outdoor café as a couple exited, she pressed the phone to her ear. "Better?"

"Much. You out walking again?"

"Yeah. Helps me think."

He scoffed. "Well, I've got something for you to think about."

"You do?"

"I figured out who your mystery men are."

Her heart jumped. "Both of them?"

"Yeah, so get this. AlexR is actually Mason Alexander Radloff. He's a former Marine."

"Holy shit," she breathed. "I knew it."

"He was medically retired eight years ago after an IED nearly killed him in Basra."

Kenzie hissed out a breath. She'd known there was something there.

"PTSD?" she asked quietly.

"Shrapnel. A lot of it. I saw the medical report. After that, he failed a psych evaluation and was discharged."

"Failed how?"

"Don't know. It's classified."

A chill swept over her that had nothing to do with the breeze. Could Alex really be the killer? Was he damaged enough to cross that line?

"Any ties to Japan?" she asked.

"None that I can find. No nationalist groups, no martial arts affiliations, nothing ideological. But there is something you'll want to hear."

"Oh?"

"His sister died when he was twenty-two. Before he enlisted."

Kenzie frowned. "How?"

"The official cause was a drug overdose. She was pulled from a canal in Doral. But Radloff never believed it. Said she didn't use. Never touched drugs."

Kenzie's stomach tightened.

She remembered a case years earlier—a teenager who'd begged her to investigate her boyfriend's death. Same story. Found in a waterway. Ruled an overdose. She'd sworn he hated drugs.

Sometimes the official version wasn't the truth.

"Is that why he joined up?" she asked.

"Possibly. He challenged the coroner's report. Said she'd been murdered. Harassed the detective in charge until a restraining order was issued."

"Murdered..." Kenzie whispered.

"Looks like that's when he signed up."

Kenzie let out a breath. "Wow. I wasn't expecting that."

"I know." He sounded proud of himself. Kenzie stared out of the window at the sea. She had to digest this, let it sit for a while. Her brain felt like it was going to explode. What did any of it mean?

Did it mean anything, or was it just a tragic story?

"There's more," Raoul said.

"I'm not sure I can take much more," she muttered.

He laughed. "It's not as exciting. ThirdWitness, your true crime junkie, is just that."

"An addict?"

"No, silly. He's just a fan. He belongs to a dozen true crime groups on Facebook with the same username. His real name is Wiley Allen. He's from Minnesota."

Kenzie blinked against the breeze. "Wiley Allen?"

"Yeah. He lives in University Park, which is near Tamiami Park where Burton-Holmes was found. He's an amateur photographer. Posts on Instagram as *ThirdLens*."

"I'm sensing a theme."

"Subtlety's not his strength," Raoul agreed. "I think he's harmless."

Kenzie had to admit—it sounded that way.

"So he's just a fanatic."

"Yep. Garden-variety."

"Well, that kills that theory."

He laughed. "I'd say that's a win. At least you're not in danger."

There was still the teensy matter of the other night's tail.

"Hey, Raoul. What vehicle does he drive?"

"Who? ThirdWitness?"

"Both of them."

"ThirdWitness owns a brown pickup, and Alex drives a black SUV."

"I thought that was a rental?"

"What was a rental?"

"The car Alex drove to the warehouse that night. I'm sure Reid told me it was a hire."

"Well, he owns one too. What can I tell you? He likes SUVs."

The rental was only for the purposes of the stakeout, then. Another reason to suspect Alex had done this kind of thing before.

She'd been wrong in her assumptions about the two men. ThirdWitness was harmless. Alex was the one carrying trauma—and secrets.

"Thanks, Raoul. I owe you."

"No, Lieutenant Garrett owes me, and I'll be invoicing him as soon as this is over."

She smiled despite herself.

The reason she hadn't spotted the car, Kenzie decided later, was because she'd been so deep in thought.

It appeared seemingly out of nowhere—a flash of silver to her right, hurtling down the beach road. She turned, realized it was about to hit her, and... froze.

It was as if her brain had short-circuited. Her body refused to respond. No sound came from her throat despite the impending doom. Time seemed to slow down.

Then someone barreled into her and tackled her toward the curb.

They both went flying, rolling across the asphalt. Pain flared as she grazed the skin on her elbows and knees. Her lip split on impact.

Stunned, she stared up at her savior. He was a man in his fifties, dark hair graying at the temples, his face etched with concern as he hovered over her.

"Are you all right?" he asked, carefully shifting off her.

She blinked, did a quick mental inventory of her limbs—everything seemed to be working—and nodded. "I think so."

He offered a hand. "Here. Let me help you up."

A small crowd had gathered.

"I saw the whole thing," a woman said, hurrying over with a shopping basket tucked under her arm. "That car was heading straight for you. You were a goner."

"Thanks," Kenzie said, frowning as she touched her lip with her tongue. She tasted blood.

"Here," another woman offered, pressing a napkin into her hand.

Kenzie stared at it, still trying to process what had just happened. Had someone really just tried to kill her?

She looked back at the woman with the basket. "What color did you say the car was?"

"Gray. A light gray."

"Do you know the driver?" her rescuer asked, scanning the street.

She shook her head and clutched his arm as she stepped onto the sidewalk. "No. I don't think so."

He nodded. "Do you want me to call an ambulance?"

"I'm fine," she said automatically—then her hands began to shake. "Actually... I think I just need to sit down."

"Here," said the woman with the napkin. "There's a bench."

Kenzie let the man guide her over and sat heavily. "Thank you," she said, really looking at him now. "If you hadn't—" Her voice caught. "You saved my life."

"I'm just glad I was there," he said. "What an imbecile. He could have killed you."

Privately, Kenzie thought that might have been the point.

She pressed the napkin to her lip. Her T-shirt was stained bright red where the blood had dripped onto the fabric.

"You sure you're okay?" the man asked. "I should get going—my wife's waiting for me."

"Yes. I'm fine. Thank you again," she said, forcing a smile.

He nodded, satisfied, and hurried off.

The woman with the napkin lingered a moment longer, then moved away as well. The crowd dispersed, leaving Kenzie alone on the bench, her heart still hammering in her chest.

39

"What happened to you?" Reid stared at Kenzie's fat lip, the bruise running down the side of her face, and the multiple grazes on her arms and legs. "Are you okay?"

"I'm fine. Is there somewhere we can talk?"

"Sure, come into my office." He opened the door to the storeroom and ushered her inside. Everybody knew he didn't have an office, but if he did, this would be it.

She smirked and followed him in. He was glad to see she hadn't lost her sense of humor.

"Now tell me what happened?"

She perched on the edge of the printer. "Reid, I think somebody tried to kill me."

"What?" he blurted, putting his hands on his hips. "You mean this..." he waved his arm around, "wasn't an accident?"

"No. I was nearly run over this morning."

"Jesus, Kenz. Why didn't you tell me?"

"I'm here now, telling you."

He scowled at her. "You know that's not what I meant. You should have called me when it happened. I'd have come to get you."

She waved away his protestations. "It doesn't matter. I'm fine. The thing is, someone followed me home the other night. I didn't tell you because I wasn't sure, but now this—" she broke off.

He raked a hand through his hair. "Why is this the first time I'm hearing about it? For fuck's sake, Kenzie. *Two* attempts on your life and you're only telling me now?"

"The first wasn't an attempt," she corrected. "It was a tail. I spotted it on the causeway, then drove around for a while, testing the theory. It peeled off, so..." She shrugged. "I went home."

"You think this is related?" he said, frowning. Obviously, it was related.

She nodded. "Same car. Light gray, didn't get the plate."

Shit.

"It was dark the first time, and this morning I didn't see it coming. Or leaving."

He suddenly felt the need to sit down. He lowered himself onto a box of printer paper. It creaked under his weight.

"Talk me through what happened."

As Kenzie told him the story, he found himself getting more and more worked up. Who the fuck ran someone over in broad daylight?

"The good news is that road has several cameras on it. We'll find the bastard who did this," he vowed, not sure if he was reassuring Kenzie or himself.

She gave a little nod, and he grimaced as he again inspected her lip and the purple coloring on her cheek.

"I think it's the killer," she whispered.

He stared at her.

"How—? What makes you say that?"

"Because I'm getting close, Reid. I know it." She paused, and he saw her lick her lip. Her voice was slightly slurred as she tried to talk over the swelling.

"I don't think it's a member of the Heritage Preservation Coalition. I think it's someone in my true crime group. They're the only people who know what I've been thinking."

He shook his head. "I don't understand. The armchair detectives?"

"Yes." She nodded, then winced. "I should have seen it before, but we were all looking at the ideologues. The swords and the symbols and the hate mail—none of that was real. It was all designed to get us to look the other way."

Reid stared at her.

"What do you mean?" he said quietly. Something inside him was beginning to shift. To ease.

"Well, I went over the three murders. In the first one, the scene was impeccably staged, the katana positioned just so, the lighting arranged to highlight the act, and so on..."

He nodded. "So?"

"In the second, the sword was the feature—again. But this time there was a cloth positioned beside the body."

"The silk cloth with the symbolism on it," he said. "We deciphered it. It was just bushido symbols."

"I know, it was a decoy. It was supposed to make you think the murder had something to do with the Heritage Preservation Coalition or a similar fanatical group."

He frowned. "It was pretty convincing."

"I know. But in the third scene, the killer went totally over the top. That whole decapitation stunt. The planter. The festival. The publicity. It was too much."

Reid slanted his gaze. He didn't disagree. "You're saying it doesn't align with their belief system?"

"Exactly. It's not the way of the warrior, or whatever you want to call it. It's chaotic, extreme, overly violent. Showy. That's not what the coalition believes."

He exhaled softly, letting that percolate. She wasn't wrong. He hadn't gotten that vibe from Nakamura either. That's what had been bugging him.

"I voiced this in the private chat. Everyone was there. I mean the core group. I said I thought the killer wanted to make it look like it was the HPC who was responsible."

Reid drew in a sharp breath. "Let me guess, that's when the hit-and-run occurred."

"Right." She looked up at him with her clear, blue gaze now laced with fear and he fought the urge to take her in his arms and comfort her, except he knew she wouldn't like that. Not while she still had things to say.

"Someone in that group tried to stop me, Reid. The problem is, I don't know who it was."

There was a pause as Reid tried to get his head around it.

"Let me get this straight," he said slowly. "The killer commits three murders, then joins a true crime group so he can help solve them. And when you actually get close to the truth, he tries to take you out?"

"That's about it. I mean, it's not uncommon for a psychopathic killer to want to be involved in solving their own crimes. There are plenty of documented cases where they contact police, come forward as witnesses, even revisit the crime scenes."

He knew that was true. It didn't make this any less fucked up.

"What about AlexR?" he said, mentioning the first member of the group who sprang to mind. "You suspected he had a law enforcement background. He used a rental to attend the meeting, hid his true identity."

"It's possible," she said vaguely, and he could tell she wasn't convinced. "Anyway, we found out who he is. His real name is Mason Alexander Radloff. He's got a military background. United States Marine Corps." She paused, then added, "He also has a history of harassment and was discharged on medical grounds after an IED nearly blew him up."

"Jesus Christ," Reid snapped. "Then we should bring him in. Talk to him."

"I'm just not sure he did this," she said. "He drives a black SUV, not a gray car. And he doesn't strike me as the type to go all Kill Bill on a victim. He's way too reserved for that."

"He could still be unhinged," Reid pressed.

"I don't think so. You know why he joined the Marines? His sister died when he was in his early twenties. According to the police report, she overdosed and ended up in a canal. He never believed it. He always thought it was murder."

"I suppose that's why he's a true crime nut," Reid said with a snort. "Trying to solve his sister's death."

"I'd like to see the original police files," she said hesitantly. "Maybe they'd give us some clarity on his motives."

Reid narrowed his gaze. "You're not cleared to see those files."

"Do I need clearance? I'm a vetted consultant."

She was twisting his goddamn arm.

"Besides, it's not an active case," she added. "It was closed after the coroner ruled it a drug overdose."

Reid let out a long breath and folded his arms across his chest. "I guess we could take a look. But I'm still bringing him in. Even if he's not guilty, he's been in that group longer than you. He might help us solve this—and catch the bastard who did that to you."

40

KENZIE WATCHED AS ALEX, or rather Mason Alexander Radloff was brought into the police department. As Morales handed him over to Hamilton, he turned and met Kenzie's eye.

"Fancy seeing you here," he said with a sardonic grin.

She knew straight away that he knew exactly who she was.

"You've known from the start, haven't you?" she said, walking over to him. Reid got up and followed, a scowl on his face.

Hamilton's grip tightened around Alex's arm.

"It's okay," Kenzie said, and Reid nodded.

Hamilton relaxed, but just fractionally.

"*Almost* from the start," he corrected, his eyes lingering on her lip and the bruise on her cheek. "I thought the way you joined was suspicious. And then you asked me to vouch for you with RedCairn. I suspected you had an agenda, I just didn't know what it was. Then I took down your license plate at the warehouse and it all made sense. Kenzie Gilmore, investigative reporter and podcaster."

Reid grunted, but Kenzie pursed her lips. "Very smart."

"What happened?" Alex nodded to her swollen lip.

"Had a run in with a hit-and-run driver." She watched as his eyes widened.

"When?"

"We'll get to that," Reid said.

Alex fixed his gaze on him for a beat, then turned back to Kenzie. "What am I doing here?"

"Lieutenant Garrett," Reid cut in, before she had a chance to answer. "Thanks for coming in."

Alex tossed his head in Hamilton's direction. "Not like I had much of a choice."

"You used a rental at the warehouse," Kenzie said, wanting to get back to their original discussion.

Alex's lips quirked. "I knew you'd check. Some people just can't help themselves."

She felt herself flush.

"Do the others know who I am?" she asked.

He shrugged. "Don't think so. RedCairn definitely doesn't because he asked if I knew. Thought you might have told me your real identity when we met."

Reid put up a hand. "Let's hold it there and carry on in the interview room. Hamilton, take Mr. Radloff through."

Alex raised his eyebrows at the use of his real last name but went without complaint.

"I'm coming too," Kenzie said before Reid had a chance to tell her she couldn't. "He's not under arrest. This is a voluntary interview and I have history with him. We have a rapport. He's more likely to open up to me than you."

Reid opened his mouth to speak, but she cut him off. "He doesn't trust the police because of what happened to his sister."

He put a hand on her shoulder. "I know. Relax. I was going to suggest that anyway."

She stared up at him. "You were?"

"Yeah. Let's go talk to him on the record and see what he knows. I *am* going to caution him though, so if he trips up, we can use his testimony in court."

"He won't trip up," she reassured him. "He's not guilty of anything."

Reid smirked. "We'll see."

Alex sat at the table, his hands now free of the cuffs and folded neatly in front of him. He seemed relaxed, but his gaze was... cautious. That's the only way Kenzie could describe it.

As she pulled out a chair, he said, "You weren't joking when you said you worked closely with the police. I didn't realize how close."

She shrugged. "I didn't realize you were U.S. Marine."

He grinned. "You've done your homework. Anyway, it's not something you bring up in casual conversation."

Fair enough.

Reid came in and sat beside her, his chair scraping on the concrete floor.

Alex tensed. "Am I under arrest?"

"Not yet." Reid set a notebook on the table, along with a closed manila case file. "But you've been advised of your rights, and this interview is being recorded."

"We're hoping you can help us identify the Samurai Killer," Kenzie said, hoping to ease the tension in the room. Why did men always have to be so confrontational?

His gaze turned to her. "Why would I be able to help?"

"Because he's in our group."

Alex blacked. "The Evidence Room? You're kidding?"

"No, I'm serious." She pointed to her face. "He has to be. It was only when I said the killer was trying to put the blame on a member of the HPC that things started getting dangerous."

Alex nodded to her lip. "That was this morning?"

"Yeah, and I was followed home the other night." She smiled. "And not by you."

He shrugged. "You're right about that. I had no need to follow you. Once I had your plate, it was easy to find out where you lived."

Beside her, she felt Reid stiffen.

Alex noticed too. "Don't worry. I had nothing to do with any of this."

Reid's gaze narrowed. "So you say."

Alex turned back to Kenzie. "I don't expect the cops to believe me, but you know none of this was me."

She gave a quick nod, hoping Reid wouldn't hold it against her.

"Besides, I have an alibi for two of the three murders."

"You do?"

"Yeah. I was having dinner at my parents' place in Kendall when Hargreave was killed. I stayed over and heard it on my mom's old radio the next morning."

"We'll need their number to verify," Reid said.

He nodded but kept his gaze on Kenzie.

"Which other murder do you have an alibi for?" Kenzie asked.

"Arthur Whitmore. I was at my girlfriend's house that night."

"She'll vouch for you?" Kenzie asked.

"Yeah."

"But nothing for the night Burton-Holmes was abducted?" Reid asked.

"No, I was at home, but my neighbor can vouch for me. She saw me go in and asked me to change the bulb in her bathroom. It had gone out."

Kenzie glanced at Reid, who gave a reluctant nod.

Reid scribbled a note on his pad. "Do you know who any of the other members are?"

Alex hesitated. "By telling you, I'm breaking the agreement of the group."

"It says we'll never try to find out each other's identities," Kenzie explained.

Reid's jaw tightened. "This is a murder inquiry. If you know and you don't tell us, you'll be withholding information."

He sighed. "Okay, I get it. I know the drill."

Kenzie knew he was talking about his experience with the police after his sister died.

He folded his arms across his chest. "ThirdWitness is actually Derek Wilder, a delivery driver and freelance photographer. He lives in University Park and spends his free time listening to police radio frequencies and trying to get to crime scenes to take photographs he can sell to the media."

Reid bristled. Law enforcement generally despised those kinds of people.

"He was at two of the crime scenes," Kenzie pointed out.

"I know, but he's harmless. I can't see him doing this. He's not a planner, nor would he be able to pull it off without making a mess of the crime scenes." He lowered his voice. "I've seen inside his house."

Reid frowned. "You broke in?"

"I peeked through the window."

Kenzie masked a grin.

"What about RedCairn?" Reid asked, ignoring Alex's smug tone. "You mentioned him before."

"Yeah, he's the only one I don't know," Alex admitted. "Doesn't say much other than to direct the flow of conversation in the group and vet new joiners. He's conscious of the law, which makes me think he might be a lawyer or a judge—or something in the legal arena."

"Interesting," Kenzie mused. "I can actually see that about him."

"RedCairn must have some relevance," Alex continued. "Maybe he's got red hair, or he's Scottish. I don't know."

All good guesses.

"Are all these users in America?" Reid asked.

"It's a prerequisite to joining the group," Alex confirmed. "It's in our bylaws. It states clearly that we only investigate U.S. cases, that members are subject to U.S. law and that we don't allow international users."

"How is that enforced?" Reid asked.

"It's not enforced as such," Alex explained. "When a user joins, they go through a vetting process. Part of that is to check their IP address, and that has to be in America."

"There are ways to mask that," Kenzie said, thinking of VPNs and the like.

"Sure, but nobody bothers. There's no interest in speculating on cases that aren't in your own country."

Reid agreed. "I guess so."

"CrossCheck and GrayAtlas?" Kenzie asked, naming the other two core members of the group.

"CrossCheck is Marcus Yeh, a data analyst. Works at a financial firm in New York. GrayAtlas is Vince Williams. He used to work as a beat cop in Philly. He's retired now but still lives in his old neighborhood."

"You've been busy," Reid muttered, but Kenzie could tell he was impressed, and a little relieved. Alex had just saved them a ton of work.

"What about FieldNotes?" she asked, deciding to keep quiet about her little expedition to his house.

"Jeff Oliver. Lives with his wife and two kids in Miami. Checked him out after the warehouse stakeout too, although I knew he was local. He'd mentioned it a few times before."

"That's all of them?" Reid asked.

Kenzie nodded, rubbing her now-throbbing cheek. "Yeah. That's it."

He leaned forward on the table, his head tilted to the side so he could look at her.

"Then which one of them is our killer?"

41

Reid didn't like Alex Radloff. He was too familiar with Kenzie, and there was an easy mutual admiration between them that grated—but that wasn't really it. It was the quiet confidence. The sense that Alex thought he was smarter than everyone else. Smarter than the police.

He'd skimmed Alex's sister's file earlier, and while the speed with which the case had been closed surprised him—it had been ruled an accidental death within forty-eight hours—it didn't automatically mean the investigators had been wrong. Toxicology showed opioids and benzodiazepines in her system. She had a prior possession arrest. Even her friends admitted she "partied." On paper, it looked like a straightforward overdose followed by an accidental fall into the canal.

Kenzie, however, had been less convinced. She'd flagged inconsistencies almost immediately, so Reid had handed the file over to her to go through properly. If there was something there, they'd circle back to it later.

Right now, though, he had a serial killer to catch.

Whoever was responsible had to know Kenzie was closing in. It was only a matter of time before she worked out exactly which member of that group was behind it all—and that made her a liability.

"Derek Wilder. Marcus Yeh. Vince Williams. Jeff Oliver," Reid said, writing each name on the whiteboard and adding their known aliases beneath them. "I want all four brought in for questioning."

Diaz stepped closer, scanning the board. "We don't have the space to hold all of them."

"I know," Reid said. "Wilder and Oliver come here. Sweetwater PD will handle them. Yeh is in Philadelphia—get PD there to bring him in. Williams is based in New York. NYPD can do the initial interview. I want timelines, alibis, and phone data for the nights of all three murders."

Diaz nodded. "Vargas and I will take Wilder and Oliver."

"Good," Reid said. "Find out exactly where they were, who they were with, and what vehicles they were using. No assumptions."

She turned back to her desk to grab her badge and weapon. Vargas was already moving.

"And I need driver's license photos," Reid called out to Martinez and Hamilton. "Send them straight to my phone as soon as you get them."

Vargas paused at the door. "Where are you headed?"

Reid didn't hesitate. "There's one person who's already seen the killer. I just need her to tell me who it is."

Diaz lowered her voice. "Mambo Solange."

Reid gave a stiff nod and headed for the exit.

Reid pushed through the doorway of Solange's botanica, the familiar scent of incense and crushed herbs thick in the air. Bells chimed softly above him, but there was no one behind the counter. No ledger. No Solange.

"Madam Solange?" he called.

A pause. Then the faint rustle of fabric.

From the back of the shop, a curtain of beads shifted. Solange appeared between its folds, her expression unreadable, dark eyes fixed on him as if she'd been expecting him all along.

"I knew you'd come back," she said calmly.

Reid frowned. "How?"

She didn't answer. Instead, she lifted one long finger and crooked it, beckoning him closer. "Come. We talk in the back."

He hesitated only a moment before following her through the curtain. The room beyond was dim, lit by a single bare bulb and the glow of votive candles arranged in uneven rows. Shelves lined the walls, cluttered with jars, bundles of dried plants, and objects Reid didn't want to guess at. Solange moved with practiced ease, settling onto a low stool opposite a narrow table.

Reid remained standing.

"I know you can't give me a name, but will you look at some photographs for me?"

She studied him for a long beat, then nodded once.

He blinked, expecting more resistance. "You've heard about the other murders?" he asked.

She averted her gaze.

"You know it's him, don't you?" he said quietly.

Again, she didn't reply.

He pulled out his phone and brought up the first photograph—a DMV shot of Derek Wilder. Angling the phone towards her, he asked, "Is this him?"

Solange leaned forward, peered at it for a long moment, then shook her head. "No."

Reid swiped to the next. Marcus Yeh.

Another slow shake.

Alex Radloff. Vince Williams.

Each time, the same response. No hesitation. No uncertainty. Just a quiet, absolute refusal.

Reid felt his patience thinning. "You're sure?"

Her gaze lifted to his. "I am sure."

He let out a frustrated breath and scrolled again. "What about this one?"

Jeff Oliver's photo filled the screen. Solange studied it longer than the others. Her head tilted slightly, as if listening for something only she could hear.

Reid leaned forward despite himself. "You recognize him?"

She shook her head. "No. Not him."

"Goddammit," Reid snapped, then sucked in a breath. "Sorry."

To his surprise, she patted his hand. "You are close, but you are not there yet."

No shit.

"That's not very helpful," he muttered.

"Truth is not always helpful," she said mildly. "But it is still truth."

He ran a hand through his hair. Now she was just talking in riddles.

"I've got one more for you," he said, holding up his phone again.

Kenji Nakamura. It was a last-ditch attempt, a vague thought that maybe the Japanese academic had been playing them all this time.

She shook her head and gave a definitive "No."

He let out a long sigh. Then it had to be RedCairn. The one person they didn't have a picture of. Typical.

She waited, watching him.

Reid straightened, anger and helplessness knotting in his gut. This had all been for nothing.

Were they ever going to catch this guy?

He turned to the curtain, then stopped.

"Why did you help me?" he said, suddenly. "Last time you refused."

"The reason has changed," she said softly. "It is no longer pure."

42

Kenzie looked up from the case files, a feeling of righteous indignation growing in her chest. Alex had been right to question this verdict. It was shocking how the police had mishandled the case.

Alex's sister, Emily Radloff, age twenty-one, had been found floating in a drainage canal on the edge of an industrial area. The tox screen showed opioids and benzodiazepines in her system. She had a prior possession charge, and her friends admitted she was a party girl. That was enough for the police.

The death was ruled an accidental overdose within forty-eight hours. No homicide detective was even assigned. No full canvass was done. The case never really got off the ground before it was shut down.

Reading the file now, Kenzie could see how much had been missed. There was foreign DNA under Emily's fingernails, for goodness' sake. It had been logged and dismissed as secondary transfer.

The medical examiner mentioned faint bruising on her upper arms that didn't match a simple collapse, but it was never followed up on. She'd been wearing a sweatshirt that wasn't hers, yet that was never tested either.

She exhaled noisily, causing Martinez to glance over at her.

None of it fit the overdose narrative, so none of it mattered.

Getting up, she stretched and strolled over to where Hamilton was sitting at his desk. "Is Alex still here?"

"Yeah, the Lieutenant wants to keep him here until he gets back."

"Have you verified his alibis yet?"

Hamilton nodded. "Yes. Both his parents and his girlfriend confirm he was with them the nights of those two murders."

"So can I see him?" She held up the file. "Reid let me read this, but there are some things I want to clarify with Alex."

Hamilton shrugged. "I don't see why not. He's not under arrest."

"You'll find him in the interview room," Monroe said, walking past. "I'll take you there now."

"Thanks." She glanced behind her as the front door opened and a man in his late twenties was escorted in by Diaz. He wore a faded courier jacket over a plain T-shirt, practical sneakers scuffed from use, and a camera bag slung diagonally across his chest. His hair was unremarkable—short, hastily styled—and he had the look of someone used to being on the move, in and out of places without being noticed.

"I demand to know why I've been arrested," he said, indignant rather than afraid, his hands cuffed in front of him.

"We need to ask you a few questions," Diaz replied, her tone clipped. Kenzie caught the edge beneath it—Diaz wasn't known for her patience, and this guy was already testing it.

It had to be ThirdWitness. Jeff Oliver—FieldNotes—hadn't arrived yet.

Kenzie darted through the door behind Monroe that led to the interview rooms, before ThirdWitness spotted her.

Monroe opened the door to the interview room, which wasn't locked. Alex glanced up and broke into a smile when he saw her.

"I wondered where you'd got to."

She held up the file. "I was reading about your sister's case."

The smile faded.

"I'll leave you to it," Monroe said, nodding at Kenzie and walking off.

"What do you think?" he said, and she read the apprehension in his eyes.

"I think it was handled very badly."

Alex exhaled. "Right? Forty-eight hours. It wasn't even handed over to the homicide division. When I complained, I was told the case had been closed."

He laughed bitterly.

"You appealed the decision?"

"I tried, but they kept giving me the cold shoulder. I started going into the station, demanding to speak to the Captain. Eventually they slammed me with a restraining order. They didn't want to know."

"I'm so sorry," she whispered. "That shouldn't have happened to you."

"What do you care?" he asked, studying her. "You're not a cop."

"No, but I wanted to be," she admitted. She told him about the academy and how a car accident had dashed her dreams of joining the Force.

"I became an investigative reporter instead," she said with a shrug. "I figured it was the next best thing."

"I joined the Marines." He chuckled. "Seems we have more in common than I thought."

"I'd like to help you reopen this case." She nodded to the folder on the table.

He stared at her. "You can do that?"

"No, but Reid can. I mean, Lieutenant Garrett. New evidence has come to light, which means he'll have grounds to reopen it."

"New evidence?"

"Yeah, like the DNA found under Emily's fingernails. Samples were taken but it was never tested."

"Wait. That's in there?" Alex reached for the file.

"Yes. You haven't seen it?" She'd just assumed he'd read the police incident report.

"No, I only know what they told me, which wasn't much. I knew it didn't add up, but I didn't know there was DNA."

"Yes, and possibly more on the sweatshirt she was wearing. I'm betting that didn't belong to her."

"That's right," he said, straightening up. "I'd never seen it before. They said that didn't mean anything, but it was two sizes too big for her. I don't know whose sweatshirt that was, but it didn't belong to Emily."

"Did she have a boyfriend?" Kenzie asked, taking a seat opposite him.

"Not that I knew of. Her friends also said she was single."

Kenzie didn't remember seeing the names of Emily's friends in the file. "Do you remember who you spoke to?"

"Er, Katie, maybe. Becca?" He frowned. "It was a long time ago."

Kenzie glanced at the date on the file. "Fourteen years, to be exact."

He nodded. "Exactly."

Kenzie frowned, thinking. "The report mentions bruising on her upper arms. Do you know where that could have come from?"

"I noticed them when I ID'd her body." He swallowed, his voice croaky. "But when I questioned them, they said it was due to falling into the canal."

Bullshit. Those were finger marks.

Except overdoses often came with unexplained bruising, and no one wanted to question the verdict.

"Well, in my opinion, this case was mishandled. It should have gone to homicide, should have been treated as a suspicious death, at the very least."

"Thank you," he murmured. "Really."

"When Reid gets back, I'll talk to him," she promised.

"What's happening out there?" Alex asked, leaning back in his chair. "Have the others come in yet?"

"ThirdWitness is here now, complaining loudly," she said.

He laughed.

"I don't pity whoever gets him."

Kenzie looked across at him. "Alex, what if it's RedCairn? Do you know anything about him that could help us find him?"

He thought for a moment. "To be honest, I don't even know if it's a him. We've never spoken on comms, only ever messaged in the chat."

Kenzie frowned. "You know, it does sound like it might be a woman. RedCairn is organized, careful, and conscientious. I'm not saying those are solely feminine traits, but even the way they talk is measured and careful."

"That's right," Alex said, warming to the idea. "RedCairn doesn't like violence. Is always steering us away from direct action or anything illegal. I was surprised he—or she—agreed to the warehouse stakeout, to be honest."

Kenzie nodded. "How did you meet?"

"I was one of the first recruits. I was looking for something to do in my spare time after I came out of the military. I wanted to help people solve crimes they felt hadn't been solved by the police."

She could understand that. After what he'd been through with his sister... She would have been tempted to do the same thing.

"I met RedCairn in a true crime Facebook group. They mentioned that they'd just set up a private chat and asked if I wanted to join. Said they wanted to get justice for the victims of crime. Said we'd solve murders the police couldn't—or wouldn't. Often it just boils down to budget limitations or resourcing constraints. It sounded good to me, so I said yes."

Kenzie could see exactly why it would have appealed to him.

"So let's just say RedCairn is a female legal professional. It's unlikely she's also the type of person who would go around decapitating innocent art collectors."

"True," Alex shrugged. "Problem is, we don't know who they are."

"Kenzie," called Reid's voice down the corridor.

"In here," she said, getting up and going to the door. It was ajar, so she poked her head out. Reid came striding down the corridor.

"How'd it go?" she asked.

"Not good. Can I talk to you?"

"Sure." She shot an apologetic smile at Alex and followed Reid out into the bullpen. "Are any of the suspects hanging around?" she asked.

"They're both in the holding cells."

She nodded.

"I showed Mambo Solange photographs of all our suspects. She said it's not any of them."

Kenzie frowned. "The killer could have sent someone else to buy the toxin. I mean, if they were about to commit a series of murders, they probably wouldn't have gone and picked it up themself."

He massaged his forehead.

"She seemed to think it was him. All that nonsense about his motive being pure. Or not pure, as it turns out."

"Can I see the photographs?"

"Sure." He pulled them up on his phone and handed it to her. "Here, take a look."

She scrolled through one by one, trying to put the faces to the handles. "This doesn't make sense," she said, frowning.

"That's all of them other than RedCairn," Reid confirmed.

She shook her head. "FieldNotes isn't here."

Reid swiped back a couple of shots. "That's Jeff Oliver."

Kenzie stared at the photograph.

"I don't know who that is," she said slowly. "But it's not Field-Notes. At least, it's not the man I saw at the warehouse."

43

Kenzie stared at the photograph.

"What do you mean it's not him?" Reid asked.

"Well, the man who was at the warehouse with me and Alex looked similar, but it wasn't this guy." She nodded to the headshot. "Where'd you get this?"

"That is the photo from Jeff Oliver's driver's license."

Kenzie frowned. "It doesn't make any sense. His car was registered to Jeff Oliver, and when I went to his house, I saw him through the wind—"

She stopped, frowning.

"You went to his house?" Reid asked.

"Yeah, remember when you wouldn't give me his address? Well, I looked it up and went to his place and staked it out."

"For fuck's sake. When are you going to stop—" He frowned. "Kenz, what's wrong?"

She'd gone white, like she'd seen a ghost.

"Oh, God," she whispered and raised a shaky hand to her face.

"Kenz? You're freaking me out."

Her voice was a strangled whisper. "We've made a terrible mistake."

"Will you just tell me?" he almost yelled. Several of the others glanced over.

Kenzie lowered herself into his chair.

What had she really seen through that window? A figure of a woman on the phone, a man who had the same build as FieldNotes, the same hair, the same thick neck. A kid. It had looked like such a harmless family scene that she hadn't thought twice.

The car had been there too, the car that he'd driven to the warehouse, parked outside in the drive. Everything had added up—like it was meant to.

"It wasn't him," she hissed, looking up at Reid. "The man I saw through the window wasn't FieldNotes, it was Jeff Oliver."

Reid still wasn't following. "What do you mean? I've got Jeff Oliver in a holding cell. I'm about to question him."

"He won't know a thing." Kenzie rose slowly to her feet. "FieldNotes played us. He 'borrowed' Jeff Oliver's car to drive to the warehouse knowing I'd check the license plate. He deliberately chose a man who was similar in physique to him, a man with a family, who no one would suspect."

Reid stared at her. "You're serious? The man I've got in my cell isn't FieldNotes?"

"No, he's a patsy," she said, unable to shirk off the heaviness that crushed down on her. "A fall guy. The killer used his identity as a disguise, so we wouldn't suspect him."

Reid let out a slow breath. "Man, this is messed up."

Kenzie gasped. "*That's* who followed me home the other night. It was FieldNotes. He was watching Jeff Oliver's house to see if anyone would check him out, and I did. I walked right into his carefully laid trap."

Reid tightened his jaw.

"And then, once I caught onto the truth and mentioned it in the group, he tried to kill me." She dropped her head into her hands. "I feel so stupid."

Reid laid a hand on her shoulder. "You didn't know. None of us did."

She shook her head but didn't respond. What was there to say? The killer had been amongst them this entire time. She'd met him, face to freaking face. Staked out the warehouse with him, watched him take photographs of the Heritage Preservation Coalition members, all of whom were innocent.

He'd led them down that path, manipulated them every step of the way.

The worst part? She hadn't seen it.

The door opened and Alex strolled into the bullpen. He came over to where Kenzie was sitting.

"Hey, I'm going to head off now. Shit, you okay? You look terrible."

She glanced up at him and shook her head.

Alex turned to Reid. "What's happened?"

"FieldNotes is the killer," he snapped, and turned and stormed off in the direction of the holding cells.

Alex was left staring down at her. "Kenzie?"

She sighed and gestured for him to take a seat at Reid's desk. He'd gone to interview Jeff Oliver, but she knew he wouldn't find a damn thing. The poor guy likely didn't even know he'd been used by a serial killer.

"What is this about FieldNotes being the killer?"

Kenzie took a slow breath and explained. She told him about the license plate, how she'd gone to his house and checked it out. What she'd seen.

He stared at her. "I also looked it up. Got an address from the dealer where the car had been bought. I didn't see a photograph though, so I just assumed it was him."

Kenzie shook her head. "He must have known there weren't many photos of Jeff Oliver online. He did his homework."

"So who was the guy we met at the warehouse?" Alex asked, his eyes narrowing to slits.

"The killer," Kenzie whispered. "He took a chance meeting us. Once we'd seen his face, we'd know he wasn't the man he was pretending to be."

"Except neither of us had seen Jeff Oliver at that point," Alex pointed out.

"He's the one who kept suggesting there was an ideological element to the crimes," Kenzie recalled, massaging her temples. "He's the one who kept pushing us in that direction."

Alex gave a slow nod. "He was the one who mentioned the symbolism on the cloth, how it must mean something."

"He was manipulating us. He conducted us like a goddamn orchestra," Kenzie said, as the anger began to rise. She didn't appreciate being played.

"He was the last person to join before you," Alex said slowly. "But that was over ten months ago."

"He's been planning this for a long time."

Alex shook his head. "But why? Why join a true crime group and then commit these heinous crimes? I mean, what has he got against those collectors?"

Kenzie bit her lip, then winced. The pain was almost welcome, distracting her from her frustration. "I'm guessing nothing. I think he just needed targets with something in common. Some way of linking them to make it easy to cast suspicion on one person, or group."

"That's sick," Alex whispered. "And senseless."

"I think he wanted to kill for the intellectual stimulation," she said. "He wanted to create the perfect spectacle. Something that would confound the true crime community and generate endless theories. It would position him as the brilliant analyst who helped 'solve' it by steering our group toward false leads he'd deliberately planted."

"So it had nothing to do with stolen Japanese artifacts?" Alex asked.

Kenzie shook her head. "The samurai angle was pure performance. He probably looked up the aesthetics on Wikipedia. He chose victims who would trigger the nationalist narrative, then watched as we and the police ran with that theory exactly as he'd predicted."

"Well, I'll be—" Alex blew out a breath. "I did not see that one coming."

"Me neither." It hurt to admit it. She'd never been that close to a killer before and not been aware of it. She'd never been so thoroughly taken in.

"So what now?" Alex asked, just as Reid came marching back, a thunderous look on his face.

"You were right, he doesn't know a fucking thing," he growled before heading to Vargas's desk. Diaz jumped up and joined them, as did Hamilton and Martinez.

"We now know who our killer is, people. His handle is Field-Notes, and he assumed the identity of Jeff Oliver to throw us off the scent."

There was a collective murmur.

"Do we know what he looks like?" Vargas asked.

"Kenzie and Alex have seen him in real life," Reid barked. "But he looks a lot like Jeff Oliver. And he probably drives a light gray vehicle. Make?" he turned to Kenzie, who shrugged.

"Four-door hatchback, maybe a Ford or Toyota. Something normal."

Vargas cringed. "Not much to go on."

"I'll get Raoul to come in." Kenzie took out her phone. They were going to need to pull out all the stops if they were going to find this guy. And it didn't get any better than him.

Reid nodded and went back to the briefing. Alex sat in stunned silence as this unfolded in front of him. He'd never been inside the workings of a police investigation before, and while Kenzie knew he shouldn't be here, nobody thought to kick out the former Marine.

Which from Kenzie's perspective wasn't necessarily a bad thing.

It might help to change his view on the police if he saw how an efficient department was run.

She made her way outside to call Raoul. When he picked up, she quickly explained the situation and asked if he could get down to the station as soon as possible.

"FieldNotes, holy crap. Okay, I'm on it. I'll be there as soon as I can." He didn't specify when.

"Thanks, Raoul. Anything you can find out might help."

Back inside, the team was discussing next steps. The case board had been wiped clean of everything except Jeff Oliver's photograph.

"Mambo Solange said I was close, but not close enough," Reid was saying. "I didn't know what she meant at the time, but I think now she was trying to imply that the killer was a close match to Jeff Oliver, but not the same person."

"Pity she couldn't just say that," Diaz muttered, as Kenzie walked past and went back to Reid's desk.

"I could log on to the private chat and see if he's online?" Alex offered. "He doesn't know I'm involved yet, or that I know who he is."

Reid spun around. "That's a good idea. We don't want to spook him, so any usual activity is good."

Kenzie nodded. "Yes! We should log on and resume normal activity. FieldNotes doesn't know we have ThirdWitness in custody too." She took a breath. "Why don't I mention I was nearly run over, and I think I'm getting close to figuring it out. I'll DM FieldNotes and AlexR asking to meet. We met before, so FieldNotes will think I trust him. I'll say I suspect a member of the group, and hint that it's RedCairn."

"You are *not* using yourself as bait," Reid said, spinning to face her.

She put her hands on her hips. "Why not? It's a good plan."

"He's already tried to kill you twice," Reid reminded her. "You want to give him another shot at it?"

She gave a dramatic sigh. "That's exactly why he might try again.

He'll see this as his opportunity to get rid of me *and* keep his identity safe."

"Absolutely not," Reid barked, shutting it down.

"Why don't I do it?" Alex said, standing up.

All eyes turned to him.

"Why are you still here?" snapped Reid.

"Hear me out." Alex raised his hands. "I can DM FieldNotes and ReporterGirl and request the meet. I'll say I suspect RedCairn. It might be better coming from me, anyway. Less suspicious. I'm also no stranger to putting myself in the line of fire." He grimaced and glanced at Kenzie. "No offense. I'm sure you're perfectly able to take care of yourself."

She tilted her head. "None taken."

Reid paused, thinking.

"It's not a bad idea," Vargas echoed. "If it works, it'll help us catch this guy."

"You'll both be in the line of fire." Reid fixed his gaze on Kenzie. "Even if Alex makes the call, you still have to be there."

"I'll make sure she's okay," Alex promised.

"*We'll* make sure she's okay," Reid countered.

"Sounds like I'll be well protected," Kenzie quipped. She looked at Reid. "So, we're a go?"

Reid gave an uneasy nod. "Yeah. But I want a SWAT team standing by, *and* a lot of backup. This guy is a psycho killer and I'm not taking any chances."

Kenzie broke into a grin. "Excellent. Let's do this."

44

Reid still didn't like it, but he couldn't disagree that it was their best shot at catching the sick bastard.

So far, everything had gone according to plan. ThirdWitness—a stupid fucking name, in his opinion—had cooperated fully. He'd given Raoul his login details, and the tech whiz had assumed the photographer's alias in The Evidence Room group.

Annoyingly, the true crime enthusiast had also managed to whittle down the staff list at the electronics factory to a handful of possibles who could have used the Toyota pool car on the day in question, beating his own team who hadn't been able to get that far. Not that it mattered now, but it still irked.

In the chat room, the discussion proceeded as normal, and Reid had been relieved to find FieldNotes was still participating, oblivious to the fact they were on to him. Kenzie, or rather, ReporterGirl, had not mentioned the hit-and-run incident, merely said she'd had a small accident but was fine. Just the acceptable amount of sharing in a group where you didn't really know the other users.

Or so he was told.

The three of them, Raoul, Kenzie, and Alex had commandeered

his desk and were now all in the chat room on their laptops. He'd never felt so ancient or defunct. This online world wasn't new to him, but it sure as hell wasn't where his skill set lay.

Murder was real. People died IRL, not on the frigging internet. Still, he acknowledged that he had to go where the evidence was, and more and more of it these days was online.

"Alex has DM'd FieldNotes and ReporterGirl asking for a meeting," Hamilton, who was keeping tabs, told him.

Vargas was still trawling through traffic cam footage for the killer's car on the night of Burton-Holmes's murder, now that he had the color, if not the make. Diaz and Martinez were sifting through CCTV footage and eye-witness accounts taken at Wynwood Walls. Mateo and Valeria Solís's security company finally got back to them with the camera footage of the street outside Malcolm Hargreave's house, and Dwayne offered to go through that.

Monroe took charge of mobilizing the SWAT team while Reid gave Captain Perez a courtesy call, letting him know what was going on.

"Let me know the moment you have the murdering scumbag in custody," Perez had barked into the phone.

"Copy that."

Reid's stomach was in knots as he waited for the sting operation to be set up. Would FieldNotes fall for it, or would he sense a trap?

That depended on how well Alex could play his role. Fortunately, the ex-Marine seemed extremely capable. Reid had no doubt he could handle himself—he'd had plenty of combat experience, and he was smart to boot.

Obviously, Reid had pulled his military record and checked him out. If he was sending Kenzie into the field with this guy, he wanted to make damn sure there were no skeletons in his closet.

He'd found nothing.

Even the psych evaluation that Radloff had failed was because of residual anger towards losing his buddies on that dusty road in Basra. The shrink had confirmed no abnormal psychological issues, no

PTSD, and recommended outpatient therapy for six months to help him 'deal with his injuries and the loss'.

That was eight years ago, so Reid couldn't hold it against the guy now.

"We've got a time," Kenzie called, lifting her head.

Hamilton hurried over to get the particulars.

Everyone was eager to get this guy. The investigation had them all on tenterhooks. No one had slept properly in days. The shocking crime scenes were something none of them would ever forget. It didn't help that they were plastered all over the web, either.

Nobody spoke as Hamilton relayed the details.

"Location?" Reid asked.

"He suggests meeting in a public plaza."

That meant open lines of sight, benches, foot traffic, innocent bystanders. He didn't like that one bit. Predators chose places they could control. Public didn't always mean safe—it also meant witnesses, distractions, multiple exit points.

"When?" Vargas asked.

"Thirty minutes."

Reid swore under his breath. The killer wasn't giving them much time to mobilize, but maybe that was the plan. Just in case this was a setup.

"Okay. Tell the SWAT team. Let's get you wired up and then we move."

The bullpen erupted into controlled chaos. Radios crackled. Monroe confirmed SWAT was mobilizing two blocks out. Diaz and Martinez grabbed surveillance kits and headed for vantage points. Hamilton coordinated plainclothes placement, marking lines of sight and fallback routes on the map.

Reid attached a small mic to the inside of Kenzie's blouse.

"It won't be noticeable, will it?" She glanced down.

"Nope. It's hidden—and you're not going without it."

She managed a weak smile.

Reid turned to Alex. "Stick to the script. No heroics. Let's try to get through this with minimal damage."

"Copy that." Alex was calm and focused, and Reid guessed this was familiar territory for him. It may have been a while, but the former Marine still had it.

Kenzie was already shrugging back into her jacket. Reid caught her arm. "You feel something's off, you pull back. You hear me?"

She met his gaze and gave his hand a quick squeeze. "I promise."

Reid nodded, about as satisfied as he could be under the circumstances.

They rolled out in unmarked vehicles, spacing themselves evenly so as not to announce their approach.

When Reid arrived at the plaza, it looked deceptively normal. He spotted people sipping coffee, a street musician tuning a guitar, couples drifting past without a clue they were walking into the center of a live wire situation.

Kenzie and Alex waited by a low stone fountain, just as they'd arranged. Reid watched from across the street, his heart thudding, every sense sharpened.

Time crawled.

They were five minutes early.

Then—

A figure appeared at the far end of the plaza, moving with unhurried confidence, scanning just enough to look casual.

Reid leaned forward.

FieldNotes was here.

And he was heading straight for them.

45

Kenzie glanced up as FieldNotes walked over to them, a disarming smile on his face.

"Good to see you again." There was no handshaking this time, although he appeared to be pretty relaxed. He wore jeans and a checked shirt, with a white T-shirt underneath. Kenzie couldn't see a weapon but wouldn't have been surprised if he was carrying.

"Thanks for meeting us." Alex looked around like he was worried people might see them. "I know this is off-book."

"Yeah, it was a surprise. Shall we walk and talk?"

Kenzie met Alex's gaze, but he nodded. "Sure."

They couldn't tip him off.

Together, they strolled across the plaza to the riverside walk. It extended along the canal toward a landscaped park half a mile away. FieldNotes headed in that direction.

Shit.

The SWAT team wouldn't be able to get there. They were two blocks south at the end of an access road to the plaza. Now they'd be on the opposite side of the park.

At least Reid and his team would be watching, and hopefully able to follow.

"Why the urgency?" FieldNotes said.

Kenzie pointed to her swollen lip. "I think someone tried to kill me this morning."

FieldNotes stopped walking, just long enough to shoot her a worried look. "What? Jesus. Are you hurt?"

What a liar. He was damn good at it too. If she didn't know better, she'd think he was genuinely concerned.

"Yeah, I'm okay." She lowered her voice. "But I think it was someone in the group."

He frowned and resumed walking. "Who?"

She lowered her voice. "RedCairn."

For a heartbeat, FieldNotes didn't react. Then he turned to look at her. "Why would you think that?"

Alex cut in. "We don't think RedCairn is who he appears to be."

FieldNotes tilted his head, confused. "I'm not with you."

Kenzie forced herself to breathe evenly.

"How much do any of us really know about him?" Alex said conspiratorially. "He never gives away any details about himself. He didn't come to the stakeout at the warehouse. He's a ghost."

Kenzie nodded. "He also steers the discussions in the chat. Have you ever noticed that? Makes me think he's manipulating us." She pursed her lips. "I'm sensitive to that kind of thing."

FieldNotes studied her now. Really studied her. "I never thought of it like that, but I can see what you mean."

"What are we going to do?" Alex asked as they left the plaza behind. "We can't let him get away with this. If we're right, and I honestly think we are, he's a threat. Not only to ReporterGirl, but also to the general public."

FieldNotes froze, staring at them. "Whoa! Hold on. You're not saying what I think you're saying, are you?"

They all looked at each other. The silence dragged out.

Damn, he was good. No wonder he'd gotten away with this facade up until now.

"Yes," Kenzie whispered, glancing around. Reid was nowhere to be seen. She thought she spotted Diaz in a baseball cap, talking on her phone as she walked, but she couldn't be sure. She dropped her voice. "We think he's the Samurai Killer."

"Holy shit!" FieldNotes took a step back. His expression was one of sheer shock. He was so convincing, Kenzie was beginning to doubt herself. Had she got it wrong? Was he innocent all this time and just naturally paranoid?

No, of course not. The borrowed car, the assumed identity, following her home. It had to be him.

Somehow, they had to get him to admit it or to react.

"It must be someone in the group," Kenzie pointed out. "I mean, the day after I mentioned that maybe the killer was blaming the Heritage Preservation Coalition, I nearly got run over. It can't be a coincidence."

"Why are you telling me this?" FieldNotes asked, picking up the pace again.

"Because you and Alex are the only two people in the group I actually know." Kenzie had to hustle to keep up. "We've met in real life. I trust you guys."

"I think she's on to something," Alex replied, falling into step with them. "That's why I asked to meet. Together, we can bring him down."

"But how?" FieldNotes asked. "Like you said, he's a ghost."

"Has he said anything in the chat that might indicate where he's based, or who he is?" Alex asked.

FieldNotes frowned. "Why are you asking me? You've been in the group longer than I have."

"I just thought you might have noticed something that I missed," Alex said.

"No, sorry." FieldNotes stared at the ground, frowning. "Listen, I think this is too much for me. I didn't sign on for this. You guys do what you feel is right. I'm going to leave the chat."

This was going nowhere.

They needed to provoke him somehow.

"I agree, it's getting out of hand," she said to Alex. He shot her a quizzical look. "I vote we go to the police."

"Will they even believe us?" he asked skeptically.

"Well, I have a split lip and grazes on my legs. It's obvious that *something* happened. There might even be CCTV of the driver."

"That only proves the hit-and-run," Alex said. "Not the murders."

"That's right," FieldNotes agreed. "There is no actual evidence he's the killer. There's no evidence at all."

Was that a smirk she saw on his face? A private moment of smugness.

Her hands balled into fists. "That's not strictly true."

Beside her, Alex stiffened.

FieldNotes's gaze narrowed. "What do you mean?"

"Well, you know I work with the police sometimes. I heard via the grapevine that there was DNA left at one of the crime scenes. A small amount on the third victim."

"I didn't read anything like that," FieldNotes said quickly.

"They withheld it from the public." Kenzie lowered her voice. "All they need is a suspect and they can match the DNA. If we tell them about the group—about RedCairn—they might be able to trace him."

"They'll bring everyone in," FieldNotes argued. "You don't want that."

Alex shook his head. "No, but if it means catching a killer..."

Kenzie nodded. "Okay, that's it then. I'll head there now. Do you guys want to come with me? Back up my story?"

"I'm in," Alex said, glancing at FieldNotes.

The killer's hand moved. Fast. Too fast to react.

There was a flash of metal and suddenly FieldNotes was behind her, his arm locked tight around her shoulders. Kenzie felt a sharp prick against her neck and froze.

A syringe.

FieldNotes glared at Alex. “Now, you’re going to do exactly as I say, or she dies.”

46

Reid clocked the change in direction the second they left the plaza.

Shit.

The riverside path narrowed ahead as the trees closed in. He lost his line of sight as they walked around a bend, their figures briefly obscured by foliage and a curve in the path.

SWAT would be boxed out for at least another five minutes, maybe more if they tried to reposition without spooking him. Five minutes was a lifetime. People could die in five minutes.

"I'm going after them," he said into his earpiece.

He followed at a distance, keeping his pace casual, his posture loose, trying—and likely failing—to look like just another man out for a walk by the canal. His pulse had begun to thud behind his eyes, but his hands were steady. He wasn't panicking just yet, but no way was he letting them out of his sight.

Kenzie's mic crackled softly in his ear.

"—DNA left at one of the crime scenes."

FieldNotes slowed. Reid slowed with him.

Reid watched the man's body language, not his face. Faces lied. Bodies didn't. He clocked the loose shoulders, the relaxed gait, the way his hands swung freely at his sides. If he was planning something, it wasn't right now. Reid had time. How much, he wasn't sure.

Kenzie's voice again. "—they might be able to trace him."

Reid felt the shift before he saw it. A fractional hitch in FieldNotes's stride. The tiniest recalibration of balance. The kind of adjustment you made when you were lining up something in your head.

He was preparing for action.

Yet they walked on. The canal to their left ran dark and sluggish. Trees encroached to their right. There were no civilians close enough now to complicate the shot. Reid's hand brushed the grip of his weapon.

Kenzie: "Do you guys want to come with me?"

FieldNotes stopped.

Reid stopped too, using a bench as partial cover, eyes never leaving the man's hands.

Nothing yet.

There was a low murmur where the suspect said something he didn't catch—then FieldNotes sprang into motion. His arm flashed up and around Kenzie's shoulders, his body turning automatically to shield his own vitals.

Reid caught the glint of the needle just as it pressed against her neck.

A syringe.

Not a blade.

He went cold. This was worse—it was likely filled with tetrodotoxin. No cure. No room for error.

Kenzie froze.

Reid heard FieldNotes's voice. "—exactly as I say, or she dies."

Alex's voice came through the mic next, tight but controlled.

"Okay. Okay. Easy."

Reid raised his weapon, sighting down the barrel. He didn't have a clear shot, but he couldn't wait for SWAT. They wouldn't get here in time.

His finger hovered on the trigger, pressure feather-light, but he didn't fire. Not with Kenzie in the way. Not unless there was no other choice.

Reid's gaze locked onto the angle of the syringe. The tremor in FieldNotes's hand. The way the plunger hovered, waiting. Any change, and he'd have to make a decision.

The syringe pressed harder. Reid saw Kenzie's throat tighten, heard her breath catch, but she didn't move.

Alex, however, clocked Reid and shot him a pointed look.

Reid met his gaze and gave a slight nod.

The Marine turned his head, deliberately, and looked in the opposite direction, as if he'd seen something beyond the trees. A calculated move. A textbook distraction.

FieldNotes's attention snapped to him for a split second, but that was all the time Reid needed.

Kenzie dropped to her knees. Straight down.

Reid fired.

The report of the gunshot shattered the quiet, echoing off the water and the trees. The shot was clean. Center mass. The kind you trained for and hoped you'd never need.

FieldNotes staggered back, shock etched across his face, the syringe flying from his hand as he hit the ground. His breath exploded from his lungs in a wet, shocked gasp.

Reid advanced immediately, his weapon still raised, adrenaline roaring now, but Alex got there first. FieldNotes tried to reach behind his back—muscle memory, last reflex—but Alex slammed a foot down on his arm, pinning it to the path with brutal efficiency.

FieldNotes tried to speak, but blood bubbled at his lips instead.

"Don't move," Reid said, standing over him.

SWAT flooded the path seconds later, boots pounding, weapons raised, commands barking, but it was already done. They slowed as they took in the scene, saw the suspect down.

Kenzie collapsed onto the ground. Alex crouched beside her, checking her neck.

"She's good," he called. "No puncture wound."

Reid exhaled for the first time in what felt like hours. He looked down at the man who'd thought himself untouchable. The manipulator. The conductor. The ghost. And watched the light go out of his eyes.

"Game over," he said quietly.

For the first time since this case had begun, the noise in his head fell silent.

47

Kenzie got checked out by the paramedics, then headed over to where Reid was standing, talking to Alex. Both men had been brilliant, looking out for her and helping to bring the investigation to a close.

Reid had shot someone, however, and she knew that was not something he'd take lightly. Even a psycho serial killer like FieldNotes.

It struck her that they still didn't know who he was.

"You okay?" she asked, coming to a stop in front of them, her gaze on Reid.

"I'm fine," he said, but she didn't miss the flicker behind his eyes. He was dealing with it. Processing. She knew from her training at the academy—a long time ago now—that when you took a life, the effects came on slowly. It was only once the adrenaline wore off that reality kicked in and you had to live with the consequences.

Thankfully, she'd never had to experience that herself.

Reid and Alex, however, both had.

She'd seen the look in the Marine's eyes though, before Reid had taken the shot. If he hadn't pulled the trigger, he wouldn't have hesitated to take FieldNotes out either. Reid had saved him the trouble.

"Thank you," she said, smiling at Reid. "For saving my life."

He gave a stiff nod.

"It was a team effort," he said, nodding at Alex.

Kenzie was pleased they'd moved past their initial mutual mistrust.

Pruitt had arrived and was bending over the body. "This your guy?" he called to Reid.

"Yeah, we got him in the end."

"Glad to hear it. Won't waste any time crying over this one."

He checked for a pulse, inspected the bullet wound, then nodded to the waiting men to take the body to the morgue. A CSU photographer had already documented the scene, flash popping rhythmically in the fading light, and Kenzie had seen Reid hand his gun over to Captain Perez, his old boss, who was talking to the press a short distance away.

"Strange how we don't even know who he is." she said quietly.

"Actually, we do," Vargas said, coming over. He held a tablet tucked under his arm, his expression grim. "I fingerprinted him before the ME got here. Name's Arlo Brandt. Originally from Wyoming. There's a warrant out for his arrest back there."

Kenzie frowned. "For what?"

"Attempted homicide. Ten years ago. A woman he was seeing. She survived. Barely."

Kenzie felt a chill creep up her spine. "Domestic violence. Is that why he left?"

He gave a tight nod. "Timing fits."

"That's a very different crime from this," Reid said, stroking his jaw. "I wonder why he suddenly went full scale serial killer."

"And why art collectors?" Alex mused.

"He was a loner, by all accounts," Vargas continued. "I read the statement from his ex-girlfriend. She said he was distant, used to retreat inside himself. She never knew what he was thinking until he erupted."

"Why the hell would you stay with someone like that?" Reid asked, shaking his head.

"Who knows?" Vargas said. "I don't think they were together very long."

"What did he do for a living?" Kenzie asked.

"This is where the connection to the artifacts comes in," Vargas said. "He worked in museums as an archivist. Had several jobs, all over the state. Moved around a lot."

"Always adjacent to history, but never part of it," Kenzie murmured, thinking about his motive, his need for attention, to fit in.

Alex nodded. "Makes sense. He was always digging deeper, trying to find angles that weren't there. I remember we had to tell him to stop with the conspiracy theories at one point."

"You didn't think to mention that?" She raised an eyebrow.

He threw up his hands. "I've just remembered it."

Kenzie's thoughts turned back to FieldNotes. "He wanted to be someone else. Someone important. He wanted to mean something."

Reid grunted. "So he reinvented himself online. In the private chat groups, he could be anyone he wanted to be."

"Why the murders?" Vargas questioned, his brow furrowing. "I mean, I get he wanted to reinvent himself, be some crime solving genius, but why kill like that?"

"It wasn't about the killing," Kenzie said, nodding slowly. She was beginning to understand him now—not that that excused anything. If anything, it was more messed up than she could have imagined. "It was about the story. The narrative. He wanted to create the perfect mystery for the group to solve."

"He was curating it," Alex murmured.

Reid nodded toward the departing ambulance. "Narcissistic control freak."

Kenzie looked back toward the spot where it had all ended.

There was nothing there except a yellow marker to show where Arlo Brandt had died. The water flowed past, indifferent, as if it were taking the memory of what had happened with it.

"He wanted to be part of something bigger," she whispered.

Reid grunted. "But strip all that away, and he was just a pathetic loser who couldn't stand to be invisible."

Diaz came over to join them, still in her jogging gear and baseball cap. "Dwayne called from the station. He picked up a gray Ford Focus in the road outside Malcolm Hargreave's house the night of the murder. Can't see the driver, but he thinks that might be Brandt's vehicle."

"The car that tried to run me down was gray," Kenzie confirmed with a nod.

"Also, Monroe spotted a gray Ford Focus on the traffic cam footage leading to Allapattah. Looks like it's the same vehicle."

"He wasn't as smart as he thought," Reid said with a smirk.

Across the way, Captain Perez finished with the press. He came over and put a hand on Kenzie's shoulder. "Glad you're okay."

"Thanks, Captain."

He shook Reid's hand. "Good work there today, Lieutenant."

"Thanks, but I had help." He nodded to Alex, Vargas, and Diaz.

Perez turned to Alex. "I don't believe we've met, although Garrett told me about you. United States Marine Corps, is that right?"

"Yes, sir. Mason Alex Radloff."

"Well, thanks for your help, Marine. If you ever want to join the Force, you let me know."

Alex grinned. "I might actually do that, sir."

Perez nodded. "Good man. We'd be glad to have you." He turned back to Reid. "I've just let the media know the threat is over. That the Samurai Killer is dead."

Reid cringed at the moniker. "Do we have to call him that?"

"Sorry, but I don't know his real name."

"Arlo Brandt. But I guess now he's dead, it doesn't matter."

"Well, let's just put this behind us and move on. Hopefully after the news cycle dies down, the citizens of Miami will forget he ever existed."

Kenzie smiled to herself. For someone who'd wanted to be remembered, that felt like the most fitting end of all.

48

PODCAST TRANSCRIPT: EPISODE 26- GILT EDGE

(SOFT INTRO MUSIC FADES IN. *The tone is subdued, reflective.*)

Kenzie Gilmore:

If you're listening to this episode, then you already know how this story ended.

Over the past several days, Sweetwater Police have released that the individual responsible for the murders connected to what the media dubbed *the Samurai Killer* is dead. He was fatally shot during a police operation after attempting to flee and resist arrest.

There will be no trial. There will be no courtroom revelations. And for many people, that feels... unsatisfying.

So today, I want to talk about what we *do* know. What we *don't*. And why, in this particular case, restraint matters more than answers.

(*Brief pause.*)

Welcome to *Off the Record.*

I'm Kenzie Gilmore, and this is Episode Twenty-Six: The Gilt Edge.

Before we go any further, let me be very clear. I am not going to name the person responsible for these crimes. Police have not released his name to the public, and I support that decision. Not because the truth should be hidden, but because not every truth needs amplification. Especially when amplification is exactly what a killer was seeking.

What I *can* confirm is this:

There were **three murders**.

The first was a wealthy private collector, Malcolm Hargreave, who was found dead in his home in what appeared to be a ritualistic killing involving a katana. He apparently invited his killer in and showed him his collection. We now know the killer posed as a buyer, pretending to be interested in some of Hargreave's pieces.

The second, another collector, Reginald Burton-Holmes, was discovered in a public park, similarly staged, except this time the weapon was a samurai sword. A folded cloth with Japanese symbols on it was placed near the body. Burton-Holmes was abducted from a warehouse in Allapattah where he went to meet the killer, who again posed as a buyer of rare oriental artifacts.

And the third death, that of interior designer Arthur Whitmore, confirmed earlier this week, followed the same pattern. In a gruesome escalation, the victim was beheaded after being abducted from a parking garage in the building where he worked. Whitmore's body was discovered in Wynwood Walls, a public place. The placement was designed to shock.

Authorities now believe that in all three cases, the victims were killed by a lethal toxin. The swords were placed afterward, to get attention. Apart from the one used to decapitate Whitmore.

In the early days of this investigation, speculation ran wild. Some of that was understandable. When violence is staged so deliberately, we instinctively look for meaning. The swords, and the fact that the victims were collectors, pointed the finger to a cultural or ideological motive.

Was this about cultural restitution?

Was it about stolen artifacts?

Was it about nationalism, identity, or historical grievance?

The answer, we now know, is no.

Police have stated unequivocally that no cultural, nationalistic, or ideological group had any involvement in these murders. None of that was relevant. It was all a distraction. A careful ruse planned by the killer to avoid suspicion.

So what *was* the point?

According to investigators, the individual responsible was not a public figure. He was not well known. He did not hold power or influence. In fact, by most measures, he was deeply unremarkable.

And that is the point.

Because what this case ultimately revealed was not a crusade, but a hunger. A desire to be seen. To be discussed. To be important, even if that importance came at the cost of other peoples' lives.

By staging the murders with such shocking visuals, the killer ensured conversation. Online debate. News headlines. Podcasts like this one. And that is an uncomfortable truth for anyone who works in the media. Including me.

After the third murder, law enforcement officers identified the suspect and attempted to apprehend him. He fled, resisting arrest, and when confronted, he escalated the situation in a way that left officers with no safe alternatives. A single shot was fired, and the suspect was pronounced dead at the scene.

Police have confirmed that no civilians were harmed during the operation.

How do we, as a city, move on from something like this? The best way is to refuse to immortalize the person who caused it. By remembering the victims, not the spectacle. To respect their families and give them time to grieve.

There's a concept in Japanese art called kintsugi, which is the practice of repairing broken pottery with gold. Instead of hiding the cracks, the repair highlights them. The object becomes something new, shaped by its damage, but not defined by it.

I've thought about that a lot over the past week.

Miami has been cracked by this. But when we come together and repair those cracks, when we fix them with kindness, understanding, and tolerance, the final product is even more beautiful than it was before.

This will be the final episode I record on this particular case. There will be no follow-ups. No anniversary specials. No deep dives into the killer's past. His short reign of terror is over.

The most powerful thing we can do now is deny him what he wanted most. Attention.

This has been *Off the Record*. I'm Kenzie Gilmore.

Goodnight.

(*Music swells and fades out.*)

ALSO BY BIBA PEARCE

The Kenzie Gilmore Crime Series

Afterburn

Dead Heat

Heatwave

Burnout

Deep Heat

Fever Pitch

Storm Surge

Night Watch

Gilt Edge

The Dalton Savage Mystery Series by L.T. Ryan

Savage Grounds

Scorched Earth

Cold Sky

The Frost Killer

Crimson Moon

Dust Devil

Savage Season

The Detective Rob Miller Mysteries

The Thames Path Killer

The West London Murders

The Bisley Wood Murders

The Box Hill Killer

The South Bank Murders

The Soho Killer

The Marlow Murders

ALSO BY WITHOUT WARRANT

More Thriller Series from Without Warrant:

Sign up for our Without Warrant newsletter by visiting our website so you don't miss out on exclusive content, free prequels, and more!

Liquidmindpublishing.com

Dana Gray Mysteries by C.J. Cross

Girl Left Behind

Girl on the Hill

Girl in the Grave

Girl Betrayed

Girl Between

The Kenzie Gilmore Series by Biba Pearce

Afterburn

Dead Heat

Heatwave

Burnout

Deep Heat

Fever Pitch

Storm Surge

Night Watch

Gilt Edge

A Willow Grace FBI Thriller by C.C. West

Shadow of Grace

Condition of Grace

Hunt for Grace

Time for Grace

Piece of Grace

Flight of Grace

Rite of Grace

Lost Grace

Ava Cortes CBI Thrillers

Deep Dark Lies

Dark as Pitch

Join Without Warrant's private reader group on Facebook!

ABOUT THE AUTHOR

Biba Pearce is a British crime writer and author of the Kenzie Gilmore series and the DCI Rob Miller series.

Biba grew up in post-apartheid Southern Africa. As a child, she lived on the wild eastern coast and explored the sub-tropical forests and surfed in shark-infested waters.

Now a full-time writer, Biba lives in leafy Surrey and when she isn't writing, can be found walking through the countryside or kayaking on the river Thames.

Visit her at bibapearce.com and join her mailing list at https://liquidmind.media/biba-pearce-sign-up-1/ to be notified about new releases, updates and special subscriber-only deals.

facebook.com/authorbibapearce
x.com/bibapearce
instagram.com/author_blpearce

JOIN WITHOUT WARRANT'S MAILING LIST

Follow the link to stay up to date with Without Warrant!

https://BookHip.com/WKDXPAV

You'll receive a **free** copy of

Hard Line: A Kenzie Gilmore Prequel.

Printed in Dunstable, United Kingdom

81728055R00178